Just Out of Reach

DANETTE KRIEHN

iUniverse, Inc.
Bloomington

Just Out of Reach

This is a work of fiction. All of the characters, names, incidents, organizations, and dialogue in this novel are either the products of the author's imagination or are used fictitiously.

iUniverse books may be ordered through booksellers or by contacting:

iUniverse
1663 Liberty Drive
Bloomington, IN 47403
www.iuniverse.com
1-800-Authors (1-800-288-4677)

Because of the dynamic nature of the Internet, any web addresses or links contained in this book may have changed since publication and may no longer be valid. The views expressed in this work are solely those of the author and do not necessarily reflect the views of the publisher, and the publisher hereby disclaims any responsibility for them.

Any people depicted in stock imagery provided by Thinkstock are models, and such images are being used for illustrative purposes only.

Certain stock imagery © Thinkstock.

ISBN: 978-1-4620-1537-5 (sc)
ISBN: 978-1-4620-1538-2 (e)
ISBN: 978-1-4620-1539-9 (dj)

Printed in the United States of America

iUniverse rev. date: 9/30/2011

To Richard, my own true love, real-life hero and biggest champion: thank you for always encouraging me, in spite of the risks, to pursue what makes me happy; for believing without question that I can get there; and for loving me no matter what happens.

If speaking is silver, then listening is gold.

—Turkish proverb

Prologue

Smyrna, Tennessee
1993

*T*wenty, forty, fifty, sixty, sixty-one, sixty-two ... damn. Natalie sat back on her heels, staring at the bills on the floor. She still didn't have enough for the bus ticket. It was seventy dollars one way to Sarasota from this rat hole where she lived. Only eight more dollars. Maybe she could ...

"NATALIE! Get your bony ass in here, *right now!*" Claudia Brennan's cigarette-roughened voice bellowed from the kitchen, abruptly interrupting Natalie's thoughts. A stream of curses immediately followed the command, so Natalie yelled back "Coming!" and quickly grabbed her cash, stuffing it back into the secret cubbyhole she'd made in the floor of her tiny bedroom closet.

What now? she wondered, tucking the corner of the ratty carpet back into place and tossing her knapsack over it. Hadn't she just been punished for drinking the last of the vodka Claudia had thought she'd kept so skillfully hidden in the kitchen cupboard behind the pots and pans? And punished despite that fact that it was Claudia, in one of her drunken stupors, who had been the one to drain that particular stash?

Natalie stood and took one quick, deep breath. *Oh well. Here we go again.* She closed the door of her bedroom and walked resolutely down the hall, through their sparsely furnished living room and into the kitchen with its badly painted and now chipping yellow cabinets, a failed effort of previous renters to brighten up the sorry little house.

Natalie crossed the linoleum floor to stand before Claudia and tried to ignore the stale smell of cigarette smoke and stacks of dirty dishes littering the sink and counters—there was no dishwasher unless you counted Natalie. The sun slanting through the single uncovered window above the sink only served to highlight the grime-covered surfaces. Natalie had long since given up trying to keep the place clean, as her efforts had never earned her any reprieve—it wasn't done fast enough, it wasn't done often enough, it wasn't done well enough.

Claudia sat at the kitchen table, her usual spot on these late weekend mornings, her heavy mascara from the night before now smeared and her short, dark-at-the-roots blonde hair spiky from sleep. She was wearing the faded red kimono she always bragged was a thank-you gift—among others—from a rich Japanese businessman she had met and "charmed" at a bar one night. *Yeah, right,* Natalie thought—Claudia and charm went together about as well as oil and water.

An empty, stained coffee cup in front of her, Claudia inhaled deeply on the cigarette she held as she glared at Natalie, blowing the smoke out of her mouth and nose and flicking the ashes into the nearby ashtray already overflowing with butts. Waiting silently for the expected outburst, Natalie had learned years ago that the least painful route was to not say a word until Claudia calmed down and then to meekly acknowledge the mistake and accept the resulting punishment, deserved or not. Only lately, it was getting damn hard to do that.

Claudia narrowed her blood-red eyes at Natalie's suddenly clenched jaw, and she stared hard at the girl, her only child, though Natalie had long ago stopped calling her mother at Claudia's insistence. In a moment of pure insanity, Claudia had later acknowledged, she had decided to keep the kid, thinking she could finally quit her crummy waitressing job, get on welfare, and take it easy for a change. And though there were multiple possibilities as far as the father went, she had decided the baby was her real meal ticket and that she'd be better off not saddled with a man she was sure she'd only end up despising anyway.

But the life of leisure hadn't turned out like she'd planned, as a squalling baby had been more responsibility than she'd been prepared for—or wanted, as it turned out. But hell, she'd kept the worthless brat, hadn't she, and wasn't that worth a little loyalty? It was beside the point that the decision had eventually paid off for Claudia as Natalie had gotten older and was able to do more so Claudia didn't have to.

Natalie stoically withstood the silent scrutiny, unaware of how fragile and lovely she was, even at fourteen, a fact that infuriated Claudia to no end, knowing her own looks were quickly fading. Though painfully thin, Natalie's eyes were a deep, fathomless brown framed by naturally arched brows the same rich russet color as the tangled hair that fell to her waist. Her cheekbones were high, almost elegant; her nose was narrow and straight over a mouth that was beautifully shaped but rarely smiled anymore.

Her body was also beginning to show signs of development, another point against her in Claudia's distorted mind. Several of Claudia's boyfriends had been making crude remarks about it lately whenever they were around Natalie, and Claudia found herself worrying about competition from her own daughter.

Claudia broke the silence with a deceptively calm voice, her fingernails starting to rhythmically tap the scarred surface of the table. "Where's my money?"

Natalie couldn't prevent the sudden fear that flared in her eyes before she determinedly schooled her features into a blank mask. She swallowed, silently debating her reply for a second, and then decided ignorance might buy her a little more time to come up with a good answer.

"What money?"

The slap came before Natalie could avert her face and stung like the devil. But she refused to cry or make a sound, and her silence only served to enrage Claudia.

"You know damn well know what money I'm talking about!" Claudia screamed, having lost her tenuous control over her temper, now stomping across the kitchen to yank open a cupboard above the refrigerator and pull out an empty glass jar.

"The money I kept in here! *My* money! What did you do with it?" She hurled the jar against the wall where it smashed into a scattered mess of tiny, fragmented pieces.

Natalie flinched slightly at the sound of the breaking glass but remained outwardly calm and replied very slowly and carefully, "I didn't take your money." Which was true. But Natalie knew who had.

"*Bullshit!*" Claudia charged back across the kitchen, bringing her face within inches of Natalie's, and snarled viciously, "You'd better tell me right now, you little slut, or you won't be able to leave your room for a month!"

Natalie only repeated what she had just said, knowing it would only add more fuel to the fire if she told her the truth, that Claudia's boyfriend Daryl had taken the money while Claudia had been passed out on the couch the night before, after they'd done a second round of crack.

Natalie had stayed quietly in her bedroom, locking the door as she always did when Claudia's friends were over, but had come out when it had gotten quiet, having had to go pee so badly she had decided to risk leaving the safety of her room.

Sneaking down the hall to the single, dingy blue bathroom in their rental house, she had heard a clinking sound in the kitchen, so had instead turned around quietly and braved a quick look through the doorway from the hall into the living room, finding Claudia unconscious on the couch. Curiosity getting the better of her, Natalie had then tiptoed several steps farther into the living room so she could peek through to the kitchen. It was there she saw Daryl grin as he took the lid off the glass jar and pull out a thick stack of bills.

Her heart suddenly slamming in her chest, understanding immediately the consequences if he saw her, she had backed out of the living room silent as a snake, forgoing the bathroom without a second thought. As quietly as she could, she had locked her bedroom door once again, her pounding heart only starting to settle once she'd heard Daryl leave through the front door.

But she didn't tell Claudia any of that now. She almost wished she had stolen the money. Then she'd have enough to buy that Greyhound ticket to Sarasota, where she planned to start her new life—leaving Claudia and this hellhole, the sleazy boyfriends, the drugs and alcohol, and *all* the other crap forever behind her—and live in a place where the sun always shined, the water was sparkling blue, and the possibilities were endless.

Natalie had first seen the tourist brochure for Sarasota, Florida, on her teacher's desk about a year and half ago, when her teacher had planned to go there over Christmas break. The picture on the front had been so beautiful—so different from anything that Natalie had ever known or seen—that she had determined then and there she was going to go there someday. When she had asked her teacher nonstop questions after returning from the trip, the answers had only reinforced Natalie's decision.

But when things had started getting worse—much worse—at home, especially with Daryl hanging around more, Natalie had realized that "someday" would have to come sooner rather than later. So she had started doing everything she could think of to earn the money for the bus ticket without Claudia getting suspicious.

Natalie's mistake was taking her mind off of Claudia and the present situation to daydream for a few precious moments about how life might be different after she got out of there. The sudden backhand from Claudia whipped her head to the side and caused the blood to spurt from her nose, the pain exploding and intense.

"I know you took it, you little bitch; no one else knew it was there!"

Natalie slowly wiped her nose with her arm, looked down at the blood, and then looked back at Claudia, those familiar feelings of disbelief and disgust assailing her once again that this person, this ... this *monster*, was her mother. All the rage that Natalie normally kept tightly bottled up inside her started simmering to the surface.

"Maybe you should ask your *boyfriend*," Natalie ground out through clenched teeth.

Another blow, this time a fist to the stomach, caused Natalie to lose her breath and double over in pain. Though Natalie had gotten smarter as she'd gotten older, figuring out numerous ways to become virtually invisible and avoid the beatings, this morning Claudia was in rare form, her money clearly her most important asset.

Claudia suddenly laughed harshly. "Not bad, Natalie, not bad. But when you decide to point the finger at somebody else, you'd better make damn sure they won't be around to disagree with you. Daryl is coming over tonight, so we'll just see, won't we, how he likes your little *accusation*." Claudia smiled maliciously, lips wrinkled from endless years of smoking spreading to deepen the creases on either side of her mouth.

Natalie slowly straightened, the pain in her belly receding to a dull throb. She could easily predict how that scene would play out, and she knew she had to get out of the house before Daryl showed up.

"Fine. Ask him. I'll be in my room." Like hell she would, Natalie thought defiantly, but Claudia didn't need to know that. She turned to go, starting to plan her escape.

"I didn't say you could leave." Claudia's hand snaked out and clamped down hard on Natalie's thin arm, yellowed fingernails digging into pale skin.

"But since I have to go out for a bit, that's exactly where you'll stay. I'll be thinking about how you can pay me back while I'm gone." Claudia smiled again. "*And* looking forward to our little discussion tonight with Daryl." She released Natalie and sat back down to take another drag on her still-lit cigarette, apparently dismissing her completely.

Natalie didn't question the unexpected reprieve from the insults or the abuse, instead hurrying back to her room as quickly as her battered body would allow. She locked the door once again and sat down gingerly on her bed to figure out how she would disappear tonight—and wait until Claudia left before she ventured out to clean up the blood and broken glass.

※ ※ ※ ※

Natalie and Jenny giggled as they kicked off their shoes and ran barefoot across the grass, heading toward the big swings at Gregory Mill Park just down the street from where they both lived. Jenny was Natalie's best friend—her only friend, really. Only Jenny understood what life was really like for Natalie. But even then, not all of it.

They reached the row of empty swings and grabbed two next to each other, pushing off and pumping their legs as they went higher and higher, their long hair flying up and then dropping behind them with each pass. The rhythmic squeaking of the chains was a friendly companion to their uncomplicated laughter, and for now, the world was a wonderful place where they had no worries other than whether they'd skin the bottoms of their bare feet on the pea gravel when they jumped off midflight to see who could land the furthest away.

Jenny won, as she usually did, because Natalie's thin arms and legs simply weren't as strong. But Natalie didn't care because Jenny didn't care, and they dropped to the grass just beyond the swings, their laughter subsiding as they lay on their backs staring up at the beautiful, clear blue sky.

"Jenny, do you really think there's a heaven?" Natalie asked.

Jenny answered immediately, "Yes, I do." Then she grinned. "And I think it has really soft beds to sleep in, and all the candy you could ever want, and you'd never get sick from eating too much of it …"

Natalie smiled dreamily. That sounded really nice. She especially loved Goo-Goo Clusters, though she almost never got them, so to be able to have as many as she wanted would be …

A black cloud appeared suddenly over their heads, interrupting Natalie's thoughts and causing her to frown. The rumble of thunder that followed was so loud that both girls had to cover their ears, and they immediately got up and started running back to where they had left their shoes.

Just as suddenly, they both stopped, their chests heaving and their breathing heavy. Waiting for them there, holding Natalie's pair of beat-up sneakers, was Daryl. Smiling with that knowing smile that gave Natalie the creeps.

Wait a minute, Natalie thought in confusion. *Why is Daryl here?* Then his face started changing: skin turning red, brows growing dark, eyes beginning to glow. When horns slowly grew from his forehead, Natalie's mouth fell open and she blinked once, then twice, but he continued to take the shape and form of the devil.

He took Natalie's shoe and brought it to his nose, inhaling deeply, and the smile on his face grew as he started to walk toward them … beside her, Jenny screamed.

❦ ❦ ❦ ❦

Natalie bolted upright, her breathing choppy as she glanced around in a panic, until she realized with a shaky laugh that she was in her room, on her bed, and that it was only a dream—a dream of a much younger Natalie and Jenny, her best friend since kindergarten. Jenny, who was always there for her, who kept her in school, who somehow never failed to help her survive the hell that was often her life. Natalie breathed slowly and deeply. *Only a dream,* she repeated.

Then she did panic. Shit, what time was it? She looked out her window, seeing it was now almost dark. Oh God, had she fallen asleep for so long that Daryl was already there?

Her heart thumping, her breath once again shallow, Natalie quickly looked down at her bloody clothes, and then she remembered she had been able to wash up and change after Claudia left and grab something to eat from the sparse provisions in the kitchen after sweeping up the broken glass she had known Claudia would ignore. But she had gone back to her room after that because she still hadn't come up with a solid plan for leaving that wouldn't simply end up bringing more of Claudia's wrath down upon her when she finally did return. *If* she returned. If only she had enough money for that ticket. She must have dozed off while mulling it all over in her mind.

Jesus, Natalie, stop dawdling! She climbed off the bed and hastily grabbed her sneakers from the floor, shaking off the sudden, terrifying vision from the dream as she pulled them on one by one. She snuck over to the door and placed her ear against it to see if she could hear anything—and waited for what seemed like an eternity.

When no sounds emerged, Natalie figured it was safe enough to leave through the back door of the kitchen rather than try to climb through her bedroom window as she had often done in the past. Its wooden frame had just started sticking when she tried to open it, and besides being too noisy, she was almost too big now to get her head and shoulders through the narrow opening. She ever so gently unlocked her bedroom door and turned the handle with shaking hands.

Please don't let the door squeak, she pleaded silently to whoever might be listening and have power over such things. As the door noiselessly complied, she closed her eyes gratefully and issued a fervent thank-you, opening it only as far as necessary to sneak quietly though.

Tiptoeing the few steps down the hall to the living room, Natalie realized she was holding her breath and slowly exhaled through her nose as she moistened her dry lips in an effort to calm her racing heart. She scanned the living room. All clear. Now all she had to do was to make it through the kitchen to the back door, and then she could break into a run, jump the backyard gate, and sprint down the alley to freedom. Though at this exact moment in time, she didn't have a clue what, or where, freedom was.

The hand that suddenly clamped over her mouth effectively silenced the scream that rose in response from the depths of her throat. Natalie's heart instantly slammed double-time against her ribs, her hands all at once clammy as she struggled without success to pry the hand from her mouth and break free from the other arm that gripped her tightly around the waist. Natalie swore to herself if she got out of this one, she'd start lifting weights at school religiously.

"Hello there, little lady."

She instantly recognized his voice. And she could smell him—smell his terrible breath hot on her ear as he stood behind her. Daryl. He always reeked of stale sweat and greasy onions. Natalie had avoided him like the plague this past year, ever since he had started hanging out regularly at the house, as he always stared at her when Claudia wasn't looking, like he wanted to do something unspeakable to her. Filthy *creep*.

Damn it, damn it, *damn it!* Why had she fallen asleep? She had never been that careless before.

Daryl spoke slowly into her ear, snapping her attention back to the moment. "I'm gonna take my hand away if you promise you won't scream." Then he laughed softly, the sound crawling up Natalie's spine, as he whispered, "The screaming will come later."

Oh, shit, this was *bad*. Natalie had to think fast or she was probably dead.

She nodded her head jerkily in agreement. When he slowly removed his hand, she opened her mouth and bit down on the fleshy part of it as hard as she could, wrenching a satisfying howl from him as she simultaneously stomped on his foot and smashed her right fist back into his groin with everything she had. Her satisfaction was short-lived, however, as he picked her up and threw her, his obvious anger at her little trick fueling his already superior strength.

Where was Claudia? Natalie thought in a haze of pain, her shoulder now dislocated from its socket, having taken the brunt of the blow her body took as she had forcefully hit the wall. Natalie knew Claudia had never been a real mother, but she wouldn't just let Daryl kill her, would she?

Her mindless ramblings were interrupted when Daryl grabbed her by the arms and hauled her up, forcing a low, agonized moan to escape from her throat. Blackness blurred the edges of her vision as the excruciating pain in her shoulder threatened to overtake her. Daryl jerked her close to within inches of his own ugly, pockmarked features now contorted in anger. Jaw clenched, he snarled, "You like it rough?" He shook her when she didn't answer. "*I'll show you rough!*"

Her shirt easily ripped in two with one swipe of his hand. Natalie now knew, understood, what he intended. She fought like a crazy person, screaming over and over in her mind, *I'm going to Sarasota, I'm going to Sarasota,* while scratching and biting and kicking him wherever she could, until he once again threw her in a rage against the wall.

Her head hit first this time, unimaginable pain exploding behind her eyes, and she crumpled to the floor. *I'm going to die,* she thought dully as she lay unmoving on her side, the abrasive carpet under her cheek quickly absorbing the warm stickiness that flowed from her temple. She was only dimly aware of Daryl standing over her and then suddenly turning away and bellowing with renewed fury at Claudia's interruption, his hands reaching for Claudia's throat, before the black edges finally closed in and Natalie succumbed to the darkness.

Chapter One

Sarasota Springs, Florida
May 2011

"Why do you think that made you angry, Danny?" Natalie posed the question to the slender, dark-haired boy who sat across from her, watching as he intently drew designs with his fingers on the green suede fabric of the chair, only to erase them with a quick swipe of his hand.

Daniel Henderson was a sullen eight-year-old who had been referred to her by Judge Edwards of the Twelfth Circuit's Dependency Court several months earlier, and she'd just listened to him crossly recount the most recent incident in a long line of incidents that had eventually landed him here in her office. He had been in foster care for most of his life, transferring from family to family, and was quickly becoming too difficult to handle because of his ever-escalating behavioral issues. No wonder, Natalie thought. There was no stability or constancy in his life, nothing and no one he could count on.

Danny had recently been temporarily placed with Joe and Melinda Talbot, who were trying but clearly struggling to understand—and control—him. The Talbots already had two other troubled foster children in their home, and Natalie knew that wasn't always the best situation for a child like Danny. He needed less chaos, more attention. But it was the best the system could do until they could arrange for a more permanent solution. Good foster parents were few and far between, she knew.

It was one of the reasons Natalie willingly volunteered a significant portion of her time to these at-risk kids who were wards of the state or referred to her through the court system or local Community Alliance Center. At thirty-two, she had been doing this work for more than six years now, trying to help avert the train wrecks that were virtually inevitable in these young kids' lives, after having so narrowly avoided one in her own.

"Because they didn't believe me. I told them the *truth*, and they didn't believe me." Danny irritably answered her question now.

"Why do you think that upsets you so much?"

"I don't know." He slumped down further in the chair and continued to brood.

Natalie pushed a little harder. "Besides making you angry, how else did it make you feel when they didn't believe you?"

He thought for a minute, arms crossed defensively, his small hands hugging his elbows as he stared at the far wall. "I guess … I guess it feels like it doesn't matter what I say; no one really listens." He looked at her and then away again. "Or cares," he finished quietly.

And there was the heart of the matter. Unlike Natalie had been in her youth, wanting to disappear into the woodwork to avoid her mother's wrath, this child felt invisible but didn't want to *be* invisible. He wanted to be noticed, believed, loved unconditionally, and he did everything he could think of to accomplish that, even acting out.

"I can understand why you would feel that way, Danny." She sat forward in her own chair as she continued to gently talk to him. "But let's think about that for a minute. It's not totally true that *no one* listens or cares, is it? I'm listening to you right now."

He looked down at his hands. "You have to listen to me; it's your job."

Natalie smiled at his bowed head. "Well, it is true that this is my job, but I do it because I want to, Danny, not because I have to."

He glanced up at her, as if considering her words.

"Isn't it true that Mrs. Harris really cares about you? That she wanted you to stay with her, but you couldn't only because her disease was getting so much worse?" Natalie knew how hard that had been for Danny, to be moved from a home where he had just begun to feel truly wanted. "And Mr. and Mrs. Talbot must also care about you, or they wouldn't have made room for you to be a part of their family."

"They're only doing it for the money." Jaded far beyond his eight years, he looked away, discouraged again.

"No, Danny, they're not." She knew the Talbots, knew they were genuinely concerned about the well-being of the kids they took in. But she also knew that it would be awhile before anybody could convince Danny of that.

"Listen, Danny, I understand what it's like to feel invisible, like the world wouldn't even notice if you just disappeared. But we would notice, Danny. Mrs. Harris, the Talbots, and I, *we would notice*. We care about you. And I know it doesn't seem like it sometimes, but Ms. Reynolds cares about you too."

Gayle Reynolds was Danny's assigned caseworker, and she was often harried, overworked, and brisk in manner. But she was exceptionally good at what she did, and Natalie knew she would walk through fire for her kids.

"So that's five people right there. We could think of more, I'm sure." She glanced at the clock placed discreetly on the bookshelf behind Danny.

"So I'm going to give you an assignment. I want you to take a pencil and some paper and write down all the people in your life who really do care about you, despite how you feel sometimes— like your friends and your teachers. Do you think you can do that for me and bring it with you next time?"

Danny let out a big breath, though his head was still bent. "I guess."

"Look at me, Danny." He raised troubled hazel eyes to hers. She spoke with quiet conviction as she returned his gaze. "You are *not* alone. I'm here to listen, and I'll continue to be here. There are many other people in your life who also aren't going anywhere. Say it with me before you leave. *I'm not alone.*"

He rolled his eyes.

"Come on, please say it with me. *I'm not alone.*"

He grudgingly complied. "I'm not alone."

Natalie couldn't help but smile at him. "That's good, but now say it like you mean it."

She saw his gaze drop to her smile and his own lips curve ever so slightly in response.

"I'm not alone," he dutifully replied.

Her smile deepened. "See how just saying it helps? I want you to say those three words on regular basis this next week while you work on your list, okay?"

"Okay."

Natalie stood and started to walk to the door. "I'll go get Ms. Reynolds, and we'll see you next Thursday at the same time. Oh! I almost forgot!" She turned back to him. "Would you like to go to the Aquatic Center next Wednesday night? Some people I work with are having a pool party there and wanted to make sure I invited all my kids, which includes you." Natalie smiled. "In fact, Mr. and Mrs. Talbot and the whole family are invited. Lots of other kids your age will be there."

Her friend Hope Saunders at the local Victims Advocacy Center organized these pool parties three times a year using donations from the community and help from volunteers like Natalie.

Danny looked hopeful, but then his face suddenly fell. "I don't have any money to get in." He looked away. "Or a swimming suit."

"Oh, don't worry, Danny, it's free, and the Center has a stash of suits that kids can borrow. I'm sure we could find one that would fit you." She continued encouragingly, "I'll have Ms. Reynolds talk to

Mr. and Mrs. Talbot, and we'll see you all at the pool about seven o'clock next Wednesday night, okay?"

"Okay." Another timid smile snuck out in response. Natalie was determined to bring out that smile more and more.

"Okay, see you then, Danny—and don't forget your assignment." She opened her door and watched him walk over to Gayle and tell her eagerly about the swim party. It was a good sign.

Help me.

Natalie was suddenly still as Gayle and Danny waved at her and exited the small, tastefully decorated waiting room serving the suite that housed her counseling practice.

Please, help me.

Taking a deep breath, she turned and closed her office door behind her. It was time to listen again. Only this time the conversation would be with someone not of this world.

Natalie was what the parapsychology world called a mental medium. She had the gift of clairaudience, or the ability to hear the voices of those who had passed on. She couldn't see them when they talked to her, only hear them in her head.

Oh, she had definitely fought against it at first, had vainly tried to block the connection and throw up walls in her mind. It had scared her, plain and simple, until Bernie had helped her come to terms with it, to see it as something positive, one of the reasons she had been given a second chance all those years ago. Natalie still didn't fully understand why these spirits sought her out, nor was she always prepared when they did.

The first time she had been contacted had been shortly after she'd turned fifteen. She had been living with Bernie less than a year at that point. Natalie had thought she was going crazy and had even asked Bernie if she'd heard the voice. Thank God for Bernie and her pragmatic nature. She had simply asked Natalie what she'd heard, and Natalie had told her. And because Natalie had only lied to Bernie once when they'd first met, Bernie had chosen to believe her and looked into the details that Natalie had relayed, found they had potentially matched a recent crime, and told Natalie firmly that she needed to give her information to the police.

Natalie had vehemently argued with her. The police wouldn't believe her so easily, she knew. She had only been with Bernie for a short time, and Natalie was still afraid that the police, or someone else, would come and find her and take her away from Bernie.

So, when she wouldn't be swayed, they had settled on Natalie calling in an anonymous tip. Natalie had continued to handle things that way until she'd entered college, finally gaining confidence in who she was—*what* she was—and no longer feeling the need to hide it from the world. Over the years, as she had come to accept—even embrace—her psychic powers, she had learned how to keep out the negative energy and had honed her abilities to the point where not only could she hear these spirits, but they could hear her as well.

Natalie cleared her mind and channeled her thoughts to the spirit who was attempting to contact her.

I'm here, she communicated silently. Tell me how I can help you. Tell me who you are.

So cold.

I'm sorry. Why are you cold? What can I do to help you get warm?

Water … get me out of the water.

Natalie frowned. She didn't recall hearing about anyone who had recently been found in or near water.

What's your name?

Whitney. My parents … need to tell my parents.

Don't worry, Whitney, I'm sure your parents know. How old are you?

Fifteen.

Fifteen? This couldn't be the local girl who had been found just three weeks earlier, could it? Natalie recalled her name being Lauren, and she hadn't been found anywhere near water.

Please help me … it's so cold.

Natalie had a sudden vision of a small, lifeless arm, palm up and fingers slightly curled, lying upon rocks and undergrowth just above a water line, the rest of the body still submerged. Just as suddenly, the vision was gone. Had Whitney accidentally drowned, or had someone with a more sinister purpose attempted to dispose of her body in that fashion? Had her consciousness, her spirit, somehow gotten immersed in that feeling of being covered in ice-cold water?

Natalie didn't know if these souls that talked to her were trapped between their previous physical presence in this world and their spiritual presence in the next. She only knew they somehow managed to contact her wherever they were. Rarely, she might get a quick glimpse of a picture or snapshot in her head, as she did now, if their energy was strong, as it appeared Whitney's was. She could only make sense of it all by relating it to her own experience and how she had somehow managed to communicate with her friend Jenny when it had really mattered.

Talk to me, Whitney, Natalie silently urged the girl's spirit. Tell me what you know, and it will help you get warm. It will help you understand what's happening to you.

Am I dead?

Yes. I'm sorry.

I remember.

What do you remember?

Riding my bike ... a pickup following too close ... pedaling faster and faster ... it swerved and hit me. Oh God, it hurts so much. He's coming ... putting my bike in the back, lifting me ... can't fight back, but I can see him, know what he's doing ...

I know you were frightened, Whitney, but you don't have to be afraid anymore. If you can give me details, anything, we can make sure he never does this again.

Don't know who he is ... he's older, my dad's age ... greasy hair ...

That helps. Tell me anything else you can remember—how tall he was, what he was wearing, the kind of pickup he was driving— anything at all.

Black pickup, two rows of seats ... and an image, a symbol, that he ... that he ...

A symbol? Natalie frowned. That he what? Please describe the symbol to me, Whitney.

No, I can't ... I can't ...

Don't pull back yet, Natalie pleaded. I need more information. I need to know what the symbol looked like. I need to know if ...

Stark silence. Natalie knew the girl's spirit had retreated in the face of the horror that she had experienced. Despite her own troublesome thoughts, Natalie prayed that Whitney would return and provide more information that Natalie could relay to the police.

A black pickup with an extended cab. It wasn't much, but it was a start.

Add a middle-aged man with greasy hair, plus some kind of symbol—it still wasn't a lot to go on. *Unless you were Natalie Morgan,* she thought grimly.

She let out a cleansing breath, and pulled out her pen and pad, quickly noting the date, time, and details of the conversation with Whitney and her overall impressions. She then grabbed a new file folder from the drawer and labeled it, wishing not for the first time that she could just use a damn computer like everyone else. She'd even settle for a nice little digital voice recorder.

Going through the regular routine of it all helped relieve some of Natalie's underlying disquiet, though somehow she instinctively knew that this time, this case, could be more challenging than anything she'd ever dealt with.

꙰ ꙰ ꙰ ꙰

Natalie finished her notes, placed them in the file, and then placed the file in the cabinet and locked the drawer. Her last session of the day had been with Nicole—a.k.a. Nicki—Girardi, a sixteen-year-old runaway with a new juvenile record instead of the drug money she had hoped to net from the botched burglary. Now Nicki was in juvenile detention, court-ordered rehab, and mandatory counseling with Natalie.

Natalie sighed. She wished, as she so often did, that she could get to these kids *before* they reached the point where they were referred to her, so she could convince them there were better choices out there—and hope. What she did mattered, Natalie knew; it was just times like this that she had to believe it mattered enough—that it was making a difference, that it was what she was supposed to be doing.

She grabbed her purse from the bottom drawer of her desk, intent on stopping by Bernie's house to make sure she ate a good dinner before heading home to her own little bungalow a couple of blocks north on Warren. It was already after six o'clock on Thursday evening, and the staff had long since gone home, so she turned out the lights and locked the office up herself.

Morgan Counseling Services, LLC, was housed on the first floor of a two-story stately brick building that was part of a medical complex on Bee Ridge Road in Sarasota Springs. A discreet directory in the lobby informed clients and visitors of her suite number, and she still got a little thrill seeing her name—her business—listed there. When she had first looked at the space, she had loved the calming colors of the hunter green and mauve décor, and when she had learned from the property manager that a Starbucks, shopping center, *and* pizza place were within blocks of the complex, she had been sold.

Natalie exited the back doors of the building and headed to her beloved, reliable Honda waiting patiently for her in the employee parking section, her ignition key strategically gripped between her middle and forefinger, now an unconscious habit she had learned from the self-defense course she had taken years earlier at Bernie's insistence.

Bernie had insisted on a lot of things, actually. Like Natalie making her bed every morning. Drinking at least one full glass of milk a day. Eliminating all curse words—and she had not been a quick study on *that* one. Natalie grinned as she pulled out of the back lot onto Sawyer Road. Bernie was such a dear—an often cantankerous, crotchety old dear—but a dear nonetheless. And Natalie loved her with a fierceness that sometimes overwhelmed her.

It was because of Bernie that she was here, doing what she loved doing, and feeling lucky every day for it. It was because of Bernie that no matter how many times she traveled this route home, she would never stop appreciating the unique beauty and variety of palms adorning the yards on either side of the road—and all that those tropical trees had represented to her as a young girl. When she'd first escaped to Florida in search of her new place in the world, she had initially equated the trees with freedom; however, because of Bernie, they had eventually come to symbolize home to her. She had grown to love Sarasota as much as any person could love a place, and she would always associate the leafy palms with that quiet, steady sense of belonging Bernie had given her.

As Natalie turned right on Sunnyland—the street name a sure sign to her as a teenager—and into one of the more mature, tree-lined neighborhoods of the South Gate Ridge area where she and Bernie lived, she couldn't help but worry about Bernie now. She was getting on in years, having turned seventy-nine last October. Her hair was completely white now, all traces of black gone, but she was still as feisty as ever.

The memory of their very first meeting eighteen years earlier unexpectedly flooded Natalie's thoughts. It had been only days after Natalie had first arrived in Florida. She had a distinct image of the front door of the little blue house on Sloan Avenue opening, and a woman of about sixty, as best as Natalie could tell, squinting at her through dark-rimmed glasses. Her short, black hair had been only laced with gray then, her knitted sweater pulled tightly around her. She had frowned as she'd looked Natalie up and down.

"You the girl who called earlier about the room for rent?"

Natalie's mouth had instantly gone dry. "Yes, ma'am. I'm Natalie. Natalie … Smith." She had decided to change her name at the last minute when she had filled out the paperwork for the

McDonald's job only the day before, but she'd figured it was safe enough to keep her first name.

Bernie had continued to stare at Natalie with that intimidating, squinty-eyed stare. "I'm Bernice Morgan. Most people call me Bernie. I'll let you know when you can." Then she had paused for what seemed like an eternity. "You look mighty young. How old are you?"

"Eighteen, ma'am."

"Hmmmph." It had been more of a sound than a word. "You should know I don't usually rent to young people. Too much partying and drinking and drugs."

Natalie had quickly jumped on that. "Oh, you wouldn't have to worry about any of that with me. I'll be working most of the time, and I don't smoke or drink or do drugs, and I wouldn't have any friends over."

When Bernie didn't reply, Natalie had tried another tactic.

"I *really* need a place to live, ma'am." Which had been true, as her money had been quickly running out, and she had needed to get out of the Super 8 and fast. So she had put on her best doe-eyed look for Bernie and thought her voice had held just the right amount of earnest vulnerability.

"Oh, now don't go pulling that crap on me," Bernie had immediately responded. "I'm not some half-brained nitwit. If I rent the room to you, it'll be because I want to, not because you manipulated me into it."

Natalie had been totally taken aback, knowing then and there that Bernie was nothing like the suspicious police detective who had questioned her at the hospital shortly after the attack, or the caseworker she'd been assigned to as a result of her mother's death, and whom Natalie had ditched shortly after getting out of the hospital by convincing her to stop at the house so Natalie could get some "sentimental things"—namely, her stash of cash and the other unexpected, stroke-of-luck stash she'd found in her mother's room. They had been easy to fool, but not Bernie.

And apparently having decided she would take a chance on

Natalie, Bernie had held the door open wider and barked, "Well? Are you coming in or not?" So Natalie had walked through that door and into a different life.

Natalie wished now, not for the first time, that she could convince Bernie to come live with her, but Bernie staunchly held on to her independence, and knowing how important it was to her, Natalie didn't push too hard—yet. Eventually, though, it would have to happen, as Bernie's arthritis was getting worse with each passing year. Natalie hoped that when it did finally happen, Bernie would graciously—or at least as graciously as Bernie was able—let Natalie take her in as she had done for Natalie all those years ago.

Natalie pulled her Honda into the driveway of the little blue house with white trim and mature laurel oak trees, the only real home she had ever known, and parked behind the ancient Ford Fairlane Natalie had first learned to drive under Bernie's watchful eye all those years ago.

"Bernie, it's me!" she called as she opened the front door to the familiar scent of freshly cut flowers. A vase of vibrant red calla lilies sat on the coffee table in the front living room, a traditional room she had always loved with its huge picture window and dark wood floors.

"Where are you?" Natalie glanced down the hall on the left to the bedrooms as she walked through the formal dining room on her way to the vintage kitchen at the back of the house, with its sunny yellow walls, white cabinets, and recently installed dishwasher—a present from Natalie the previous Christmas. She had finally convinced Bernie that it wasn't laziness to have one, but rather a wonderful modern convenience; it had taken only a few days of using it for Bernie to harp at Natalie about why she hadn't had the decency to buy her one years earlier.

Natalie smiled at the memory as she looked out the kitchen window and saw Bernie shuffling around in the backyard among all her beloved perennials: ferns, irises, roses, and multiple varieties of lilies, among others—plants that didn't get trimmed and tended to as much as they used to but were still beautiful in their now wild, untamed glory. Though Natalie had tried, Bernie wouldn't let her hire a gardener to take regular care of the yard. It was *her* yard, she had groused, and nobody else was going to touch it.

She watched as Bernie stopped to lovingly caress a delicate pink daylily that was just starting to bloom. Those flowers were literally and figuratively a bright spot in Bernie's life. Natalie did what she could to keep that a constant, though she had never developed her own green thumb despite all of Bernie's efforts to teach her. She could identify many flowers and plants by name, but for the life of her, she couldn't make them grow and bloom like Bernie did.

Natalie opened the back door of the kitchen that led to the yard. "They're gorgeous, Bernie. You have—always did have—the magic touch."

Bernie turned at the words and smiled at Natalie. "That's right, missy, and don't you forget it. My only regret in life is that I couldn't pass it along to you."

"I know, I know. I guess my gifts lie elsewhere." Natalie gave Bernie a hand as she slowly climbed the back steps into the kitchen.

"How was your day? Did you finish the book you were reading? Did you take your pills?" Natalie started chatting as she washed her hands and then began pulling items out of the fridge and cupboards to prepare a quick dinner for them; otherwise, Bernie would likely forget to eat.

"Yes, I took my pills, child, and no, I didn't finish the book. I got sidetracked watching a movie on Lifetime." Bernie hobbled over to the coffee pot that she kept going throughout the day and poured some into the mug that sat nearby. Carefully, she carried the full mug over and sat down at the little table tucked into the alcove of the bright and cheery eat-in kitchen.

"Oh? What movie?" Natalie turned the oven on to preheat for the salmon fillets, one of Bernie's favorites, and then began preparing a quick side of prepackaged rice.

"A silly one, as it turned out. It made me mad I'd wasted my time on it." She took a sip of her coffee. "This crazy woman tried to murder her husband, and she kept messing it up, and the husband finally figured it out and worked with the police to fake his own death so she'd believe she had succeeded and they could catch her. Which of course they did, because she was an idiot." Her signature hmmmph followed. "Nobody knows how to write a good mystery anymore."

Natalie stirred the rice and grinned while her back was turned. How could you not help but love Bernie? She didn't mince words, was as brash and bold as a new copper penny, but underneath it all, she had a heart of gold that most people didn't get to see.

"Yes, sometimes the movies on Lifetime are good, and sometimes they're downright ridiculous. But that's entertainment, I guess. It runs the gamut." Natalie covered the fillets with a light sprinkling of mild spices, brown sugar, and a few dollops of soy sauce and placed them in the oven. "Why don't you just write your own and send it in?"

"Oh, don't be silly, girl. I could no more do that than fly to the moon."

"Why not? You always told me I could do anything I set my mind to." Natalie opened a ready-to-make Caesar's salad kit and poured the precut lettuce into a bowl.

"Which is true. It's just different for a grouchy old-timer like me."

This time Natalie hmmmph'd as she tossed the salad with the packets of dressing, Parmesan cheese, and croutons.

Bernie smiled behind her coffee cup, and then she suddenly sobered. "Honey, did you see the five o'clock news?"

"No, why?" Natalie glanced back at Bernie, hearing something else in her voice.

"They found another young girl today, only fifteen. The second one in three weeks."

Natalie's stomach tightened. "I suspected. A young girl contacted me today. Where did the news say they'd found her?"

"On the banks of Little Sarasota Bay near that wooded area off Highway 41."

This new victim had to be Whitney. Troubling thoughts again tumbled into Natalie's mind, but she determinedly pushed them aside.

"What else did the news say?" she asked casually, stirring the butter and herb flavored wild rice mixture. Bernie's stomach couldn't handle anything much spicier.

"Just that the police are considering this crime to be similar enough to the other one from a few weeks back to conclude that it could have been committed by the same person." Bernie watched Natalie, knowing just how difficult these cases could sometimes be for her.

Natalie placed the lid on the pot of rice and turned to Bernie. "If this is the same girl, her name is Whitney. She gave me some good information today that I'll pass along to Chief Garrett." Not wanting to worry Bernie, she pasted on a smile.

"This should be ready in just a few minutes. Let me use the restroom, then we can eat." Natalie started to leave the kitchen, and then she suddenly turned toward the table, leaned down, and gave Bernie a quick, tight hug. "I love you, Bernie."

A puzzled frown briefly crossed Bernie's face as she patted Natalie's arm. "I know, child, I know. I love you, too."

❧ ❧ ❧ ❧

The phone on Natalie's bedside table rang just before ten o'clock that night, jolting her from her musings. She could easily guess who it was, and took a deep breath. "Hello?"

"Hi, Natalie, it's Chief Garrett. Sorry to be calling you so late." Natalie would have recognized his gravelly, Sam Elliott–like voice even if he hadn't identified himself.

"Hi, Bill. It's no problem; I've actually been expecting your call." The chief of police of the Sarasota PD, Bill had also become a friend over the years.

"Yeah, I figured you would," he answered. "Listen, I'd like you to come into the station as soon as possible for a consult on this latest case. I'm sure you saw the news tonight about the second young victim."

Natalie took another slow, calming breath. "Of course. I can make it in first thing in the morning if that works for you. At eight o'clock, if that's not too early." She didn't have a session scheduled until ten.

"I'll make it work," he responded quickly. "I'm also checking to see if I can get the FBI agent assigned from their Sarasota CAC Unit to attend. We just got word today from the special agent in charge at their Tampa headquarters that they'll be lead on this."

The chief sighed, the sound clearly conveying his opinion, and frustration, at having to work with the feds. Natalie knew the chief felt their reputation was well deserved; in his words, they tended to treat local law enforcement like "hicks who had no clue" how to run an investigation.

Despite the chief's feelings, Natalie knew that the FBI, and especially the CAC—Crimes Against Children—unit in their Violent Crimes Division, was highly experienced in these matters. However, the flip side was that they didn't know her personally or know the type of support she provided to the Sarasota PD. Though the local force had reluctantly come to terms with her assistance, they were still, for the most part, uncomfortable with the whole thing and usually preferred to let the chief personally handle the cases where Natalie could provide information—and that was after five years of working with them. *A new FBI agent would not be so easily won over*, she thought wryly.

Even Chief Garrett had been understandably skeptical when the Sarasota PD Crimes Against Persons Unit had informed him of the special type of assistance Natalie provided. But she had ultimately convinced Bill that her abilities were real after he realized she was responsible for all those anonymous tips in years past, *and* after the information she had provided on the very first case they had worked on together had turned out to be spot on. Bill was now one of her staunchest allies and had come to rely without question on the information she provided.

"So I'll see you first thing in the morning, Natalie?"

"Yes, see you then. Oh, and Bill?"

"Yeah?"

"Were there ..." Natalie paused and closed her eyes, dreading to ask the question to which she suspected she already knew the answer. "Were there any markings found on either of the girls?"

Now the chief was silent for a moment. "Can we talk about it when you get here in the morning?"

Damn, damn, *damn.* "Certainly. Thanks, Bill. See you at eight."

Natalie hung up and allowed her head to fall back against the pillow—knowing tomorrow would come way too soon.

Chapter Two

Natalie quickly turned off Ringling Boulevard and into one of the few remaining visitor parking spots next to the plain, four-story brick building that housed the Sarasota Police Department. The city had tried to spruce up the exterior years ago with several strategically placed Florida red maples and Oriental arborvitae shrubs. Unfortunately, Natalie thought as she shut off her car, it still looked plain.

It was almost fifteen minutes after eight, and she was running late, having stopped at the office to take care of a few things only to receive an early morning distress call from Julia Vandermeer—of the *Parkland* Vandermeers, Julia would always emphasize—a client who'd been seeing Natalie since she'd first opened her practice. Julia had told Natalie after a couple of sessions that while it might be in a Vandermeer's blood to need psychotherapy, they also had a streak of loyalty a mile wide, and when they found a good therapist, they stuck. And Julia had. Now she was going through a rough patch with her husband, George, and he was talking divorce—and that just wasn't *done* in Parkland, Julia had tearfully told her.

Natalie had calmed her down, convinced her she didn't have to make any decisions today, and reminded her of their next scheduled session just several days later when they could talk at length. Natalie had then hustled out the door after telling Bailey, her receptionist, that she should be back by ten.

Now she was late for her meeting with the chief. Natalie grabbed her leather portfolio on the passenger seat containing her notes from the conversation with Whitney, hastily locked the car, and hurried down the sidewalk toward the front door of the building. The breeze, though welcome, wreaked havoc on her neatly styled hair as her low heels clipped at a rapid pace over the concrete. Frustrated, Natalie knew there was simply no time to use the restroom to make sure she looked halfway presentable, which she would have preferred for her first meeting with the FBI, rather than arriving late and looking like some frazzled, crazy person. But then they were probably going to end up thinking that anyway, so it really didn't matter.

Natalie reached the front entrance and paused for just a moment as she saw her reflection in the glass panels of the doors, running a hand over her shoulder-length bob and tucking the russet brown fly-aways behind her ears. She quickly tugged on the hem of her navy blazer and smoothed the fabric of her matching slim skirt, and then she took a deep breath before entering, having no idea she was being watched.

Officer Patricia Barnes sat at the front desk, a cheery fixture at the police department for as long as Natalie had been coming there.

"Hi, Pat, I have an appointment with Chief Garrett at eight. I know I'm a little late, but I got waylaid on my way out the office door. You know how it goes."

Pat smiled in response to Natalie's good-natured frustration. "Go right on up, Natalie. The chief's been expecting you."

Natalie thanked her and hurriedly walked to the door marked "Stairs."

Oh, to be young and beautiful again, *and* energetic enough to use the stairs, Pat thought wistfully as she watched the door close behind Natalie.

Pat was sixty-two with short hair that was perpetually henna red, plump in a pleasing, grandmotherly sort of way, and just about ready to retire. She had befriended Natalie early on when Natalie had started periodically coming to the station to meet with the chief, and Pat had initially been impressed that Natalie always remembered her name and had taken the time to say hi to her. But when Pat had gotten wind of the reason why Natalie was there, she had been totally won over.

Pat's own cousin in Biloxi, Mississippi, was a psychic, and the subject had always fascinated her, so Pat had felt an immediate kinship with the pretty Dr. Morgan as soon as she'd heard. Pat had even chewed out a few of the officers who had later scoffed about Natalie's "so-called" abilities, and word had gotten around that you just didn't talk about it in front of Pat unless you wanted to feel like you were back in the principal's office in grade school.

"Who was that?"

Pat turned at the brisk question to see an unfamiliar man in a conservative suit and tie. Not a bad-looking man. Actually, quite a hunk, Pat thought, the more she stared—he could easily be the January picture for the Fire Department's annual fund-raising calendar. The crisp white of his dress shirt was a stark contrast to his dark good looks, and his solid build, those arresting green eyes, and that appealing little dimple in the center of his chin only added to the package. And he was asking about Natalie, whom Pat knew was single. Now wasn't that interesting?

"I think the question is, who are *you*?" Pat asked as she looked at him pointedly.

He quickly flashed his badge. "Agent Jacob Riggs, FBI. I'm here to meet with Chief Bill Garrett." He returned her direct look, waited a moment, and then finally raised an eyebrow when she only continued to stare. "Do I pass muster?"

Pat grinned. He wasn't bashful, you had to give him that. "Lucky for you, I'm feeling particularly charitable today. I'm Officer Patricia Barnes, but you can call me Pat." Inclining her head toward the stairs, she said, "*That* was Dr. Natalie Morgan. She's a clinical psychologist, and she sometimes consults on cases for us."

Pat decided on the spur of the moment to let Agent Riggs

find out for himself the rest of the story, *and* the fact that he'd be meeting Natalie shortly. But wasn't it just the teeniest bit intriguing that he was curious enough to inquire about Natalie before he knew who she was? Pat decided to try to glean a bit more information from him.

"I detect the hint of a southern accent—where are you from, Agent Riggs?"

She noticed the quick, surreptitious glance at his watch before he politely responded. "North Carolina, originally, ma'am."

"Ah—a beautiful state," she replied, nodding. "Do you still have family there?" A wife? A girlfriend?

"My parents still live in Raleigh."

Pat smiled and bobbed her head again, but only a completely oblivious person could miss his barely veiled impatience at the conversation, and Pat had been working at this job way too long to fall into that category. "Well, I won't keep you any longer, Agent Riggs. Go right on up to the chief's office—he's on the second floor, room 215. I'm sure he's expecting you."

Pat pasted on her most professional smile as he thanked her and left. But secretly, she couldn't wait to hear the details of this meeting.

❧   ❧   ❧   ❧

Jake thanked the chief's administrative assistant on the second floor after she advised him they were waiting for him in the chief's office and walked toward the door she had pointed out. Her use of the word *they* had given Jake pause. He had understood from Special Agent in Charge Joe Stollmeyer that he was only meeting with the chief this morning to discuss the FBI assuming a lead role in the case and to request that copies of their case files be transferred to him. Who else would be attending?

He reached the partially open door of the chief's office and heard a woman's voice. Instinct had him listening a moment before announcing his presence.

"… already contacted by Whitney, Bill. Just yesterday. She told me a vehicle hit her while she was riding her bike. She was certain the driver had purposely struck her, and then he stopped and grabbed her and the bike. I got a very brief description—a middle-aged man near her father's age, maybe in his early forties, with greasy hair. She also described the vehicle as a black extended cab pickup. But then she faded before I could get anything else."

Are you *kidding* me? Jake listened in disbelief. Could this woman actually be talking about the latest young murder victim, Whitney Robertson? He knew that the parents had told authorities that their daughter had disappeared while riding her bike to a friend's house, but *come on*. Did this woman really expect them to believe that the victim had somehow just contacted her yesterday from the dead and told her that? What a crock.

Jake knocked purposefully, heard the deep, responsive "Come in," and fully opened the door, flashing his badge again, this time at the man sitting behind the large, dark wood desk. Presumably Chief Garrett, he looked to be in his early to mid-sixties and was an imposing man, even sitting down, Jake thought, with a thick head of shock white hair, matching trim mustache, and wire-rim glasses covering his startlingly blue, piercing eyes.

"Jake Riggs, FBI. Sorry I'm late." He shut the door behind him and turned and saw sitting next to the chief's desk the very woman he had earlier watched in interest hurry into the building—the clinical psychologist that the front desk officer had just identified. Shit. When he'd first seen her from across the street, he'd felt an instant and undeniable tug of attraction. She was definitely gorgeous, even more so up close, with her big brown doe eyes, smooth dark hair, and slender figure. It was just too damn bad that she'd turned out to be a gorgeous quack.

They both stood at the same time, the chief extending his hand over the top of the desk in greeting.

"Welcome, Agent Riggs. I'm Chief Garrett, but please call me Bill." The chief's deep, rough-edged voice was just as commanding as his physical appearance—Jake had no trouble imagining rank and file immediately reacting when that voice got authoritative.

The chief motioned toward the woman. "This is Dr. Morgan, Natalie Morgan. Natalie and I were just discussing the case. She's a local psychologist who provides periodic consulting services to the police department."

"Yes, I heard." Jake said this directly to her, again feeling oddly disappointed that she was so beautiful. Her deep brown eyes seemed to bore into his at his comment.

She extended her hand to him in greeting. "Nice to meet you, Agent Riggs. Please call me Natalie."

Jake lightly clasped her small hand, noticing how it all but disappeared in his, and then he felt a strange little shock, like a jolt of energy, run up his right arm, and he abruptly released her hand. What the hell was that?

The chief and Dr. Morgan sat down, so he shrugged it off and followed suit, taking the second chair next to her, and decided to jump right in.

"I overheard a portion of your discussion just before I came in. I'm not sure I completely understand." And that was about as diplomatic as he was going to get.

The chief responded first. "Ah, okay. Well, I had hoped to ease you into it a bit more slowly, but no matter. Natalie has some psychic abilities, and from time to time, victims contact her. She receives information from them that she's graciously supplied to us over the years. In fact, she's helped us solve a significant number of cases."

Jake didn't say anything, but he knew the skepticism he felt at the chief's comments was evident on his face.

Bill continued matter-of-factly, "I'm requesting that you work directly with Natalie on this case. She can provide valuable assistance to the FBI, such as grief counseling and assistance to your profilers, and she can relay any information to you that she might receive from the victims themselves. In fact, she's already received some initial information from the second victim, Whitney Robertson."

Jake finally responded after a glance at Dr. Morgan. "I have no problem with the counseling services or profiling assistance. I do, however, have a problem using or relying on information that can't be verified or proven."

"Oh, but that's where you're wrong, Agent Riggs. Natalie's information has consistently been proven accurate. Yes, it's after the fact, but it's accurate nonetheless. You'd be wise to use it in your investigation."

Jake heard the subtle command behind the chief's words. He rubbed a hand over his jaw, considering his response. Maybe he'd have to call Stollmeyer and request a reassignment. No way could he work with a self-proclaimed psychic ... *Svengali* on an investigation. He dealt in cold hard facts. Not in visions or premonitions or whatever the hell she might call them.

He cleared his throat. "No offense intended, Dr. Morgan, but I'm going to have a difficult time working with you on that aspect. As I said, I have no problem with you assisting otherwise. But maybe we could just agree that this ... other part of it be left here with the chief."

He watched Dr. Morgan slowly and deliberately cross her legs as she appeared to consider her response. "None taken, Agent Riggs. I've come across more than my fair share of close-minded individuals who just can't accept the fact that the world, and life and death, may not be so black and white." She stared at him for moment before she continued. "But here's the problem. I'm afraid I can't agree to leave this *other part* out of the arrangement. It's an essential piece of my consulting services, and you'll just have to learn to deal with it—or get another agent assigned to the case. Your choice."

Jake's eyes narrowed slightly as he considered her. She clearly wasn't a pushover. He could respect that. But he could also request that Agent Jeffery Hansen be placed on this case in his stead. Hansen was a greenhorn and much more likely to fall for this mumbo-jumbo bullshit. But in the meantime, Jake could play along.

"Understood. Why don't we table that discussion for now and talk known facts of the case and the FBI's role in it?"

The chief jumped right in. "Agreed. We should have the autopsy report shortly for Whitney Robertson. I've pulled Lauren Mackenzie's file as well—" he grabbed the two case files from his desk "—and you'll see the significant parallels between the two, age and looks for starters. It also appears that Whitney, just like Lauren, was sexually assaulted and died of strangulation, though we'll have to wait for confirmation of that from the autopsy."

He pulled a photo from each of the two files and placed them on his desk facing Natalie and Agent Riggs. "But here's the most interesting connection, though it hasn't been released to the media—and Natalie, this is what you asked about on the phone last night—each victim had a peculiar marking on her lower stomach, a symbol of sorts that we've not yet been able to identify. But the markings were very cleanly carved into the victims' skin with a sharp object, likely a small pocket or boning knife."

The chief looked directly at Agent Riggs. "You should know, Agent Riggs, that Natalie asked me this specific question on the phone last night, whether there had been any marks found on the bodies. She had no knowledge of this, no information from us that this was the case. I gathered from her question last night that one of the victims had somehow communicated this to her. Is that the case, Natalie?" They both turned to her.

Jake noticed she had gone still as a stone, her skin abnormally pale. He narrowed his eyes, instantly skeptical. Was she having some kind of psychic episode thing right now? God save him from the lunatics of the world.

"Natalie, what's wrong?" The chief was clearly concerned.

Jake watched her swallow convulsively. She was staring intently at one of the photos on the desk, and then she grabbed it and looked more closely at the picture of the symbol carved into Whitney

Robertson's stomach. "I've seen this symbol before. Or at least part of this symbol."

"Where?" Jake asked in interest as he sat forward in his seat. Now they were getting somewhere. This was the kind of fact that did solve cases.

Then she stood up and took off her suit jacket.

What in the hell? He watched in fascination as she proceeded to lay her jacket over the arm of the chair and then tug her white blouse free from the waistband of her skirt. She then reached around to lower the zipper at the back of her skirt.

The chief was apparently just as confused as Jake. "Natalie, what are you *doing?*" he asked.

"I'm showing you where I've seen that symbol." She raised her blouse out of the way and brought her skirt down to expose a broad expanse of her flat stomach.

Jake tugged at his tie, suddenly warm, wondering if he was going to see a full-blown strip tease or what. But he couldn't deny that she was sexy as hell, or that her creamy stomach looked as smooth as silk.

Then he saw it: the faint outline of an intricate scar on the lower left side of her abdomen. He jumped out of his chair and bent down beside her to get a closer look. The chief also quickly came around the desk to view the marking up close.

It was a myriad of complex lines carved into some sort of pattern and clearly not at random, but Jake could tell that it hadn't been finished. He grabbed the other photo from the desk and compared it to the scar on Natalie's stomach. To the extent that hers was complete, it matched the photo.

He and the chief both straightened up and looked at Natalie, stunned.

"I think you'd better tell us what this is all about, Natalie," Bill said as he sat down on the edge of the desk and waited while she mechanically tucked in her blouse, zipped her skirt, and sat back down.

She took several slow, deep breaths before she responded.

"When I was fourteen, I was attacked by my mother's boyfriend." Her eyes closed briefly and she took another deep, calming breath. "He ... he tried to rape me, and when I fought back, he threw me against the wall, and I hit my head and lost consciousness. He killed my mother when she got in the way, and then he started to carve this mark on my stomach with his knife." She paused and then looked directly at Jake.

"I know this because I watched him do it, watched him choke my mother to death, then engrave this ... this symbol on me while my spirit, or soul, or whatever you want to call it, had separated from my body. And while I was in that suspended state, I was somehow able to telepathically communicate with a childhood friend who quickly called 911 for me."

Her eyes all but dared Jake to challenge her statement before she continued.

"The police arrived at our house before he could finish, but he escaped out the back and was never brought to justice as far as I know. I was resuscitated by the paramedics but remained in a coma for several days afterward as a result of brain trauma. When I finally came out of it, I was told I had been clinically dead that night for at least eight minutes. The doctors were amazed that I had apparently suffered no permanent damage, other than this scar I carry. I've just been ... waiting all these years, I think, for him to find me and finish it."

Jesus. This was getting weirder by the second. Jake couldn't figure out how she could have an old scar on her stomach that clearly matched the new scars on these recent victims unless it *was* the same guy. And *if* it was, at a minimum, he'd have to be in his late thirties or early forties by now.

"When and where did this happen?" Jake figured he could at least get some hard facts out of her and pull a few strings to get a copy of that old case file.

"Eighteen years ago. I was living in Smyrna, Tennessee. It should all be there in the file when you review it, Agent Riggs, which I know you're going to. The police report, the composite sketch I helped them generate while I was in the hospital, everything I knew about him. Which wasn't much more than his first name."

She clearly wasn't stupid. She had known right away he would gravitate toward the old file. Jake looked at her closely now and could suddenly see how deeply this was affecting her. Shit. He ran a hand over his face.

"Why don't we take a break," he offered. "I'll make arrangements to get a copy of that old file, and we can meet again on Monday and finish this discussion."

The chief quickly agreed. "That's a good idea, Agent Riggs. Natalie, why don't I have one of the officers take you back to work? Or maybe you'd just rather ..." The chief stopped abruptly as he considered her for a moment, his brows furrowing.

"You realize, Natalie, that if you decide you still want to assist on this case—which I emphasize is totally up to you given this rather ... unexpected turn of events—we're going to have to keep your involvement tightly under wraps. If you *are* personally connected to this, we can't risk your safety by letting the press, or the perp, get wind of it."

Jake silently agreed with the chief on that, but Dr. Morgan hesitated for a moment before she responded.

"Thanks, Bill, but it's not necessary to have someone drive me back to the office. My car is right outside. I do appreciate your concern, but I've been taking care of myself for a long time now. I won't do anything stupid."

"Are you sure you'll be okay?" The chief asked, apprehension readily apparent on his face as he stared at her.

She smiled faintly at the chief's persistence. "I survived death all those years ago, Bill. I think I can handle this." She stood, grabbed her jacket from the chair, and pulled a business card from her portfolio, turning to Jake before leaving.

"Here's my business card with my office number. Both my home number and one other number where you can reach me are on the back. I don't use a cell phone or a pager."

Who in this day and age didn't use a cell phone? Jake wondered as he silently pulled out his wallet, placed her card there, and handed her one of his own.

Natalie accepted it and then paused as she studied his face. "Well, Agent Riggs, I think your black and white world is about to get tipped on its axis."

She turned and left, and for the life of him, he couldn't stop his eyes from briefly dropping to her unmistakably sexy ass as she exited the room. Then he suddenly realized that both she and the chief were right—this was an extremely interesting turn of events. Maybe he wouldn't request that reassignment after all.

Chapter Three

As Jake negotiated traffic on the short half-mile drive from the station back to the local FBI resident agency on Second Street in Sarasota's busy downtown district, he was torn between cynicism and fascination. Dr. Natalie Morgan was certainly not your average psychologist. She wasn't even your average woman. He could admit to himself that he was physically attracted to her. She was the kind of beautiful that had men stopping in the street to stare, only to get slugged in the arm by their companion. She was also smart and apparently tough enough to have survived the ordeal that she had. But he just couldn't get past the weird stuff. Okay, fine—the *paranormal* stuff. It just didn't fly.

But what was really fascinating to him was the inescapable connection between Dr. Morgan's incident all those years ago and the current murders. He didn't think he'd ever worked on a case where a piece of the puzzle had shown up after eighteen years.

He took a quick left from Washington onto Main, with its vibrant mixture of high rises, restaurants, shops, and nightclubs, and couldn't stop the *if only* that ran through his head without warning—*if only* this was his sister's case. What he wouldn't give to have a clue show up after all these years, a clue that would finally allow him to solve her murder and put away her killer once and for all.

Jess. Even after all these years, the pain could still slam into him like a freight train whenever he thought of her. She had been brutally raped and murdered as a young girl more than sixteen years earlier. He'd come back from college the summer of his junior year to stay with her at their family home in Raleigh, while his parents had taken a short vacation. At thirteen, she had already considered herself a woman of the world and had argued with him that she didn't *need* watching, that she could just stay with friends, and he could go back to his. He'd just laughed at her and told her to dream on, and she'd stomped off in anger. If only ... hell, it did no good to go back there now.

But he'd never given up on his quest to find her killer. The year of Jess's murder, he'd switched majors from business to criminal justice and had immediately joined the FBI upon graduation, initially being assigned to the Violent Crimes Division here in Sarasota before eventually requesting a specific assignment to the Crimes Against Children unit when he'd turned thirty. With CAC for eight years now, he was a well-respected member of the unit and a driving force behind its collaboration with local and state law enforcement agencies in quickly and effectively investigating and prosecuting crimes against children. By systematically putting these predators behind bars, Jake hoped he could somehow prove to Jess that he hadn't forgotten her, even if he couldn't put *her* killer there.

He shook off his thoughts and pulled into one of the FBI-designated ground floor spaces in the parking garage behind the multistoried brick complex that housed not only the local FBI offices, but also law firms, court reporting agencies, and other similar businesses. The light breeze that teased him as he locked his standard issue sedan and walked to the back entrance of the building was insufficient to combat the already humid heat of Sarasota in May, and he was thankful for the cool blast of air-conditioning that hit him as he walked through the back doors. Punching the ninth floor elevator button for the East Building, he intended to contact the Smyrna Police Department to request a copy of Dr. Morgan's old case file as soon as he got to his desk.

When he hung up the phone forty-five minutes later, he'd found out that not only had Natalie Morgan once been Natalie Brennan, but that her mother had, in fact, been murdered—choked to death just as she'd described—in the same incident, and that Natalie had disappeared shortly thereafter. They had found unidentified fingerprints in the home but no other forensic evidence and had never been able to track down any suspect who'd matched either the prints or the composite sketch, so the mother's murder had never been solved. After being unable to locate Natalie after she'd gotten out of the hospital, they had eventually labeled her as just another runaway and transferred the entire matter to their cold case files.

Given the change in her name and that the case had been closed for so many years, the fact that Jake had learned anything at all was a sheer stroke of luck. Captain Donohue, a veteran cop who had been on the Smyrna force at the time of the crime, happened to be there when Jake called and had remembered the case because murders in Smyrna had been few and far between back then. He had even recalled interviewing the young Natalie in the hospital when she'd regained consciousness several days after the attack. He had not been able to get anything worthwhile out of her at the time, but she had agreed to work with the sketch artist and they had generated a composite drawing of the suspect. When they'd gone back to interview her a second time after she'd fully recovered, she had been nowhere to be found.

Captain Donohue had advised Jake that he'd pull the old case file from their unsolved archives and send a scanned copy to him, and Jake was waiting for the e-mail with the attached documents now. His thoughts turned back to Captain Donohue's comments about Natalie when she had been Natalie Brennan.

Apparently, she'd had a hard home life. No identified father, and an absentee, addict mother who had likely physically abused her for many years. Jake's respect for her raised a notch, as she had clearly turned her life around from that dismal situation to where she was now. He wondered how she had managed to accomplish it. Running away at fourteen and not ending up a prostitute or hooked on drugs was a major miracle. He realized he'd be interested in hearing her story.

At least the part *after* she had supposedly floated around like a damn ghost while the perp had marked her. Why did the woman have to throw all that psychic bullshit at him? There was just no way she could have remained conscious through that kind of trauma. She had probably just hallucinated while she was losing consciousness and had convinced herself she had actually seen the guy carve that bizarre symbol on her stomach.

On her sexy-as-hell stomach, he amended. An image of that smooth expanse of skin flashed through his mind, his own hand slowly sliding across …

The beep on his computer interrupted that troubling train of thought, indicating the e-mail had finally come in. He quickly opened the message and clicked on the attachment. The police report came up first, which he skimmed for now and then scrolled to the next document. It was a grainy picture of Natalie at fourteen. Jesus, she'd been skinny. With huge dark eyes and long brown hair. Something stirred in him that he couldn't quite recognize. Pity? He didn't think so. But he felt it grab hold of him as he stared at the picture of this slip of a girl that she had been.

He picked up the phone before he realized what he was doing and dialed the chief.

"Chief Garrett."

"Chief, it's Agent Riggs. We need to coordinate some protection for Dr. Morgan. I've reviewed the old police report, and this is just a little too coincidental for my comfort. I don't want to take any chances. I'll see what strings I can pull to get some protection from the Bureau. If you could help, we could probably manage sufficient coverage between the two of us."

"Agreed. I'll get to work on it right now," the chief responded. "But Agent Riggs, if I were you, I wouldn't mention this to Natalie.

I know her, and I know she'd object to our taking such a paternal attitude."

"Thanks for the heads up. I'll be in touch." Jake hung up and felt oddly relieved. Then he went back to the file, pulled up the old composite sketch and unidentified fingerprints, and forwarded them on to Agent Hansen to have the prints run back through IAFIS, the FBI's Integrated Automated Fingerprint Identification System, just in case this guy had messed up somewhere down the road. Then he'd get Frank Bronstein, their sketch artist, to create an updated, aged drawing. Stay busy with the facts, he told himself as he dialed Frank's number, and just ignore the psychic bullshit.

Back at the police station, the chief replaced the telephone receiver in its cradle, and realized he was worried—really worried—about Natalie, both professionally *and* personally. Though he didn't make it known around the station, he had somehow allowed her to worm her way into his tough old heart over these past few years and because of it, had no doubt this new development in the case would cause him some serious heartburn in the coming weeks.

Smoothing his mustache with his thumb and forefinger—a nervous habit he'd never been able to break—he decided he'd have a cruiser follow Natalie home tonight, though technically, she lived just outside their patrol area in the County Sheriff's jurisdiction. But hell—he was chief of police, wasn't he, and authorized to exercise his reasonable discretion when warranted? He felt the first twinge of pain in his esophagus, and pulled the role of antacids from his pocket before he went to work arranging for the extra coverage.

❧ ❧ ❧ ❧

Natalie was still irritated on her way to Bernie's that evening, but the smell of Chinese takeout permeating the Honda was helping. A little, anyway. What she couldn't figure out was *why* she was still irritated. It wasn't like she hadn't come across people like

Agent Riggs before. She knew firsthand that there were plenty of individuals in the world who, if they couldn't observe something with one of their five senses, simply assumed it didn't—or couldn't—exist. It was just her luck that Jake Riggs appeared to be one of those people.

As she thought back on their meeting, Natalie wasn't entirely sure she had detected a southern accent in his voice, subtle as it had been, but there had been nothing subtle about the derision she'd heard there. Hadn't she told herself that very morning to expect such a response?

But did the man have to be so ... overwhelmingly male? He had been tall, several inches over six feet, she'd estimated, and with shoulders so broad his suit jacket had pulled tightly against them when he'd shaken the chief's hand. His thick, black hair had been trimmed military short, his shrewd green eyes framed by brows of the same deep ebony. The faint cleft she'd noticed in his chin had only served to further highlight his firm mouth and strong jaw. His face had just been entirely too rugged, too masculine, for any woman's peace of mind.

In the chief's office this morning, however, his striking features had been schooled in an expression that could not entirely hide his disdain. God, she had wanted to blow his condescending attitude—and ignorance—right out of the water. But she had never used her abilities to impress people or for shock value, so she had done her best to remain professional in his presence. Unfortunately, she hadn't been as successful the rest of the day, as bits and pieces of the conversation had continued to intrude into her thoughts after she'd gone back to work.

Pulling into Bernie's driveway, she made the conscious decision to put it all out of her mind, have a nice meal with Bernie, and then go home, kick back, and continue with the latest Ken Follett novel she had recently started. She grabbed the still-warm bags of food and went inside.

"Bernie, I've got sesame chicken, just how you like it!" Natalie walked into the kitchen to find Bernie sitting at the table concentrating fiercely on a crossword puzzle and chewing on the end of her pencil.

"Boy, that smells good. What's a five-letter word for 'annoyed' and starts with an 'R'?"

Natalie had to laugh. "Riled?"

Bernie glanced up at her. "What's so funny?"

"Oh, only that that's exactly how I felt at the police station today." Natalie unpacked the cartons, chopsticks, and paper napkins and placed them on the table, and then grabbed some plates and glasses out of the cupboard.

"Really? Why?" Bernie put down her pencil and gave Natalie her full attention.

"Well, I met with the chief this morning about the case, to let him know what I'd learned from Whitney yesterday, and while I was there, I had the pleasure of meeting the FBI agent who will be handling the case." Natalie put the plates and glasses on the table and returned to the fridge for the pitcher of tea.

Bernie opened the cartons of aromatic chicken and started dishing up. "Why do I get the distinct impression that there was nothing pleasurable about it?"

Natalie smiled as she sat down and filled their glasses. "You know me too well. He was just so ... so ..."

Bernie raised an eyebrow. "So *what?*"

"Irritating. Obnoxious. Arrogant. Take your pick." Natalie grabbed her chopsticks and forcefully grabbed a piece of chicken. "He made it clear he doesn't believe in psychics or the paranormal, or anything that isn't a cold hard fact he can wrap his big hands around. And he had the gall to say that he couldn't—or maybe wouldn't, I'm not sure—work with me on that aspect of the case."

Bernie watched as Natalie stabbed at another piece of chicken. "So was he cute?"

Natalie stopped and gaped at her. "*What?*"

Bernie replied calmly, "I said, was he cute?"

Natalie sputtered for a moment. "I ... he ... what kind of question is that? Why does that matter?"

"If you can't answer the question, child, maybe it matters more than you think." Bernie smiled placidly as she scooped up a mouthful of pork-fried rice.

The ringing of the telephone hanging on the kitchen wall interrupted Natalie's response, and she got up to answer. The caller ID read "Private."

"Hello?"

"Dr. Morgan?"

"Who's calling, please?"

"This is Agent Riggs, FBI. I tried calling your home number first." He paused. "It's good to know you field your calls like a cautious woman." When Natalie didn't say anything, he cleared his throat and continued.

"Listen, we need to schedule a time tomorrow to meet with the chief again. I know it's a Saturday, but I've thoroughly reviewed your old file and the current files, and we have a lot to discuss. I don't want to waste anymore time."

Natalie almost rolled her eyes but managed to stop herself just in time. She wouldn't allow herself that little bit of childish satisfaction. Besides, Bernie would see and wonder why, and question her to no end.

"Fine. What time?" She knew she sounded brisk.

"We can work around your schedule, Dr. Morgan. You tell me what's good for you."

What's good for me? Natalie thought with a silent laugh. What's good for me is if you suddenly developed a severe case of poison ivy and …

"Dr. Morgan?"

Natalie jerked and glanced over at Bernie, who was munching on her food and watching Natalie with interest. Oh brother. It was inevitable. Bernie was going to question her to no end.

"Uh, sorry, I'm a bit distracted tonight. How about right after lunch—say one o'clock?"

"Okay, fine, we'll see you then at the chief's office. Oh, and Dr. Morgan?"

Natalie couldn't help but bristle. "Agent Riggs, I thought I told you to call me Natalie."

There was another slight pause on the other end. "All right. I just wanted to clarify, *Natalie*, that we won't be discussing any of that … that mind reading stuff tomorrow. Just so you know."

Oh, *really?* "Well, I should also clarify, Agent Riggs, that I don't technically *do* mind reading stuff, or tell the future or bend spoons. Just so you know. Good night." She hung up.

She looked over at Bernie and saw her smirk. "Don't even go there."

Bernie raised her hands in mock surrender. "I didn't say a thing."

Natalie sat back down and attacked her chicken.

❧ ❧ ❧ ❧

Pat Barnes was not at the front desk when Natalie got to the station on Saturday afternoon. Instead, a distracted uniformed officer who was talking on the phone waved her through without so much as a smile. As she climbed the stairs, Natalie made a mental note to tell the chief what a gem he had in Pat.

Walking toward the chief's open door, she heard a low voice and realized Agent Riggs was already there. Damn. She'd hoped to have a conversation with Bill about him first—well, it just would have to come later. She tugged on the hem of her crisp pink blouse to make sure it lay smoothly over the casual gray slacks she wore, checked the tortoiseshell clip holding her hair in place at the nape of her neck, and then knocked lightly and entered the room.

"Good afternoon, Bill. Agent Riggs." She sat down and immediately noticed the large chart that lay across the chief's desk and looked at Bill expectantly.

"Hi, Natalie, thanks for coming in on a Saturday." He smiled apologetically. "Agent Riggs was just advising me that their sketch artist is working as we speak on aging the composite drawing of the suspect that you helped generate eighteen years ago. It should be ready shortly, and then we'll send both sketches out to all the FBI field offices as well as local, county, and state law enforcement."

He then pointed to the chart.

"Jake also prepared this last night to document the specific parallels between the three cases, yours included. This is what he'd like to discuss today."

Natalie finally turned to Agent Riggs—she wasn't quite ready to acknowledge him as Jake, as Bill just had—only to find him staring at her with narrowed eyes. Her chin raised a notch and she held his gaze even as she felt her cheeks uncharacteristically heat.

He finally broke the eye contact and turned to the chief. "That's correct, Bill," he said as he propped up the chart and began to go through the information.

"As you can see, I've listed the pertinent categories that I examined last night in going over the files. Age appears to be a critical factor for this guy, as two victims were fourteen and the third had just turned fifteen at the time of attack." He stopped and looked at Natalie. "And pardon me, Dr. Morgan—Natalie—if I appear to refer to you as though you're not in the room. It's not intentional; it's just easier to discuss the facts that way."

He went back to his chart before Natalie could respond. *Fine,* she thought irritably.

"Additionally, you'll see these photos clearly indicate that he has a 'type,' which includes long dark hair, dark eyes, and generally similar facial features, as well as comparable body height and weight."

Jake continued matter-of-factly as Natalie watched him knowledgeably articulate his points. "The sexual assault and cause of death—strangulation—are also interesting correlations and will have some meaning to him, though he clearly didn't get that far with Natalie." He briefly glanced at her again.

"Now let's talk about the symbol. I've already sent the photo image of it as it appeared on the two recent victims to all the regional FBI field offices and law enforcement agencies with a request to be contacted immediately if it shows up in any way, shape, or form. This symbol is the clear signature of the suspect, and to him it represents something intimately connected to his motivation to kill these girls. I believe if we find out what the symbol represents, or where it comes from, we find our killer."

Jake laid the chart back down. "Our profiler is currently working with all of this information to generate a profile we can use—which, as I indicated previously, Natalie, you're more than welcome to assist on. I've also got another agent checking our system for any cases in the southeastern United States within the past twenty years with a similar set of facts. Finally, you should know that in Natalie's old case file, there were some unidentified fingerprints from the scene, and we ran those back through IAFIS, but unfortunately, there's still no match. This guy's either been very lucky, or very careful."

"Thanks, Jake," the chief replied. "Did you find anything at this second crime scene? I know our unit was extremely frustrated at the distinct lack of evidence recovered from the scene of the first victim."

"So far, our forensic team has found nothing of any value," Jake responded. "This perp appears to know what he's doing, especially if he's somehow managed to avoid detection for almost twenty years."

Natalie sat listening to this exchange, knowing it wasn't necessary to contribute and that even if she did, Agent Riggs would probably …

Go to the scene.

Her thoughts abruptly cleared. Whitney?

Yes. Go to the scene. It's there.

What's there?

The evidence they need.

What evidence? She waited, but heard nothing further, so she turned to Bill and Agent Riggs and quickly interrupted their conversation.

"Agent Riggs, I need to go back to the scene where Whitney Robertson was found. Today. Right now."

Jake stopped talking and looked at her warily. "I don't think that's necessary."

Bill jumped in. "Actually, Jake, it might help. Natalie can sometimes get valuable information when she's at the location where the victim is found."

Natalie watched as Jake rubbed the back of his neck in obvious frustration.

"Fine. I'll take you there," he said briskly. He grabbed the chart and looked impatiently at Natalie. "Ready?"

Natalie stood up and glanced at Bill, silently communicating an "Oh, brother" and telling him thanks with her eyes. The chief winked back.

❧ ❧ ❧ ❧

Thankful she was wearing her flats, Natalie navigated slowly back and forth among the rocks, dirt, and underbrush at the edge of Little Sarasota Bay where they'd found Whitney's body. After a tense ride there in Jake's car, during which she had stared out the window while feeling the waves of animosity rolling off of him, it was almost a welcome relief to be out into the fresh air—even if it had involved a hike of several hundred feet through dense foliage and uneven ground to get to the actual crime scene. She could certainly see why the killer had chosen this site, as the thick cover of trees and lack of nearby homes or businesses made it the perfect site to dump a body.

Natalie had no idea what she was looking for; she was just hoping to see something, anything, and waiting for some additional communication or direction from Whitney. She had been here for fifteen minutes and knew Agent Riggs was prowling around in frustration at her unquestionable lack of success.

She knew she should give up. She just wasn't getting anything. But she did *not* want to admit that to him. If only she could …

The sudden image flashed through her mind and was gone just as quickly—an image of the symbol, the killer's signature, only in glowing, shining gold. What did that mean? She started looking at everything more closely, the ground, the shrubbery, the trees, going through the possibilities in her mind, totally oblivious to Agent Riggs now.

Jake had realized on the drive to the crime scene that he just wasn't going to be able to avoid this weird shit. Fine. So be it. He'd let her do her chanting or rituals or whatever it was she needed to do. He just didn't have to like it.

As he stood at a distance and watched her pace back and forth over the rough ground, he recognized that part of his frustration stemmed from the fact that he just couldn't figure her out. She looked about as fresh and pure as a bowl of strawberries and cream, but she obviously had the mind of a psych ward patient. It just didn't add up—or maybe, he acknowledged, he just didn't want it to add up. He wanted her to be a regular, ordinary, run-of-the-mill woman, so he could …

Jake suddenly realized she was muttering to herself and wondered what in the hell had gotten into her now. Had the girl's ghost talked to her again? *Please*. He was beginning to feel just a bit fed up with this entire charade and decided to call her on it.

"Are you getting anything?" he called to her.

Natalie stopped and turned to look at him suspiciously. "Yes, actually I am."

"Do you need to perform a ceremony or something?" He tried to maintain an innocent look, but knew he'd failed when she growled in frustration and turned away.

"Just calling 'em like I see 'em, sweetheart." He couldn't resist that final dig, though he wasn't sure why he felt compelled to needle her.

Natalie turned on him at the comment, her sudden anger palpable.

"Don't you call me *sweetheart*, you arrogant ass!" She walked purposefully over to him and thumped his chest soundly with her forefinger. "You have no *idea* what it's like to have to live with this, to feel obligated to use it to help people, only to have those very people you try to help throw it back in your face!"

Jake's eyes widened a bit at her unexpected vehemence, and he quickly raised his hands and called a truce. "You're right, you're right—that was uncalled for. Please accept my apologies." He smiled ruefully. "It's just that this whole thing is so far outside my frame of reference, I don't know how to respond to it."

She turned away for a moment, inhaling deeply. "Please accept my apologies as well," she responded finally. "I'm not sure what just came over me." She turned back to him, her eyes puzzled.

Jake watched as her gaze moved slowly over his face, her beautiful brown eyes clearly reflecting some thought process going on in her mind. Damn it, she *was* beautiful. His right hand suddenly itched to reach up and stroke her smooth cheek, to rub the pad of his thumb across her lower lip. Her lips. His eyes stopped there. Soft, generous, slightly parted lips that looked like they were just waiting to be kissed.

The atmosphere around them suddenly changed, as if the air had become charged with electricity. As they stared at each other, Jake realized there had just been a subtle shift of some kind, a silent acknowledgement of sorts from her of the underlying, unspoken attraction he felt. Then Natalie cleared her throat and the moment was gone.

"Again, I'm sorry for my unacceptable behavior, Agent Riggs. I promise it won't happen again—if you promise to keep your comments to yourself." She smiled wryly at him and stuck out her hand. "Deal?"

He took her hand. "Deal." But damned if there wasn't that small little jolt that ran up his arm again. He wondered what the hell would happen if he really did kiss her.

Natalie dropped her hand and looked back out over the scene. "Look, Jake, here's the truth. I saw an image of the symbol in my head, only it was carved in gold. I'm not sure what that means, but I know something is here that Whitney wants me to find. I guess

I just won't be finding it today." She sighed. "We should go." She turned to walk back to his car.

Jake heard both the sincerity and disappointment in her voice and suddenly realized that she truly believed what she was saying. He felt compelled to make one more peace offering.

"I'll tell you what—I'll have a couple of folks from forensics comb the area one more time just to make sure."

She stopped and turned to look at him in surprise. "You'd do that?"

"Sure—who knows? We might uncover some more cold, hard facts." He grinned and winked at her as they walked back to the car together.

Chapter Four

Natalie booted up her office computer that Monday morning and clicked on the calendar, saying a tiny prayer for it to cooperate. She kept everything she did backed up with hard copies, even her calendar, because she couldn't always rely on electronic equipment to work properly around her. Some days, things went more smoothly than others, but this apparently wasn't going to be one of them, as the calendar blinked once and then froze in the middle of opening.

She resignedly got out her day-timer and checked her schedule for the day, and then she suddenly smirked at the unbidden thought that flashed through her mind—if only Jake Riggs could be more appreciative of her magnetic qualities.

She leaned back in her chair. Why couldn't she stop thinking about him? Yesterday, Bernie had peppered her with questions when they'd taken an early morning walk around the neighborhood to avoid the heat of the day, asking her about the case and the FBI agent who'd put her in such a "twitter" after the phone call on Friday evening. Natalie had downplayed the whole thing, replying vaguely that they were trying to work through their differences and treat each other professionally.

Only Natalie knew it was her personal and not professional thoughts of Jake that were causing the problems. She couldn't get his face out of her mind—the image of those glittering green eyes surrounded by thick, inky lashes looking at her as they had on Saturday was permanently imprinted on her brain.

She still couldn't quite believe he had been able to get such an intense, angry reaction from her at the crime scene. As she had puzzled over it on Saturday immediately following his apparently sincere apology, she had chastised herself—she was a psychologist, for crying out loud. She was in the *business* of understanding people. How could she have just lost control like that? Then she had suddenly realized that one of the things that drew her to him was his competence and ability to make her feel safe—and she had at once understood that his ridicule bothered her so much because she believed in his competence, and she wanted him to believe in hers as well.

But when his eyes had suddenly darkened, and he'd looked at her that way—in a way no woman could misinterpret—she had felt an immediate, reckless response vibrate through her. She had known instantly, however, that a relationship of that kind just couldn't happen. They were professionals working together on a case. That was all.

And she had continued to tell herself that over the weekend. But last night, as she had thought once again of his parting offer on Saturday, and how he could definitely be just the teeniest bit charming when he wanted to be, she had finally admitted to herself she would be in serious trouble if he ever turned that charm on her in full force. Especially given that she didn't have that much experience with men.

Sure, she had found other men attractive, and had even dated a few of them, but once they got to know her and realized she was "special," as one gentleman had awkwardly put it, they pretty much turned tail and ran one hundred and eighty degrees in the other direction. She had eventually given up on ever finding someone to accept her for who she really was and had learned to content herself with Bernie, her friends, and her work.

The fact that Jake was having the same reaction to her abilities as everyone else had but couldn't turn and run because of his commitment to the case didn't make her feel any better. If only they had assigned an agent with more of an open mind.

Ironically, she realized it was just as Danny had said—she'd told the truth and still hadn't been believed. It really did leave a person feeling as though the other person wasn't truly listening—or just didn't care. She'd just have to remain true to herself and show Jake that she wasn't a fraud or a fluke. Maybe if she was instrumental in solving the case, he'd look at her in a different light.

And the symbol was the key to the case, he'd said.

She took out a pad and pen and drew the full mark from memory over and over again. She broke it down by drawing each line separately and then layering them one over another in different orders, trying to decipher a pattern from within the strange design.

It was no use—it just didn't mean anything to her. Yet. She glanced at her clock on the shelf across the room and realized she'd better get to work. One thing she absolutely couldn't let happen was for the case to interfere with her clients.

❧ ❧ ❧ ❧

"Why the hell don't you carry a cell phone? If you're working on this case, I need to be able to reach you at all times." Natalie replayed Jake's impatient message once again that afternoon, which said he'd called every number she'd given him without success, and that she was to call him back "immediately" upon getting the message. She couldn't help but smile at his obvious frustration. It would do him good to find out that not everyone asked "how high" as soon as he yelled "jump."

She pulled out his card and dialed his cell number from her office landline. He answered on the first ring.

"Jake Riggs."

"Agent Riggs, it's Natalie Morgan returning your call."

"It's about damn time. I've been trying to get in touch with you for the last two hours."

"I'm sorry. I do work for a living, you know." She bit her lip to try to keep from smiling, though she couldn't have said why she found it so funny.

"We need to get you a cell phone, at least while you're working on this case. I need to be assured that I can reach everyone at the drop of a hat if necessary."

Interesting. She was being included with "everyone" who worked on the case. It could be deemed progress. Unfortunately, her next statement would probably negate that progress. "I'm afraid that's not possible, Jake," she replied. "Cell phones don't work, at least not reliably, around me."

"What do you mean?"

"I mean just that, they don't work. I'd be happy to give you a demonstration sometime if you'd like."

There was silence on the other end for a moment. "We'll have to discuss that later. In the meantime, I need you to meet me at the Robertson crime scene again. Can you get away?"

"Certainly, if you feel it's important. I can be there within the hour."

"Fine, I'll see you then." He hung up, and Natalie grabbed her khaki blazer and purse, wondering at the tone in his voice.

❧ ❧ ❧ ❧

"Is this what you were babbling about on Saturday?" Jake held up a baggie to her, having shoved it in front of her as soon as she got there, without so much as a "hello" or "thanks for coming so quickly." Inside she saw a dirty but clearly gold pendant necklace that was an exact replica of the symbol that had been carved on the victims' stomachs, including hers.

She looked back at Jake. He was clearly frustrated about something. "First of all, I take exception to your use of the word 'babbling.'" She glanced down at the necklace again. "But this has to be what Whitney wanted me to find. She said—"

Jake interrupted her. "I don't want to know what Whitney supposedly said. I want to know how you knew it would be here."

Natalie sighed. Apparently, they had taken more than one step backward from their tenuous truce on Saturday. "If you understood anything, Jake, you'd know that the first is the answer to second."

"What kind of psycho-babble BS is that?" When Natalie glared at him over his use of the word "babble" again, he started over as he laid the evidence bag back in the mobile forensics kit.

"It's just that when I told you I'd have the guys comb the area one more time, I never in a million years expected that we'd find something that matched your little 'vision' quite so accurately. It's just a bit too coincidental for me."

She knew her mouth gaped open, but she couldn't close it, she was so shocked by his veiled accusation. "Are you saying I *planted* this here? Or that I'm ... I'm somehow *involved* in the crime?"

She was going to lose it. She was really going to lose it. She had to do something, say something, but she was so *pissed* at him she was pretty sure she could no longer speak in intelligent sentences. She saw he was carrying his cell phone in his hand and without thought, she grabbed it from him and held it tightly for several seconds, concentrating fiercely on the feel and shape of it in her hand.

When he finally said, "What the hell are you doing?" she shoved the phone back in his hand and said, "Explain that, Mr. BS," and immediately turned to leave. She was going straight to the chief's office and tell him that she couldn't work with this ... this *jerk* a second longer.

Jake quickly followed and grabbed her arm. "Hang on. Wait just a minute. That's not what I'm saying." When he saw her stare down with a clenched jaw at his hand holding her arm, he immediately let go and shoved his hands, including his cell phone, into his pockets.

"What I'm saying is that I can't wrap my mind around it. I can't understand how you could know what you did unless it was just some bizarre coincidence, or you had some prior knowledge of it being here. And I'm usually not a big believer in coincidence."

Natalie filled her lungs and slowly exhaled, trying to get a better grip on her temper and salvage some of her offended dignity. "But that's just it, Jake," she said slowly and distinctively. "I *did* have prior knowledge; I just didn't get that knowledge from the sources you use to get yours. I didn't know *what* I was looking for when we came here, just that she told me I *should* look."

She saw him scowl and pleaded with her eyes for understanding. "Look it up, Jake. I'm a psychic medium. Spirits speak to me. It's called clairaudience. On rare occasions, they send me images as Whitney did. Do a little research first, then maybe you'll find you can wrap your mind around it."

She turned to leave and then stopped once more. "You know, I'm going to give you the benefit of the doubt, as I'm pretty sure that deep down, you don't believe that I'm capable of whatever it is you think could have happened here. But until you can accept that I am what I say I am, and that I don't lie, it's probably best that we steer clear of each other." With that, she turned and left.

As he watched Natalie start to make her way back through the wooded area to her car, Jake was surprised to find he was troubled. He really had been too hard on her. It was just so difficult to fathom that she was for real, that any of that supernatural … voodoo stuff was for real. Maybe he'd have to take her up on her challenge to research the matter.

Jake pulled out his cell phone to call the chief. Natalie was obviously upset, and Jake knew that if she was on her way back to the station, he'd better give Bill a warning.

He started to punch in the number and realized his screen was black. What the devil? He shook the phone a bit, hit the on/off button. Nothing. His battery was completely dead.

He looked back up with narrowed eyes as Natalie walked out of sight.

❧ ❧ ❧ ❧

The smell of chlorine and steady shouts of laughter from the one hundred plus kids splashing and playing in the indoor pools at the Aquatic Center went a long way toward helping Natalie find her center again. Ever since Jake's accusation on Monday afternoon, she had been feeling … unsettled.

Her friend Hope Saunders sat beside her in one of the numerous green and white striped lounge chairs that surrounded the pools, including the shallow kiddie pool with its turtle slide and spraying fountains, and the bigger lap pool the older kids used. Hope and Natalie always volunteered to supervise, as both were trained in CPR and first aid, and each was lifeguard-certified. Natalie always looked forward to these events, which were held at least three times a year, more if they could get the donations. Many of these kids rarely got to go swimming, and it never ceased to make Natalie smile to see their unadulterated joy at the simple experience.

Hope worked tirelessly as the director of the Victims Advocacy Center, a local nonprofit that acted as an independent advocate for victims of all kinds: domestic violence, rape, the foster care system—you name it, the center could handle it. Natalie had met Hope five years earlier when one of Hope's clients had been referred to Natalie for counseling, and they had developed a friendship outside of work.

Hope was petite and pretty with naturally curly blonde hair and had a husband and two-year-old daughter who both adored her and kept her very busy, but she still somehow always managed to make time for Natalie.

"I'm telling you, Hope," Natalie reflected now as she watched the kids, "I don't remember when I've ever been that angry. It's like I suddenly have this big red button inside of me that says 'Warning!' and whenever I'm around him, no matter what gets said, he pushes it and I lose it."

Hope smiled at her friend. "That doesn't sound at all like

you." Which it didn't, since Natalie was about as levelheaded and sensible as they came—her conservative one-piece navy swimsuit a clear reflection of that trait. Hope wondered if this FBI agent Natalie was describing was someone who could possibly bring a little excitement into her carefully ordered world.

Natalie frowned slightly as she kept an eye on the older kids in the big pool. "The thing is, I suspect that deep down he's probably a decent guy, it just doesn't come out around me because he can't get past the fact that *I talk to dead people.*" She made quotation marks with her fingers and then rolled her eyes.

Hope laughed. "A lot of people can't get past that. Not everyone is as open-minded as you and I are." She winked at Natalie and then quickly wagged a finger and shook her head at a boy nearby who was attempting to dunk a younger child.

"I've basically told myself that already," Natalie said. "That I should just stay true to myself and eventually, I would win him over."

Hope turned back to Natalie with a curious look. "Why, I wonder, is it so important that you win him over?"

Natalie opened her mouth to reply, and then she stopped. "I don't know." She thought about it for a moment. "You know, I had congratulated myself last Saturday on having a breakthrough of sorts on this, that since I saw him as totally competent and good at what he does, it only made sense that I would want him to see me the same way."

Natalie quickly blew her whistle when she saw a couple of older kids start running beside the lap pool. They immediately stopped when they heard the whistle and jumped in to avoid getting into trouble.

Natalie smiled at their tactics and turned back to Hope. "But you're making me think, why *is* that important to me? Would it really matter if he *never* thought I was competent or that my abilities were real?" She stared out at a group of kids playing water basketball and then suddenly looked back at Hope. "I really care what this guy thinks about me. Why has that never really happened before?"

Hope smiled hugely. "Oh, maybe because *you've* never really cared about a guy before?"

Natalie let out an indelicate snort. "Please. That's ridiculous. I've known him less than a week."

"The heart has a mind of its own, I'm afraid. Time means nothing to it. I met Charlie on a Friday night, and he proposed two days later." Hope sat back in her chair smugly.

"Well, that's different. You and Charlie …"

"Me and Charlie what?"

"Well … you and Charlie are just two of a kind, that's all. Jake and I are as different as night and day."

"Different can be good."

"Different can be exasperating."

This time Hope laughed. "Well, Nat, I think that maybe you should just continue to take your own advice, stay true to who you are, and he'll eventually see the light." She smiled ruefully. "Sorry, unintended—and bad—pun."

Natalie grinned at Hope's joking reference to her long-ago near-death experience. What would she do without her friends?

Hope suddenly jumped up, a blur in her pink and turquoise striped suit. "Whoa, whoa, whoa," she yelled as she ran over to where several young boys were getting into a scuffle in the shallow water. "What's the problem?"

Several voices responded in unison.

"It's Danny …"

"He's splashing everyone in the face …"

"He won't stop …"

Natalie had followed and realized it was Danny Henderson, her client. She crouched down by the side of the pool, motioned him over, and asked what was going on.

"I don't know." He moved his arms back and forth through the water, not looking at her.

"Come on, Danny, out with it. Unless you want to get out of the pool and go sit on the sidelines for a while?"

He looked at her then, his lower lip starting to quiver until he bit down on it with his teeth. "They were playing a game, and it looked like fun, but they wouldn't let me play. I asked a bunch of times, but they just kept saying no. Finally they said, 'Take a hike, weasel.' So I got mad and started splashing them." His little chin jutted out in silent defiance, his eyes full of rebellion.

Oh dear. Why was it that kids were so cruel to one another? Natalie wondered. But were adults any better when it came right down to it? Maybe she'd anonymously bounce Danny's case off Bernie later and get her opinion; in the meantime, she talked to him in a quiet voice so the other boys wouldn't hear.

"I'm sure you know, Danny, that splashing someone in anger is not the best choice. A better choice might have been to start your own game and make them want to join *you*." She winked at him and then whispered, "So I'll take care of it for you."

She stood up and loudly blew her whistle, and all the kids stopped what they were doing and looked up at her expectantly.

"All right, everybody. We're going to play a group game now and divide up into four teams. I want … you, you, you, and you to be team captains." Danny beamed when she pointed at him.

"Okay, hop to it, captains, select your players, and then I'll explain the rules."

Hope mouthed *nice job* to her as the kids scrambled out of the pools to get selected for a team.

❦ ❦ ❦ ❦

Jake rubbed his neck in frustration as he sat at his desk on the ninth floor of the FBI offices, his tie loosened and shirtsleeves rolled up, the fatigue starting to set in. The pale orange glow of dusk outside his window was quickly vanishing as heavy rain clouds started to roll in.

Damn it, what did the necklace mean? Did it, or the symbol

itself, come first in the killer's mind? Had the necklace belonged to someone the guy had loved and lost? Was there only one necklace or many? It didn't look like a manufactured piece as he studied it closely, but rather something that someone had painstakingly created by hand.

Hell, there were just too many questions and not enough answers. He had searched the Internet for anything remotely resembling the piece, for exclusive jewelry makers and jewelry designers. Nothing. Though it looked to be a one-of-a-kind, he was nevertheless going to put Hansen on generating a list of regional jewelry designers, manufacturers, and retailers and then methodically go through them one by one to see if any of them recognized the design or knew if it had been sold anywhere commercially.

Nor was he sure if the necklace was somehow connected to Natalie from all those years ago, or if it was it a piece of the puzzle that had come up more recently. Something, some instinct, told him it went clear back to Natalie and before, and that it *was* the key to tying everything together.

Natalie. He stretched back in his chair, linking his hands behind head, and stared at the ceiling as he heard the first fat drops of rain hit the window. He had thought of Natalie—dreamt of her if he was totally honest with himself—entirely too much these past two days since the scene at Little Sarasota Bay on Monday.

What had possessed him to be so hard on her? To essentially accuse her of being a fraud or worse? He had been just as unable to control his anger when they'd found the necklace as he had been when he'd lashed out at her about it. When her eyes had openly reflected the hurt, then fury, she had clearly felt at his words, he had felt like a total ass. Yet his stupid pride had not let him retreat.

He just wanted so damn badly for her not to be ... different. God, if she had been just another woman he had met somewhere along the way, he'd have already had her in his arms and in his bed, and not just for one night. And it wasn't just her beauty that drew him to her. From everything he knew about her, she was intelligent, determined … resilient.

It made him question his own objectivity. How could he feel this way about her—be almost consumed by thoughts of her—when she represented everything that he was not? His whole life was based on the concrete, the tangible. His entire career had been built on systematically compiling the physical evidence necessary for convictions. How could he be so damned attracted to someone who was the antithesis of that?

But in all fairness, was she *really?* He acknowledged that she had never indicated she was opposed to physical or forensic evidence or building a case against a suspect. She just—how had she put it?—used different sources to obtain the information she gave to the police in building that case.

Well, she had challenged him to do some research, hadn't she? He looked at his computer, considering. Would it help if he understood it a bit better? Or would it only make him more frustrated once he fully realized that she was not, would never be, what he wanted or needed her to be?

As the rain fell in earnest now, he made his decision and got to work.

Chapter Five

On the drive to Gary and Loretta Robertson's on Thursday morning, Natalie debated over whether to reveal to the couple that Whitney had been in contact with her. Some people were reassured by such things, others got uncomfortable or angry. She usually played things by ear depending upon what she knew about the individuals and how receptive they were.

But Bill had told her nothing about their beliefs, other than that they were struggling desperately to deal with their grief over the tragic and unexpected loss of their daughter, and that they had agreed to talk to Natalie at the chief's suggestion.

Natalie drove down Wisteria Street in Sarasota Heights looking for the Robertson's house number, noting that the houses here, though older, were well cared for by their owners, with box elder trees and butterfly palms common staples in yards that were still a bit moist from last night's typical May rainstorm. Finally seeing the Robertson's house number, she pulled into the drive of their tidy beige rancher, parked her Honda, and grabbed her tote bag. She was immediately assailed by the relentless humidity as she got out of the car.

"Are you the lady that's going to talk to my mommy about Whitney?"

Natalie turned as she shut the car door to see a pair of huge dark eyes fringed by too-long bangs staring up at her earnestly.

The girl gripping the handlebars of the small pink bike appeared to be about six, so Natalie knew she must be Whitney's younger sister, Allison.

"Yes, I am. I'm Dr. Morgan. And you must be Allison?" Natalie smiled gently and was pleased to see the girl return the smile.

"Uh-huh. You can call me Allie if you want. My mommy said Whitney died and isn't coming home. Is she in heaven?"

"Yes, honey, I believe she is. What do you think?"

Allison wrinkled her brow. "I'm not sure. I thought she was, but when I talk to her, she doesn't answer."

Natalie bent down to crouch beside her. "You know what I think? I think she can hear you even if she doesn't answer—and I think it makes her feel good when you talk to her, because then she knows you haven't forgotten her, *and* she gets to hear how you're doing. So I think you should keep right on talking to her." Natalie smiled again as Allison appeared to be seriously considering her words.

"But how do I *really* know she's there if she doesn't answer?"

Oh, the curiosity of youth. And how to best answer that one? Natalie wondered. Maybe the best answer was not really an answer at all.

"Well, that's something you'll just have to decide for yourself. We don't *really* know for sure that the people we love are in heaven, because we're not there yet, but we have to decide what we believe. So you'll have to decide if you want to believe that Whitney's in heaven. I personally think it's a really nice thing to believe in."

The front door opened, and Mrs. Robertson stepped out. "Allie, sweetie, I thought I told you not to go outside unless you told me first. Hi, you must be Dr. Morgan. I'm Loretta Robertson. Sorry, I'm a bit of a wreck. I hope Allison hasn't been pestering you." Wrapped in a bulky sweater, her light brown hair was pulled back into a messy ponytail, and she was pale and without make-up. She looked exhausted, Natalie thought.

"Not at all. We were just having some girl talk." Natalie winked at Allison, who grinned in return, clearly pleased that a grown-up had decided their talk was important enough to be kept be a secret.

Natalie held out her hand. "It's very nice to meet you, Loretta. Please call me Natalie."

"Thank you, Natalie, come in. I'm sorry—Gary couldn't be here this morning. He's at his parents' house. They're … struggling, too." Loretta held open the front door and said, "Allison, why don't you run to your room and pop in one of your Barbie DVDs? We'll be in the kitchen having a grown-up talk, okay?"

"Okay, Mom!" Allison sprinted through the door, her bike forgotten, and disappeared just as quickly through the arched opening on the other side of the living room.

Natalie smiled as she entered and followed Loretta through the neat-as-a-pin living room into the kitchen. "I don't remember ever having that much energy."

"I know; there are some days she wears me out."

"You have a son, too, right?" Natalie asked as she sat down on the wooden bar stool at the kitchen counter where Loretta indicated.

"Yes, Seth, he's ten. He's over at his friend's house next door. It seems to help him. Coffee?" She grabbed two mugs from the cupboard when Natalie nodded.

"How are they both handling things?"

"As well as can be expected, I suppose," Loretta sighed as she poured the coffee. "They ask questions that we can't answer, or won't answer, I guess. I don't want them to know how … how Whitney died."

"That's understandable," Natalie replied quietly. "They're young, and you're probably wise to explain things to them in general terms for now."

Loretta handed Natalie a full cup, placed cream and sugar in front of her, and then came around and sat down on the stool next to her, wrapping her own hands tightly around her mug as if she were desperately trying to absorb its warmth. "It's too hard even for *me* to think about." She closed her eyes for a moment and let out a shuddering breath. "All I do all day is clean, or cook, or just try to stay as busy as I can, so I don't think about it."

Natalie placed a gentle hand on Loretta's arm. "I'm so sorry, Loretta. I can't imagine anything more difficult than losing a child." She reached into her tote and pulled out a book, placing it on the counter. "I brought something for you to read when you're ready. I've found in my practice that it's helped quite a number of my patients cope with an unexpected death."

"Thank you, I appreciate it." Loretta glanced at the book and then turned and stared out her kitchen window, a faraway look coming into her eyes. "Sometimes—and I hope you won't think I'm crazy when I say this, but sometimes—I think Whitney is trying to tell me something." She turned back to Natalie with a sad, resigned look. "Then I lecture myself, saying it's just my imagination, that she's really gone, and I just can't let her go."

Was Whitney really trying to communicate with her mother? Natalie wondered. Whitney's energy was strong, Natalie knew, stronger than most of the spirits who contacted her. It was entirely possible that Whitney was attempting to talk to her mother, but Loretta just hadn't quite come to believe that she could really hear her. Natalie decided to find out.

"Did you and Whitney have a close relationship?"

Loretta's eyes welled with unshed tears. "Amazingly, we did. I know she was a teenager, and everyone always says the teenage years are some of the hardest in raising a child, but Whitney and I … we could relate. Oh, we had our disagreements, don't get me wrong, but she could talk to me about what was bothering her, and she knew I would listen without judgment, and that I loved her unconditionally. And we had fun together, you know, shopping and going to movies and things. She wasn't embarrassed to be seen with her mother." The tears rolled silently and freely now.

"Loretta, do you believe in heaven or an afterlife? Do you believe that Whitney has gone on to a better place?"

Loretta turned her red-rimmed eyes to Natalie's, pulling a tissue from a nearby box and dabbing at her eyes. "I want to. So badly. We're not a religious family, really, but I just … feel in my heart, somehow, that she *is* in a better place."

Natalie decided to take a chance. "Loretta, I hope what I'm about to say doesn't scare you, or make you question my professionalism. Instead, I hope you find that it helps you."

She held Loretta's eyes with her own, wanting her to not only hear the truth of the words Natalie was about to say, but to *see* it in her eyes.

"I had a near-death experience when I was fourteen. I was clinically dead and … crossed over, if you will, for a brief period of time before I was resuscitated. I *know* firsthand that there is life after death. I *felt* the incredible love that was waiting there for me—that I know is there for Whitney."

Loretta remained silent, but she appeared totally absorbed in what Natalie was saying. Encouraged, Natalie continued, "I also now have some psychic abilities as a result of that experience. The spirits of those who have died sometimes talk to me. In fact, when I was separated from my body during my near-death experience, I was told by someone I like to think of as an angel that I needed to learn to listen with my head *and* my heart. So that's what I try to do. I listen to these spirits and try to help." Natalie gripped Loretta's hands between her own. "And Whitney has talked to me, and so I'm trying to help her, too."

Loretta's eyes widened, and the tears started to fall again.

"In fact, one of the first things she said to me was that she needed to tell her parents where she was. That told me that Whitney loved you and her father very much."

Loretta started crying in earnest now.

"You need to know that Whitney is helping me, and the police, solve this case by communicating to me some of the details of what happened. You should be very proud of her." Natalie's heart was breaking at the depth of Loretta's grief, but she continued, needing to tell her this one last thing, perhaps the most important thing of all.

"Listen to me, Loretta," Natalie said gently, but gave her a moment to try to gain control of her emotions. Loretta wiped her eyes and took several deep, hiccupping breaths, and then she looked at Natalie with eyes that for the first time appeared to contain a glimmer of hope.

"If you think Whitney is trying to tell you something," Natalie said, "I believe, truly believe, that she is. You need to believe that too, and open your heart, open your mind, to the possibility that she *can* communicate with you from where she is. I think it would also help Whitney come to terms with everything, if she knew her mother truly heard her, knew she was in a better place, and could let her go in peace."

Loretta smiled tremulously at Natalie and took another deep, calming breath. "Okay. I'll listen."

❧ ❧ ❧ ❧

What a day, Natalie thought as she poured herself some orange juice and sat down at her own kitchen table to go through the mail. The long, soulful sound of the saxophone was coming from the radio mounted under her kitchen cabinets, and she had just called Bernie to make sure she was settled in for the night.

The stark grief in Loretta Robertson's eyes, in her voice, that morning, had affected Natalie more than she'd anticipated. But maybe, just maybe, Loretta would now be able to open the channels of communication and really talk to her beloved Whitney. Then let her go, so she could focus on the two children and husband that needed her now. Natalie fervently hoped so.

She had been mulling over just those possibilities when her tire had gone as flat as a board on the drive back to her office. Because Bernie had insisted she learn when she'd first started driving, she'd been able to put the spare on herself with a bit of elbow grease, a great deal of sweat, and a few choice curse words that Bernie would never know about, and then had made her way to the tire shop for the repair.

Once the tire was fixed and in place and the spare returned

to the trunk, she'd driven back to the office for Danny's weekly session, followed by a call for an unscheduled, emergency session from a newer client, Ronald Julian, whom she'd seen a couple of times in the past two months. Ronald was struggling to cope with the changes in his life after being tragically blinded in an industrial accident. She'd somehow managed to fit him into her calendar late that afternoon when she realized the emotionally unstable state he was in, even taking some extra time with him after he'd questioned whether she could really help him if she'd never had to overcome anything similar in her own life.

Finally, she'd received a call from Dr. Ben Zimmerman, the cardiologist at Sarasota Memorial Hospital, requesting she visit a patient who'd just reported having a near-death experience during heart surgery at the hospital.

Death. So difficult to accept, much less understand. Natalie took another sip of juice and tossed aside some junk mail. To some it seemed so final; to others, just another transition in one's overall existence. For most people, it was easier to accept death if one believed there was life *after* death. For those who didn't believe that, death was frightening. It was the final frontier, the end of the line, the last hurrah.

Natalie wholeheartedly believed that when she did eventually die and her human form ceased to exist, she would continue on in spirit and rejoin that higher power that had so graciously given her a second chance at fourteen. Natalie was not afraid of death. It was no longer an unknown to her. She embraced life, but she was not afraid of dying when all was said and done. Having the near-death experience, or NDE as it was commonly referred to, had made her come to understand that her spirit could, and eventually would, exist independently of her human form.

When Natalie had done some initial research years earlier at Bernie's suggestion, what she had found had been remarkable, and it had so fascinated her that she had eventually written her PhD dissertation on the subject. She had found that many mainstream disciplines had already contributed significantly to the research on the subject, including medicine, psychology, psychiatry, and parapsychology. Natalie's own research had uncovered statistics indicating that more than eight million people had reported having experienced an NDE, and that the basic elements of the classic NDE were surprisingly consistent among the reports: an awareness of being dead, a sense of peace or well-being, an out-of-body experience, a feeling of moving through a tunnel or passageway, movement toward a light or communicating with a light, being reunited with deceased loved ones, and being given a life review, among others.

Natalie had found especially fascinating the biological explanations of the phenomena supplied by those skeptical of NDEs, including theories such as a massive release of chemicals in the brain at death stimulating aural or visual hallucinations, extreme stress to the body triggering something akin to REM sleep or lucid dreaming, or neuronal death contributing to the generation of false memories.

But the primary focus of her dissertation had been on the psychological effects the NDE had on the individuals experiencing them, specifically, the changes to their values and belief systems—and Natalie could personally identify with this—including a greater appreciation for life, greater compassion for others, and a heightened sense of purpose.

Bernie had happened to mention all this to Dr. Zimmerman one day when Bernie had been volunteering at the hospital, and Ben, intrigued, had contacted Natalie to discuss it. Now Natalie had a contract with the hospital to provide counseling services to their patients experiencing NDEs—and an admirer in Ben.

She had long suspected he had a bit of a crush on her, but she didn't encourage it. He was forty-two, divorced, and still a good catch, she knew. But she had never felt the slightest hint of attraction for him, despite his bookish good looks, kind blue eyes, and gentle manner. She had tried several different ways to subtly communicate that she wasn't interested in anything other than a friendship, but he had continued to flirt with her. At least he had stopped asking her out quite so much, so that was progress. Natalie just wasn't interested in pursuing a romantic relationship when there was no spark.

And she definitely had sparks with Jake. She could have full-blown ignition with Jake, if she was honest with herself. *Why couldn't Jake be more like Ben* and accept that there were things in life that defied logical explanation? How wonderful would it feel to be that wildly attracted to someone who really and truly believed in all that she was?

Damn. She had to stop thinking about Jake. Today had been so busy, it had helped keep her mind off of him and their last unpleasant encounter, and Natalie knew that the grief counseling, her clients, and helping NDE patients make sense of their experience was where she was really needed. It was what she should be focusing on, what she was good at, and what made her feel good about herself. Not some insensitive, close-minded, jerk of an FBI agent—no matter how attractive he was.

※　※　※　※

Friday morning, Jake left his downtown condo on Central Avenue and headed to the Sarasota PD for a status meeting at the chief's request. He knew the chief also intended to call Natalie, but Jake highly doubted Natalie would show if she knew he would be there.

She had made it pretty clear at their last disastrous confrontation that until he could come to terms with her supposed abilities, they should stay away from each other. He had tried to honor her request for the last four days. But until this morning, when the chief had mentioned that he would now be requiring these Friday morning status meetings as a matter of course, and Natalie would also be required to attend them, Jake hadn't realized how much he was looking forward to seeing her again.

He parked and entered the building, his thoughts on Natalie and how he might be able to diffuse the inevitable tension of this morning's meeting if she did show up, and didn't notice Pat Barnes waving at him.

"Agent Riggs!" He turned at the sound of his name and saw her talking to another visitor while gesturing him over. Wondering at her intent, he made his way over there and waited patiently while Pat finished telling the elderly lady what she could do about her neighbor's dog leaving unwanted and "malodorous deposits" in her yard. Jake tried to hide his grin as he stood behind her.

After the woman finished her business and slowly shuffled away, Jake asked, "What can I do for you, Pat?"

Pat gave him a huge smile. "How's the case coming?"

"Now, Pat, you *know* I'm not going to disclose details of the case out here with you. Of course, you could go to dinner with me, and we could discuss it further." He winked at her.

Pat giggled like a schoolgirl. "How are you and Natalie working together?" she asked, her grin still wide and curiously innocent looking.

Jake smiled faintly in response, wishing he had a better answer for her. "At the moment, we're not. Let's just say we don't see eye to eye on everything." He glanced at his watch. "I'm sorry, Pat; I have to get upstairs for a meeting with the chief. I'm sure I'll see you again."

She nodded and watched him go, a speculative look on her face.

~ ~ ~ ~

Natalie kept telling herself she was a professional. She could handle this. She could put her personal feelings aside and focus on the case. She had told Bill that very thing on the phone this morning when he'd called and asked her—ordered was actually a better term—to attend this status meeting and the subsequent ones he was requesting every Friday morning until the case was solved, leads or no leads.

She'd patiently explained to him her feelings on the matter

after Jake's behavior last Saturday and again on Monday, and Bill had just as patiently requested that she put those feelings aside and think about the victims and their families. Natalie had instantly felt awful. Completely selfish. So she had swallowed her pride and agreed to be there, even rearranging her regular schedule for Friday mornings to accommodate these status meetings.

Yet when she walked into Bill's office and saw Jake already there—looking as attractive as ever in his dark gray suit and red-striped tie—her newfound resolve flew right out the window, and she wanted to walk right up to him, pound him on the chest, and yell, why, *why* won't you believe me?

So much for professionalism.

"Good morning, Bill." She quickly inclined her head toward Jake. "Agent Riggs." She sat down, smoothed the moss green fabric of her ankle-length sundress, and looked expectantly at the chief.

"Thank you both for coming, I appreciate it." Bill leaned forward and placed his elbows on the desk, clasping his hands and tapping the pads of his thumbs together with nervous energy as he considered them for a moment. "You should know I'm getting some pressure from the local press on this case, and I wanted an update, from you especially, Jake, on any new developments. Natalie, I was wondering if you'd received any additional information." He looked at each of them in turn.

Jake looked at Natalie; Natalie looked at Jake. He gestured silently that she respond to the chief first.

Odd, the strange little pang she felt at that gesture. They couldn't even find a way to talk civilly to one another but instead were reduced to head nods and hand gestures. She tried to ignore it and called once again upon her steadily evaporating professionalism.

"I'm sorry, Bill, I've heard nothing from Lauren and had no contact from Whitney since Monday. I did meet yesterday with Loretta Robertson, Whitney's mother, and I think it went well. She seemed to be receptive to ..." Natalie glanced at Jake. "Or, rather, she seemed to be doing okay." She nodded to Jake that it was now his turn.

Jake stared at her for a brief moment before turning to the chief.

"We did receive some preliminary results from the lab regarding their metallurgy tests on the necklace. It appears to be made up of several alloys …"

The intercom on the chief's phone buzzed insistently, and then his assistant came on. "Sorry to interrupt, Chief Garrett, but I have a Gayle Reynolds on the line who's frantically trying to reach Dr. Morgan. She said it's urgent that she talk to her."

Natalie immediately spoke up. "I'm here. Where can I take the call?"

"I'll put her through right now," the assistant replied. The phone rang, and the chief punched the appropriate line and handed the receiver to Natalie.

"Hi, Gayle, this is Natalie. What's going on?"

"I'm sorry to bother you, Natalie, but it's Danny. I just got the call from Melinda Talbot that he's at Sarasota Memorial. He fell from a tree and broke his arm and is asking for you. She said he's just come out of surgery and is a bit unruly, and the doctor has requested that if you can get over there, he thinks it would help calm him down."

"I'm on my way." She hung up, grabbed her purse, and turned to the chief. "I'm sorry, Bill, I have to go to the hospital. One of my patients, a little eight-year-old boy, has broken his arm and is asking for me."

"I'll take you." Jake immediately stood up.

Natalie paused, a little startled. "That's really not necessary."

The chief interceded. "I think that's a good idea, Jake. I won't worry so much that way." He smiled at Natalie's widened eyes and shrugged his shoulders. "So sue me. I worry about you."

She looked back and forth between them. "I … really, it's not …"

"It's settled. We'll take my car." Jake shook Bill's hand and gestured for Natalie to precede him out the door. It looked as though she was outnumbered, and she didn't want to waste any more time arguing the point. She just wanted to make sure Danny was all right.

She sighed. "Fine, let's go."

❧ ❧ ❧ ❧

The full skirt of Natalie's sundress billowed behind her, her low-heeled sandals clicking steadily as she hurried down the main floor hall at Sarasota Memorial to the nurse's station after being directed there by the polite elderly lady at the Information Desk. Jake followed, though she tried to ignore him.

A nurse—a very young, blonde, and *tanned* nurse, Natalie noted irrationally—was working at the computer behind the counter. "Can you tell me what room Daniel Henderson is in? He's only eight. He may still be in recovery. I'm told he just had surgery for a broken arm and was asking for me. I'm Natalie Morgan." Natalie glanced back at Jake and knew she really *was* babbling this time, but he remained silent, standing at a respectful distance.

The nurse looked down to consult her chart when Natalie heard her name being called. She turned to see Ben coming down the hall toward her.

"Natalie, how are you? Are you here to see Mr. Carter?" He smiled and grabbed her hand when he reached her, his blue eyes crinkling with pleasure.

"Hi, Ben." Mr. Carter? Natalie scoured her memory. Oh yes, the patient they'd spoken about yesterday who'd just had the NDE during cardiac surgery.

"No, I've scheduled him for early next week. I'm here to see one of my patients, Danny Henderson. I'm trying to find out what room he's in. He just broke his arm."

Ben finally let go of Natalie's hand and turned to the nurse. "Trisha, can you help us?" He turned back to Natalie. "When you're done, have me paged, and if I have a minute, we can go have a cup of coffee in the cafeteria." He smiled and winked, and then walked off.

Natalie watched him leave and then turned back to the counter as the nurse spoke. "Daniel Henderson has been moved from Recovery to room 429. The elevators are over there—" Trisha pointed further down the hall "—and when the doors open on the fourth floor, it's just down the hall to your left." As she finished, Trisha smiled appreciatively at Jake.

Oh, *please*. Natalie walked off toward the elevators, determined *not* to notice that the young nurse's eyes had all but invited Jake to her place for a romp in the … she stopped herself midthought. What the devil was *wrong* with her? She was in the middle of a murder case, one of her patients had just been injured, and all she could think of was Jake and some hot-to-trot …

She punched the elevator button and then jabbed it a second time when it didn't light up. Get a *grip*, Natalie. Jake is standing right behind you, and you look like an idiot. Focus. You're here to see *Danny*. Right now, this is about Danny.

Natalie could not remember a more uncomfortably silent elevator ride. Or a time when she had been so surprised at the direction of her own thoughts. She breathed a sigh of relief as the doors opened, and she quickly headed left to Danny's room, determined to put the whole thing out of her mind and give Danny the attention he deserved.

"I'll wait out here," Jake said as she knocked on the door of room 429. She nodded gratefully to him as Melinda Talbot opened the door and welcomed her in, her smile genuine.

"Thank you for coming so quickly, Dr. Morgan. Danny simply wouldn't rest until you got here." Melinda looked over at him all but swallowed up in the big hospital bed, her eyes clearly concerned. "I'll go get some coffee and be right back—okay, Danny?"

He nodded but kept his eyes on Natalie as Melinda left.

Natalie walked over to the bed with a smile. "Hi, Danny. How are you feeling?" She glanced at his arm. "That's quite a cast—do I get to sign it?"

She noticed his eyes remained locked on her face and that something was clearly troubling him. "What's the matter, Danny?"

She sat down in the chair next the bed. "Do you want to talk about it?"

He nodded mutely as his eyes welled and a single tear rolled down his cheek.

Natalie laid her hand gently over his. "I imagine it was scary, falling out of the tree like that."

He swallowed convulsively. "That's just it," he whispered, "I didn't fall. I jumped. On purpose. Only I didn't mean to break my arm. I just wanted Mrs. Talbot to watch me 'cause I'm really, really good at climbing trees. But she was so busy with Aaron and Samantha that she wasn't paying any attention to me. She never does."

The second tear fell.

"Now I'm in the hospital, and I know she's upset, and I know it's going to cost money, and … I know I'm gonna be in trouble when she finds out … and … and they're gonna move me again." The tears started to fall in earnest.

"Oh, Danny, honey, you don't have worry about the money, and you're not going to be transferred again just because of this, I promise. But let's talk about trying to get Mrs. Talbot's attention that way …"

Jake knew he shouldn't have, but he had stayed right outside the door and listened to the exchange. He continued to listen as Natalie explained to the young boy about how it was nice to be the center of attention, but that no one could have *all* the attention all of the time, and that you had to learn this lesson if you were going to be part of a family.

He was surprised at how good she was at this. How good she was with the boy. Despite her obvious other issues, she clearly had a knack with kids. It didn't negate her appeal to him in the least. Nor, he imagined, her appeal to the good Dr. Zimmerman.

Jake had noticed several things from their brief encounter: Natalie calling the doctor by his first name, though his nametag had just said *Dr. Zimmerman*; the good doctor holding on to

Natalie's hand a bit longer than was appropriate; and that the guy clearly had a major thing for Natalie. Jake wondered if she knew.

Now why was he even going there? He shouldn't care that another man found Natalie attractive. Hell, every man probably found Natalie attractive. But if he was entirely honest with himself, what Jake was really worried about was whether Natalie found the good doctor attractive.

His thoughts were interrupted when Melinda Talbot returned and Natalie exited the room, turning and waving at her patient one last time.

She cocked her head slightly toward Jake. "Ready? I need to get to the office, so if you could drive me back to my car, I'd appreciate it." Without waiting for a reply, she turned and walked back down the hall to the elevators. He watched her for a second before following.

In the car, the silence on the way back to the station was again almost oppressive. Jake, frustrated, finally decided to cut the tension with the proverbial knife. "So you didn't have time to have coffee with Dr. Zimmerman? You're dating, I take it?"

Natalie turned from staring out the window to stare at Jake. "*What?*"

"I'm just commenting on what was fairly obvious back there at the hospital."

"I don't see how that's any of your business," she replied coolly.

Jake knew it wasn't his business, damn it, but he wanted her to say it *wasn't* obvious, that it *wasn't* how it appeared.

"Never said it was. Just making conversation." He turned right onto Ringling from Washington Boulevard, irritated as hell that he was letting this situation piss him off. He *couldn't* be jealous, didn't even recall the last time he *had* been jealous, but the way he felt, it was looking like that's exactly what he was.

"Oh, well, if you're just making conversation," Natalie retorted, "then I'd like to point out that it was *fairly obvious* back there that Miss Nurse What's-Her-Face would have followed you around like a dog salivating after a bone if you'd so much as ..." She trailed off and Jake saw her cheeks flush before she quickly averted her head to stare out the window again.

Jake grinned as he turned into the station. Well, I'll be damned. Could it be that she was jealous too, and over someone he could barely recall? Maybe there wasn't anything going on with Zimmerman after all. Jake pulled into an available parking spot, shut off the car, and turned in the bucket seat toward Natalie as she immediately reached for the door handle.

"Natalie, wait." She stilled but didn't look at him. "Please, just give me a minute. Let me explain." When she finally turned to him, Jake's gaze was intent on her beautiful, wary brown eyes.

He took a deep breath and jumped right in. "I'm finding that it's getting harder and harder to ignore this ... attraction I feel for you, and it's making me say and do things that I wouldn't normally say or do." There, he'd finally said it. Now it was up to her to decide what she wanted to do about it.

As Natalie stared back at Jake after his pronouncement, she was suddenly aware of her heart pulsating in her chest. "Jake ... I ..." She faltered, unsure how to respond.

She unconsciously moistened her lips and saw Jake's eyes lower to her mouth and watch. When he raised them back to hers, Natalie forgot to breathe. A frisson of heat curled low in her belly at his look—at those intense green eyes as they began to glitter again, mesmerizing her, silently beckoning her to eliminate the distance between them and let this overwhelming force take over.

Her breathing suddenly uneven, Natalie's own eyes were compellingly drawn down to Jake's firm, masculine lips, the bottom slightly fuller than the top, and she wondered what it would be like to kiss him, *really* kiss him. Explosive. She raised her eyes back to his.

In less than a heartbeat, he spanned the gap between them and captured her face in his hands and her lips with his own in a kiss so unrestrained that it instantly ignited them both. It was hot, wet, with tongues mating, retreating, mating again. Natalie moaned and grabbed the back of Jake's neck, intent only on hanging on and assuaging this sudden, blindingly intense need that overtook her.

She could not refuse his demanding lips or his hands as they lowered to her shoulders, her arms, under her arms, and then suddenly, shockingly, lifted her over and across his lap without effort. He swallowed her sudden gasp with another searing kiss and laid her back over his supporting arm as his mouth continued its sensual onslaught. Natalie was helpless to stop her own hands from sliding over his broad shoulders to pull him closer, this new, more intimate position making her instantly and achingly aware of his arousal pressing against her backside. And his hands, oh God, his hands were doing things to her, grazing and then lightly kneading her breast, his thumb rubbing back and forth over the material of her dress where her taut nipple was straining through the confines of her lacy bra ...

The sudden blaring of the horn from a car nearby jolted them both back to awareness, breaking them apart. Natalie's breathing was short and choppy, and Jake's chest was swiftly rising and falling with his own as they stared at one another for several heartbeats. Natalie was amazed at their loss of control, at the intensity of what had just happened.

She glanced away for a second and was suddenly and immediately mortified. They were in the parking lot of the police station, for crying out loud. Anyone, *anyone* could have walked up on them. What had come over her? She scrambled off of Jake and back across the seat, her face flushing hotly. This just *couldn't* happen. She knew better than to get involved with the people she worked with. *Especially* when those people thought she was a fake.

"Jesus, Natalie, I'm sorry." Jake rubbed a hand over the back of his neck as she struggled to straighten her dress. "I usually don't ..."

Natalie grabbed the door handle, not looking at him, intent only on escaping. "Jake, this can't happen. We're working together.

It's unprofessional. It's …" She faltered. "I'm sorry, I have to go."
She grabbed her purse, slammed the car door, and hurried to her
own car across the lot.

Jake watched her go, rubbing his lips with his hand, acutely
aware of his own body still on fire from a simple kiss. Hell, there'd
been nothing simple about that kiss. *Damn*, he thought. This was
getting way too complicated.

Chapter Six

S aturday morning, after a restless night spent stewing over what she refused to think about any further, Natalie was out bright and early weeding in her front yard in a concerted effort to release some tension. Bernie had always said that weeding was good for the soul, but Natalie had never been able to figure out why. All she had found was that it was good for a sore back—which was why her pitiful flower bed looked as it did.

After starting on one side of the big planter under her front window and carefully and deliberately pulling the weeds from the blooms, she had eventually given up on the methodical approach after realizing she had made pathetically little progress after an entire hour. She had then just starting yanking here and there in an effort to at least make the planter look a little less overcrowded, a little more … purposeful.

She glanced up, now sweating, as a car drove slowly by and noticed it was a police cruiser. That was odd. She didn't think she had ever seen one come through this neighborhood, a relatively safe residential area filled with older, well-maintained homes, mature trees, and inhabited by retired couples and single professionals like Natalie.

Why would a cruiser be making the rounds here? She decided to call the chief about it as she reached for another persistent, irritating weed.

I can see the pickup.

Natalie immediately sat back on her heels. Whitney? Is that you? Do you mean the black pickup? Where? She waited, closing her eyes and opening her mind.

Yes ... parked at the edge of a big, open area ... it's very noisy.

That's good, Whitney. Do you see anything else? Any street signs?

Smokestacks ... some large buildings ... don't know the area. But I know it's the same pickup ... remember the bumper sticker on the front ... I'M NOT FOLLOWING TOO CLOSE, YOU'RE GOING TOO SLOW.

Good girl, Natalie responded. That helps. You're doing great.

Natalie's heart suddenly constricted, and she knew without question the girl's spirit was suddenly sad. This was the hardest part for Natalie, sometimes feeling the pain of these spirits and not always being able to ease it. But she always tried.

Whitney, I hope you can hear me. I talked to your mom.

Natalie did her best to convey not only the thoughts to Whitney, but also the emotions that she had felt from Loretta.

She loves you so much, Whitney. She wants to be able to hear you. Can you try again with her? Let her know that you'll be okay? I told her what a wonderful thing it is that you're doing, helping us with this case. I think you're meant to, Whitney. I think you're meant to help us find him. Then you'll be at peace. But help your mom find peace, too, okay?

But Natalie heard no more.

She took a deep breath and was surprised to find her face wet with tears. Whitney's energy was truly strong. She must have been an amazing girl.

Natalie took off her gardening gloves and wiped her cheeks, surveying the still minimal progress she had made with this flower bed. Oh well, maybe she could invite Bernie over to dinner, and she could finish it while Bernie directed. Bernie was good at that.

She got up to go inside, record her impressions, and call the chief. And of course, continue to refuse to think about Jake and that volatile kiss. Damn it, anyway.

❀ ❀ ❀ ❀

"Who found it?" Jake barked at Officer Petrone from the Sarasota PD Sunday evening, listening as the officer indicated he didn't know, just that a call on an abandoned vehicle had come in when he'd been on duty, and it had generally matched the description of the vehicle they were searching for in the FBI's case, so he thought he'd give Agent Riggs a heads up.

Jake had just finished a solitary dinner at his condo and was *not* looking forward to a long, drawn-out evening sure to be filled with tangled thoughts of Natalie. He had been planning to head to the gym—for the second time that day. But this would provide another distraction. If it was, in fact, the vehicle used in the Robertson crime, which Jake still didn't totally buy into. Yet he knew the chief hadn't questioned Natalie's original information from more than a week ago and had previously dispatched her general description of the truck to all local and regional units.

"Have they touched anything? Tell them *not* to touch anything. I'll call the FBI team right now and send them over, and I'll be over myself shortly."

He quickly pulled a pair of jogging pants over his workout shorts and grabbed his running shoes—then wondered how he was going to feel if this particular pickup did turn out to be the vehicle used to run Whitney off the road.

❀ ❀ ❀ ❀

As Jake headed to the chief's office Monday morning to let him know about the black, late-nineties Dodge Ram that was still being dissected by the FBI, his thoughts once again turned to Natalie. It seemed that over the last three nights, he had been unable to control them and had eventually given up, allowing them free rein.

He still had trouble believing the incredible sexual potency behind the kiss they had shared. He had never gone from zero to sixty and then out of control with a woman so quickly. What was it about Natalie that affected him so powerfully?

There was no denying she was beautiful, but it was a willowy, almost delicate beauty. The image of her at fourteen flashed through Jake's mind. Though she was a grown woman now, she had not lost that fragile air. He thought of the smallness of her hand in his. That kind of vulnerability tended to bring out the protective side of a man rather than the heat.

She was slender, with gentle curves—and his body tightened in response as he recalled the curves he had held and stroked—but they were not the voluptuous curves of a centerfold that a man might typically picture when he thought of hot, sweaty sex.

And though her face was unquestionably stunning with those deep brown, fathomless eyes that held mysteries he could not explain, that slim, graceful nose, and those lips—God, those lips— hers was not the face of a practiced seductress who was skilled in bringing out a man's baser instincts.

Yet Jake admitted to himself, in spite of the fact that Natalie did not come across that way, he was more sexually drawn to her than he had been to any other woman in his life. He was drawn to her despite their differences, despite … *her* differences.

He knew she was feisty, spirited. She had proven that to him on more than one occasion. He knew she was intelligent and compassionate. All those things only added to the intense pull he felt every time he was around her.

He also knew she was psychic—or at least claimed to be. Hell.

Could he figure out a way to separate that part of Natalie from the mix and just have a relationship with the rest of her? Jesus, that sounded ridiculous, even to himself. Besides, Natalie had point blank told him any relationship between the two of them would *not* be happening.

He suddenly realized he was at the station and had no memory of the drive there. Holy Christ. He was going to have to figure out a better way to deal with this. Otherwise he might end up inadvertently killing someone in the process.

He parked and hustled into the building on his way to the chief's office, only smiling briefly at Pat as he strode by pointing at his watch, knowing full well she wanted him to stop. He just knew he was in no shape this time to be able to successfully avoid her pointed questions about Natalie.

When he reached Bill's office, he knocked once and entered when he heard the gruff response. The chief's glasses were on the desk, and he was pinching the bridge of his nose with his thumb and forefinger. He looked up finally. "Hi, Jake. What did you want to see me about?"

Jake paused. "Everything all right, Bill?"

"Sure, fine—just dealing with a wife who's still mad at me for forgetting our forty-second wedding anniversary this weekend." He replaced his glasses. "Whatever you do, don't forget your anniversary." He smiled wryly. "Now, what's going on with the case?"

Jake sat down and switched gears. "I wanted to update you on the vehicle that was found yesterday out near the Wellcraft Marine Plant at the Sarasota-Bradenton International Airport. A black, 98 Dodge Ram, extended cab. It's been processed, and I've got the lab running tests on everything as we speak."

"I know about the truck, Jake."

Jake stopped. "You do?"

"I just read the initial report from Officer Petrone. And Natalie called me Saturday morning."

"But the truck wasn't found until late yesterday," Jake said, frowning.

"Natalie's information was the reason we found the truck at all. She received some fragments of details from Whitney that she relayed to me, and we pieced them together and came up with a likely location. Sure enough, there it was."

Jake sat back, stunned. He had already been grappling with

how he would respond if the truck ultimately proved to be the vehicle used in the crime. But now to be told that Natalie had provided the information on *where* the truck was located? First the necklace, now this. *Two* coincidences? He didn't know what the hell to think anymore.

"How is that possible, Bill?"

"How is what possible?"

Jake rubbed a frustrated hand over his jaw. "How is it possible that Natalie had information on the whereabouts of that truck before it was found? There are only two rational explanations. That she *knew* it was there, or that it was just a coincidence, and she made an educated guess."

The chief sat back in his chair, steepled his hands, and considered Jake in silence for a moment. "Do you view me as an intelligent man, Jake?"

Jake looked surprised. "Of course I do, Bill. What are you getting at?"

"Then how is it that, being intelligent, I can believe in Natalie, can trust that she is the real thing, when you can't?"

"I admit, she's good and makes a person want to believe her," Jake acknowledged. "But I think she's got you fooled, Bill. I think she's got everybody fooled." Jake may ultimately be a fool over her, but he wasn't going to be fooled *by* her.

"Look Jake, I know there are a lot of fakes out there—scammers, charlatans, whatever you want to call them. But Natalie is not one of them." He paused a moment, his piercing blue eyes locked on Jake's. "Do you know that she described a bumper sticker to me she said we would find on the truck, and it was exactly where she said it would be, and it said exactly what she said it would say. Can you explain that logically, Jake?"

Jake remained silent, though he had seen the damn bumper sticker himself.

"Natalie is not trying to fool us, Jake. She is one of the most genuine people I've ever met. She does what she does because she feels compelled to help others. If you took the time to get to know her, you'd find that out, and you'd find out why. And if you took the time to learn about *what* it is she can do, you'd find yourself a bit amazed."

Jake felt the need to defend himself. "I did do a little research, Bill. I looked into exactly what she said she has, something called clairaudience. I can admit that the overall subject might be a bit more mainstream than I'd expected, but I also discovered that even though the scientific community has looked into it, into all the alleged paranormal abilities, they have yet to be able to conclusively prove they exist. I saw a lot of studies and reports showing percentages or ratios of accuracy by these self-proclaimed psychics, but nothing definitive. I'm just not convinced." Jake recalled how he had been strangely disappointed at what he had read that night, questioning whether deep down, he had wanted to be convinced. The problem was, he just wasn't.

The chief looked at Jake resignedly. "I hope someday you will be, Jake. I'm an old man now, but I wish I'd learned earlier on to be more open to life's possibilities. You'd be surprised at how much richer your life can be for it."

Bill abruptly thumped his desk with both hands. "But enough of that. Let's talk about this pickup. Tell me what you do know."

Jake determinedly dismissed the chief's words for the time being and relayed the details he had—that the pickup had been stolen several weeks earlier; that it had slight dents and marks on the right front fender consistent with hitting a bicycle; that the minuscule paint chips they'd found on that fender were being processed to see if they might match the type of paint the manufacturer used on the particular bicycle Whitney had been riding; that luminal had revealed tiny specks of blood on the front seat; and that they were conducting tests to see if the blood matched Whitney's. Other than that, no discernable fingerprints were found, no foreign fibers or any other forensic evidence.

Jake agreed to keep the chief informed if anything else came up and confirmed he'd be back on Friday morning for their weekly status meeting. As he left the building, Jake pondered the conversation and Bill's unquestioning support of Natalie.

❧ ❧ ❧ ❧

She was under close watch, Bill had said, not technically surveillance. For her protection. How was it that Natalie had not noticed that? She was a bit put out at Bill's explanation that he hadn't told her because he had thought she'd object. Which she would have, but that wasn't the point. He'd made a decision about her welfare and hadn't consulted her.

Okay, fine—it did make her feel a bit safer, knowing there was a law enforcement officer regularly cruising past her house at night, and she knew that Bill had acted solely out of concern for her welfare. But why was it that men always seemed to think they knew what was best for a woman without ever asking the woman?

Her office phone rang, and she picked it up, still feeling a bit miffed, but knowing she needed to get back to work and stop stewing.

"Natalie Morgan."

"Natalie, I'm so glad I caught you. It's Jenny."

"Jenny Patterson, oh my God!" Natalie squealed. Her frustration went right out the window at the sound of her childhood friend's voice. "It's been—what? Almost a year since I've talked to you? How are you? *Where* are you?"

Jenny laughed on the other end. "I'm at a continuing education conference in Atlanta and just noticed that the sponsoring company is also holding another one later this summer in Sarasota that I need to go to, and I thought of you. Then I had this brilliant idea that I'd call and see if you were around then, and maybe we could arrange to spend that weekend together."

"Yes! Absolutely! Just tell me when, and I'll make the time. We can spend the day at the beach, go shopping ... oh, Jen, I've missed you."

"Me too, Nat. What have you been up to?"

"Oh, the same old stuff, counseling clients, talking to dead people ... kissing FBI agents ..."

"*What? You* kissed a guy? And an FBI agent at that? The last guy I heard you kissed was about three years ago, and he had that weird ... tongue thing going on."

Natalie giggled, and Jenny joined in. "I know, I know, I'm pathetic. But this guy ... I'm telling you, Jenny, I felt it right down to my toes." Natalie sobered a bit. "But the really discouraging part is that he doesn't believe in the paranormal at all, and he pretty much thinks I'm a fake."

"Well, if he kissed you all the way down to your toes, he must be thinking something else, too. You're too wonderful, Natalie, for him not to eventually come around."

What would a girl do without her close friends? Natalie wondered. They talked some more, and Natalie wrote the date of the conference on her calendar and promised to meet Jenny that weekend at the hotel where it was being held.

Hanging up, Natalie felt better, content. Her friends, Bernie—they were the people who really mattered in her life. They had stuck by her through thick and thin, and they believed in her without reservation.

Jenny had proven it from the very beginning, when, on the first day of kindergarten, Natalie had been sitting alone at the edge of the playground, all the kids laughing and running by her as though she wasn't even there, and Jenny had walked right up to her and asked if she wanted to play hopscotch. Then years later, on the night Natalie had almost died, when she had somehow been able to telepathically contact Jenny and ask for her help, Jenny hadn't hesitated. Jenny's call to 911 was the reason the paramedics had arrived in time to save Natalie.

Natalie remembered the secret call she'd made to Jenny the day she'd woken up in the hospital after the attack, when all the nurses and doctors were gone; how she'd told Jenny what had really happened and how Jenny had cried for Natalie as she'd heard the truth, accepting without question when Natalie had described in a whisper how she'd temporarily left her body when she'd ask Jenny for help.

Natalie also recalled how they'd come up with the story Jenny would give the police—simply a vivid dream—if they ever questioned Jenny about what had prompted her to call them that night.

Natalie remembered how terrible she had felt not telling Jenny about her plans to run away, but she just hadn't wanted Jenny to get into any more trouble by having to lie about where Natalie had gone if she had known. Natalie had sworn to herself then that she'd somehow keep in touch with Jenny, no matter what happened, and that's exactly what she had done.

Now they did their best to stay in regular contact in spite of their busy lives, and Natalie knew how difficult it was for Jenny to do so. She was a successful attorney in a huge firm in Nashville, putting in sixty hours a week practicing family law *and* doing pro bono work for many child advocacy groups, like the CASA—Court Appointed Special Advocates—program, as a direct result of what Jenny had seen Natalie go through.

Natalie knew her life had been blessed the moment Jenny had come into it, and she said a quick thank-you that she was still a part of it.

Chapter Seven

S miling on the way home Wednesday night after dropping
Bernie off at her house, Natalie realized she had enjoyed
Bernie's cackles throughout the Sandra Bullock movie
they'd just seen almost as much as she had enjoyed the movie
itself. She loved going to the movies with Bernie, a tradition they
had started early on when Bernie had been shocked to hear that
Natalie had never been to the movie theatre before coming to live
with Bernie.

So Natalie had suggested the film tonight, hoping Bernie would
accept it as routine and not see through the ruse, that Natalie
was trying everything she could think of to keep her mind off of
Jake. Only the plan hadn't worked as well as Natalie had hoped,
as she kept seeing Jake in the male lead character. Bernie's laugh
would then pull her back to reality. Unfortunately, when she was
alone as she was now, it was almost impossible to prevent her
traitorous thoughts from gravitating back toward him, including
his remarkable ability to kiss her senseless, to the point where she
had been blissfully unaware that she had been in the middle of a
public parking lot. Her cheeks still heated at the memory.

She parked her Honda in the driveway, and as she got out of
the car, she noticed the plain brown package on the front steps. She
looked around quickly but couldn't see anything or anyone. It was
nine thirty—and dark.

She slowly made her way toward the box, her instantly thudding heart not listening to the admonitions in her head to slow down and remain calm. She swallowed, telling herself it was nothing, probably just a package left by the UPS man. But when she got close enough, she could see there was no writing on it.

She stood there in indecision. Where was the cruiser when she needed it? She made a split-second decision and steadily backed away from the box as though it might suddenly jump up and bite her, and then she turned and ran to the back of house, unlocking the back door and immediately locking it behind her once inside. She pulled her wallet from her purse, grabbed the business card and then the phone, and dialed.

"Jake Riggs."

Natalie suddenly couldn't speak over the roaring sound in her ears. "Jake." It came out as a hoarse whisper.

"Natalie, is that you? What's wrong?"

She swallowed again, trying to find some tiny bit of moisture in her mouth. Suddenly the words came rushing out. "Jake, I just got home, and there's a box on my doorstep. I don't recognize it. It doesn't have any writing on it, and I'm not sure who left it. I … I don't know what to do." *Can you please come?*

"Don't touch it. Where are you right now?"

"Inside my house, in my kitchen."

"I assume all the doors and windows were locked before you left?" At her affirmative response, he continued, "Don't go back outside. Keep the doors locked, and I'll be there as fast as I can. I'll call it in on my way over." He waited a heartbeat. "Sit tight, Natalie. I promise I'll be there, and we'll take care of it."

"Okay." *But hurry.*

❧ ❧ ❧ ❧

Lieutenant Greg Harris of the Sarasota County Sheriff's Office was on nearby patrol duty and heard the call come in, diverting to Natalie's house within a minute. When he showed up, her fear eased greatly. But Jake wasn't there yet. Where was he? She was waiting in her living room looking out the window and biting her nails—Bernie would never know—as the officer stood sentry-like on the front steps communicating with his captain and relaying the details of the unmarked box.

Headlights suddenly appeared on the street and quickly turned into Natalie's drive. Natalie saw Jake jump out and jog over to Lieutenant Harris, and she hurriedly went to the front door, suddenly needing to be near him and not questioning why.

When she opened the door, Jake was crouching down to scan the box, and Natalie immediately felt better as she looked down upon his now-familiar dark head. He glanced up at her, his eyes intense. "Hey. You all right?"

"I am now. Thank you for coming." She let out a silent breath. "I've just realized tonight that I'm a big scaredy-cat. I would never have thought it, considering I hear dead people talk." She smiled shakily, trying to make light of the situation.

"Anyone would have been scared, Natalie." Jake looked back down at the box, listening quietly for a moment before he stood up. "Thanks for responding so quickly, Lieutenant. My team is on their way. Just to be on the safe side, I'm going to call the Hazardous Devices Unit at the Sheriff's Office—they owe me a favor." He grilled the officer with one final question. "Nothing was touched, correct?"

Lieutenant Harris confirmed the integrity of the scene and then headed back to his patrol car. Jake got out his cell phone to make the call while Natalie remained near him, absorbing his competence, his sureness, and letting it calm her racing heart.

"Damn it, what the hell's wrong with this thing?" Jake shook his phone as the screen started to go haywire.

Oh boy, Natalie thought. Now appeared to be as good a time as any to tell Jake about her other little ... talent. "Um, Jake?"

He half turned to her while still fiddling with his phone, frowning. "Yes?"

"It's probably my fault your phone isn't working." He stopped and looked at her directly, his frown deepening.

"How so?" he asked slowly, as if he realized he wasn't entirely prepared for the answer—which Natalie knew he wouldn't be. Oh well.

"You see, I have this … this electrostatic or electromagnetic energy … thing going on in my body. I got it after my near-death experience, I suspect from the paramedics using the defibrillator so many times to try to shock my heart back to life." She searched his face for any signs of skepticism. So far, so good.

"The problem is, if I'm too close to something electronic, or especially if I'm touching it, I either make it malfunction somehow or drain the power. Anything made of metal gets magnetized when I touch it. Which is why I can't use a cell phone or a pager, or wear a watch, or use any battery-powered equipment. I regularly blow out light bulbs in my house when I flip the switch. And I can drain the battery on a cell phone faster than you can say … well, you get my meaning." She smiled faintly and then continued.

"Anyway, as you can imagine, it's a real pain in the butt for me, not to mention the people who happen to be standing too close to me trying to use said electronic devices."

Natalie watched as Jake's mouth lifted slightly in response to her wry humor, and then his lips slowly curved into a full-blown smile as he continued to stare at her. A genuine smile. Taken aback, her heart did a funny little dance in her chest.

Multiple headlights indicating several other cars were arriving jarred Jake into action. "Natalie, will you wait inside while we take care of this? I'll be in shortly." He stopped for moment. "You sure you're all right?"

Natalie nodded, her eyes dark and luminous and glued to his until he winked quickly at her and went to meet the arriving officers.

❧ ❧ ❧ ❧

Jake was furious. Who the hell was this creep? They'd better find him and nail his ass soon, because Jake wasn't taking any more chances. It appeared that Natalie's life could be at stake.

The technician from HDU had come and gone, confirming that no bomb or other incendiary device had been inside. But they'd just slowly opened the box, and what they'd found inside, in Jake's opinion, was worse. Far worse. Another necklace, just like the one from the Robertson crime scene. And a lock of long, straight brown hair that looked like it matched Natalie's hair. What kind of message was this bastard trying to send?

As Jake silently stewed while he knelt next to the box, Natalie opened the door, asking him if she could see. She must have been looking through the front window. Damn.

"It's really not a good idea, Natalie."

She instantly bristled. "Jake, if this affects me, I have a right to see." Ignoring his advice, she stepped forward and bent over the open box. Her face immediately drained of color.

"Is it mine?" she whispered.

He expelled a breath, ran a hand over his hair in frustration. "We'll have to test it to make sure, but … it's possible."

"When would he have taken some of my hair?" Her voice remained at a whisper.

Jake reached up and grabbed her hand and squeezed, trying to reassure her. "I imagine it was all those years ago. Sometime during the attack when you were unconscious."

She looked at him for a moment. "Is that really any better, Jake?" she asked unsteadily. "That he didn't just recently sneak into my house while I was asleep, but instead, kept a lock of my hair all these years?"

Her voice had given her away, but Jake could easily see just how frightened Natalie was—her eyes were a bit too bright and she was now biting down on her lower lip to keep it from trembling. He wanted to take her in his arms then and there. He finally stood, retaining his hold on her hand, now icy cold.

"Hansen, finish up with the scene, and make sure this gets taken into evidence. *No* mistakes."

"Yes, sir," Agent Hansen replied, and he directed the remaining crew and forensic team to start wrapping things up.

Jake led Natalie through the front door and into her living room, forcing her to sit down on the couch and taking a seat next to her. "How about if I make some coffee?" he volunteered.

Natalie stared down at his hand over hers for a moment before raising anxious eyes to his. "Stay. Tonight. Please."

"Natalie, I don't know if that's a good idea. I can call—"

She interrupted him. "I don't want you to call anyone else. You can sleep here on the couch. I don't … I just …" She looked away, closing her eyes. "I just feel safer when you're around."

How could he refuse that? She was clearly afraid, and he was just as concerned that she might be in real danger. Did he really trust anyone else to keep her safe?

"Okay, I'll stay—but on one condition."

Natalie opened her eyes and turned back to him.

"I like pancakes for breakfast, with lots of syrup."

She smiled softly. "Deal."

❧ ❧ ❧ ❧

Natalie jerked awake at the sensation of being thrown across the room. She frantically looked around and then blew out a breath. It's okay, it's okay, she repeated silently; it was just a dream. Focus on your parasympathetic nervous system—in and out, long slow breaths. Suddenly, she became aware of a light tapping sound. At her window. Oh God.

She quickly glanced at the window, saw nothing. Think logically, she told herself. How could someone tap at a second floor window? They couldn't, unless they were throwing something from the ground. Or they were on the roof.

Natalie immediately jumped out of bed and hurried downstairs. Jake was downstairs. Jake would figure it out.

She reached the bottom of the stairs and entered the kitchen, and then she realized she hadn't grabbed her robe. She looked down at her sleep shirt that fell midthigh, with Tweety Bird on the front, and groaned inwardly. But she was *not* going back up those stairs to get her robe.

Her bare feet making no sound, she padded through the kitchen and into the living room, expecting to find Jake asleep on the couch. But he was already sitting up, the blanket she had given him earlier tossed aside—and he was shirtless.

Natalie stopped dead in her tracks, all her earlier thoughts instantly evaporating from her head. He was simply magnificent. Beautifully formed. Like some chiseled Greek god with firmly muscled shoulders and arms, a smattering of hair in the middle of his chest, and a darker, thin trail of it running down his flat stomach ...

"Natalie, what's wrong?"

She swallowed, trying to ignore her thumping heart, not sure if the reason now was Jake or the sound she had heard. "I heard something. Upstairs. It sounded like a tapping at my window."

He immediately got up, threw on his shirt without buttoning it, pulled on his shoes, and grabbed his gun from his holster lying on the floor next to the couch.

He had a gun, Natalie thought with some surprise. She had never seen it.

"Stay right here; I'm going outside to check it out."

"Okay." *Be careful.* Her heart in her throat, she watched him quickly walk over to stand next to the front window, surveying the front yard, the street, the neighbors' houses, and then he opened the front door and proceeded out, arm bent, gun raised to shoulder level.

Natalie waited. And waited. What was taking so long? What if he'd been attacked from behind? What if Daryl was out there and Jake was lying unconscious somewhere, or worse ...

The front door suddenly opened and Natalie gasped, and then she let out a huge breath of relief when she saw it was Jake. "Oh, thank God. Are you okay? What took so long?" She immediately went over to him, needing to be near him again, needing to feel his warmth.

"I checked out the entire property and didn't see anything, or anyone. I'm not sure what you heard, Natalie, but whoever or whatever it was, it's gone now."

"Oh. Well. That's good." She ran her hands through her hair, suddenly conscious of how she must look as Jake stared at her, hair mussed, no make-up, half-dressed. She looked down, anywhere but his eyes, and her gaze landed on the narrow expanse of solid chest still revealed through his open shirt. Her mouth went dry.

Jake turned away, instantly aware of that look in Natalie's eyes, the same look he had seen in the car that had led to instantaneous combustion. He busied himself replacing his Glock 23 in his holster, lecturing himself as he did so that she was vulnerable right now, that it was *not* the right time to be thinking of burying his hands in that sexy, tousled hair, seizing those eminently kissable lips with his own, taking unfair advantage of the easy access that short T-shirt provided ... his body instantly responded to the uncontrollable, illicit thoughts. Hell.

"Jake."

He continued to focus his attention on the Glock to avoid looking at her. "Natalie, you'd better go upstairs. We can talk in the morning."

"Jake, I ..."

"Natalie, *go upstairs*. Please. Or I might do something that you'll regret later."

He felt her tentative touch on his back. "I don't want to go upstairs," she whispered. "I want ... I want you to turn around, Jake."

He couldn't stop himself. He finally put the gun down and turned and saw her looking up at him, her head barely coming to his chin in her bare feet. Saw the heat and the yearning in her eyes. He closed his own eyes to try to evade it, to try to settle his disobedient body, to try to remain professional. Just like she'd requested.

"Natalie, I don't think you know what you want."

Her hands slid up the front of his shirt and then parted the material so she could touch his bare skin. *Scorch* his bare skin.

"You're wrong, Jake." He opened his eyes to see her watch her own hands as they slid up to his shoulders and then back down over the muscles of his chest. Then she raised those dark, slumberous eyes to his. "I *do* know what I want. You. I want ..."

It was enough for him. He didn't wait for her to finish, simply hauled her close and imprisoned her mouth with his own and felt the heat implode into him again. Christ, what was it about her? He couldn't get enough of her, her moist, pliant lips just as impatient as his, her sexy as hell curves underneath that short damn T-shirt.

He couldn't stop his hands from clutching her narrow waist, sliding down the slope of her hips and then around to cup her softly curving ass. Sweet Jesus ... inflamed, he pulled her forcefully against his own hardness, continuing to ravage her mouth, stopping only to draw in a ragged breath and drag his lips across her smooth cheek and down to nip at her softly scented neck. She whimpered, and his need shot straight through the roof.

He forcefully grabbed her behind and lifted her up to him, guiding her legs around his waist, and then turned to fall onto the couch with her sitting on his lap. She settled fully against him, her softness nestling his hardness, and then she moved her hips and drove him insane.

Shoving her T-shirt up and out of the way, he captured one rosy, puckered crest in his mouth. He heard the sudden, sharp intake of her breath and then the whisper of his name over and over ...

The sound of something hitting the front window jerked Jake's head up. What the hell? He looked into Natalie's wide, startled eyes, lifted her off of him, and said through clenched teeth, "Don't move." He grabbed his gun once again and proceeded quickly but cautiously out the front door.

❧ ❧ ❧ ❧

Jake found the small, lone rock in the flower bed directly beneath the front window. Leaving it there, he continued stealthily over the lawn to the street, looking for any evidence, footprints, a suspicious car, someone fleeing on foot, anything.

Shit, he was an absolute idiot. There had been someone outside the house, and he had been so wrapped up in Natalie that he had forgotten he was there to protect her. He was sure as hell doing a piss-poor job of it.

He turned and circled around the side of the house to check the back again and saw the still-smoldering cigarette butt just outside the back door. God *damn* it! He'd have to call it in, get the crew out here to fully check it out, take the butt into evidence. This guy was one cocky son of a bitch, that was for sure. He had to know they'd get his DNA from the cigarette.

The guy clearly had just been there if the thing was still warm. But why was the butt back here, when the rock had been thrown from the front? Though it raised the possibility of two individuals, Jake knew in his gut it was only one sick bastard. Something else told him that while the son of a bitch had meant for them to find the cigarette, the rock ... the rock had not been part of his plan. It was too ... juvenile. Jake suspected it was probably thrown in anger or some other uncontrollable emotion.

Thinking back to that moment, Jake recalled what he and Natalie had been doing. Had the perp seen them through the window? Did he have some sort of sick fascination with Natalie or some feeling of ownership over her because of the past? Jake would not rest until he found out.

He wondered if the asshole was still watching. "Why don't you show yourself, you little chickenshit?" he muttered as he scanned the darkness. Frustrated, he left the scene intact and went back around the house to the front door to check on Natalie and call it in.

When he opened the door, she was still on the couch but was wrapped in the blanket and staring sightlessly at the wall.

"Natalie."

She jerked and tensed until she realized it was only Jake. Her eyes closed briefly in relief. Damn, he hated that she had to go through this, had to be terrorized by some wack-job who'd decided he wanted to play a few sick games with her. But Jake had to remain professional now.

"Do you have a plastic sandwich bag and some tweezers?"

She frowned but didn't question him. "Yes, I'll get them right now." Still wrapped in the blanket, she hurried upstairs, came back down to the kitchen, and opened a drawer. Meeting her in there, he took the tools and went out the back door to focus on his job.

Natalie's eyes followed Jake as he went outside, watching him as he wiped the end of the tweezers clean and then carefully pick up a cigarette butt and place it in the bag. A *cigarette* butt? Someone had been smoking right outside while she and Jake … while she and Jake … Natalie swallowed convulsively.

Jake came back in and placed the bag on the counter, and then he grabbed the phone from the wall and dialed, advising someone on the other end of the situation and requesting an immediate response.

When he hung up, Natalie just stood there, the blanket enveloping her. She wished it were Jake's arms that were around her instead, that he would tell her everything was going to be okay.

Instead, he just rubbed a hand over his neck in obvious frustration.

"Natalie …"

"Jake …"

Resigned, Natalie walked over and sat down at the kitchen table. "You first."

He sat down in the chair next to her, clearly struggling with what he wanted to say, and then he turned to her. "I'm sorry."

She was thunderstruck. "You're *sorry?* For what?"

"For taking advantage of you like that. Especially on a night like tonight. I'll understand if you'd like to request that I be reassigned, that—"

"Now, wait just a minute, Jake. If anybody took advantage of the situation, I did. I was the one who ... it doesn't really matter anyway. I make my own decisions, and I chose, Jake, *I chose*. But are you ... are you saying you're sorry it happened at all?"

He hesitated. "Natalie, look. I compromised your safety tonight. It's an unforgivable thing for an agent to do. I let my ... personal feelings override my professional judgment, and it put you at risk."

He looked out the window for a moment before he continued.

"So yes, it shouldn't have happened. But you can rest assured that it won't happen again. I'll get another agent to stay with you, or we'll put you up in a hotel or a safe house, but I won't compromise your safety again."

He got up and went into the living room, leaving Natalie staring after him with an odd little ache in her chest. She understood his dedication, she really did. She could even appreciate it and be grateful for his obvious concern for her well-being.

But couldn't he have at least said it meant something to him? Couldn't he have told her that he wasn't sorry about the incredible experience they'd just shared? Where she had given herself to him without hesitation, without a second thought?

Natalie covered her face with her hands. What was the matter with her? She had never felt anything for a man even remotely close to what she felt for Jake. How could that be? He didn't even believe in who she really was. How could she have such intense feelings for this man when he couldn't even tell her that what they had just done had been ... mind-blowing? Earth-shattering?

Hope was right. The heart had a mind of its own. Natalie could no more tell her heart to stop what it was feeling than she could force Jake to admit his own feelings for her. If he even had them.

Her heart suddenly felt like it was being squeezed. Was that why he hadn't said anything? Because it *hadn't* really meant the same thing to him? Maybe to him it was simply ... recreational sex, a way to satisfy a basic need that really had nothing to do with her personally.

Natalie was suddenly furious at the tears that threatened to spill over. She would *not* cry over him, damn it. She got up and walked upstairs, *with* the blanket. He could sleep without the damn thing for the rest of the night.

Chapter Eight

The buzzing of the alarm slowly penetrated the fog in Natalie's brain, and she rolled over and slammed her hand down on the top of the wind-up clock on her bedside table. Six thirty. Ugh. Rubbing her eyes, she lay back against the pillow and was immediately hit with the memory of last night—with Jake. Her stomach plummeted.

Was he still here? Suddenly infused with energy, she hurriedly got up, grabbed her robe, and stopped in the bathroom to pee— okay, and to check her hair and face, she admitted—then walked slowly down the stairs. The conversation she had with herself on the way down did not ease her trepidation about seeing Jake again.

Reaching the kitchen, she noted it was abnormally quiet and padded through the dining room and into the living room. There was no sign of Jake. Natalie's gray high-backed couch looked as it normally did, the cushions straight, the burgundy accent pillows plumped and in place.

The abrupt image of herself as she sat astride Jake while he tormented her with his clever mouth hit Natalie with the force of an F-5 tornado. Heart tripping, she closed her eyes, amazed at the intensity of the feeling with Jake not even here. Get hold of yourself, Natalie. It was just … a moment in time. It doesn't have to *mean* anything.

Taking a deep breath, she walked over to the front door and

peered out one of the two slender panes on either side. A cruiser sat curbside in front of her house with an officer clearly inside. Turning away, oddly disappointed, Natalie went to get ready for work.

When she got to her office, after having been followed there by the patrol car, she immediately sat down and dialed Bill's direct line.

"Chief Garrett here."

His familiar, sandpaper-rough voice was like an instant salve, easing some of the strain. "Hi, Bill, it's Natalie."

"Natalie, how are you doing?" the chief quickly asked, concern lacing his voice. "Jake contacted me early this morning and let me know what happened last night. Are you all right? Where are you?"

Was she all right? Natalie didn't really know. She wasn't half as bothered by the unwanted gift left on her doorstep as she had been by Jake's rejection of her. "I'm okay—I'm at work now. Thanks for asking." She swallowed. "Where is Jake?"

"He's with the FBI's profiler right now, trying to get something we can use to nail this bastard." The last word was underscored with anger. "We need to take this seriously, Natalie, very seriously. You'll need to come in as soon as you can and provide a blood and hair sample, and we also need to talk about having you temporarily stay somewhere else. Is Bernie—"

"Absolutely not!" Natalie jumped in. "Bernie does *not* come into this. I will *not* put her at risk. In fact, I want you to arrange for some protection for her as well. If he knows where I live, it's entirely likely that he also knows about Bernie." Natalie suddenly realized she was very afraid. She didn't know how she would—*if* she would—survive if anything happened to Bernie.

"Calm down, I agree with you," Bill replied patiently, knowing of Natalie's protectiveness of Bernie and the history there. "I was just attempting to ask if Bernie was aware of what had happened. I'll take care of getting her some protection, but we have to discuss where you'll stay. We can either put you up in a hotel or in one of our safe houses. Either way, you need to be placed in protective custody."

Natalie closed her eyes. Had it really come to this? Being forced out of her own home by a maniac who thought he was calling the shots? To slink away in fear while someone else took care of closing the book on the details of her past?

Not today, she thought with a sudden flare of anger.

"I'm not going to run and hide, Bill, nor am I going to let this creep push me out of my own home. I'm going to stay and fight, and he's going to rue the day he decided to look me up again." She felt better just saying the words. "I think the continued close surveillance is important, and I don't have a problem with that. I'd like to think of this guy screaming in frustration when he sees the fortress we create."

"All right. For now we can do it that way." The chief said goodbye and hung up, but he was still worried. He knew that even though it would make things safer for Natalie to have the authorities constantly watch over her, it was not a guarantee if she chose to stay put. But he also knew Natalie. She might not look like she had a backbone of steel, but he knew it was there.

He made a spur-of-the-moment decision to talk to Jake and make a personal request that Jake stay in the house with Natalie each night. Though Natalie didn't need to know about the sleeping arrangements just yet, it was the only thing that would make the chief comfortable with the situation and help ease the heartburn that he knew wouldn't be going away until they caught this asshole. He grabbed another roll of Tums from his desk drawer.

❧ ❧ ❧ ❧

Danny was looking at Natalie a bit peculiarly as they talked during their regular Thursday session. She finally gave up. "Okay, Danny, out with it. What's up?"

He frowned a little. "I'm not sure." He twisted his hands. "It just seems like you're upset. You're not upset with me, are you?"

"Of course not! What makes you think that?" Natalie smiled at him, but even she knew it wasn't a totally natural smile.

"My stomach hurts. It feels like you're scared or sad, and I don't know why. I just don't want you to be sad."

Natalie was amazed. Was Danny a Sensitive? Someone who was acutely attuned to the emotions of others, even residual emotion from those long gone? It had never come up in their sessions before. But it was clear he was picking up cues from the tension she was feeling about the case. Maybe even about Jake.

"I'm sorry your stomach hurts, Danny. You know what? I guess I *am* a little scared. I'm working on a case right now, and it's possible that a person I love very much could get hurt. And it makes me frightened and sad at the same time. So you're exactly right."

His eyes got big and round. "Get hurt? Like, are they in *danger*? You're not in danger, are you?"

Oh, dear. She probably shouldn't have been so blunt. Normally, Natalie believed the truth was the best option, and the next best option was just not telling the whole truth. But actually *lying* was hardly ever a good option for her. Until now.

"No, Danny, I'm not in any real danger. At least not danger like you mean, like … being attacked by a lion, or … or … falling off a cliff." Oh, that was bad, Natalie. If he buys that, you've got a career in acting. "You don't have to worry, okay?"

Danny just sat there staring at her, appearing to consider her words. Then he spoke slowly. "But … what if something *happened* to you? Who would listen to me?" His eyes suddenly filled, and he whispered, "You're the only one that I … that I really talk to."

"Oh, Danny." Natalie got up and went to kneel in front of him, covering his hands with her own. "I'm not going anywhere." Natalie prayed she was telling the truth this time. "You can talk to me for as long as you want." She smiled. "I'm so glad you *like* talking to me. It makes my heart swell—" she placed her hands over her heart and puffed them out "—like in *The Grinch Who Stole Christmas*, you know?"

Danny's quickly smothered grin told her she had made it past the worst of his fear. He was probably imagining her with a big green head and body. *Whatever it took*, she thought.

"Listen, Danny, I am going to take a couple of weeks off from work. You know, like a vacation? So I won't see you until a week from next Thursday, okay?"

She got up and went to her desk, pulling out a pen and piece of paper. "I'm going to give you my home telephone number, so you can call me anytime you feel like it. Just don't give it out to anyone else—it'll be our little secret." She winked at him.

He took the paper she handed to him and stared down at the numbers for a moment, and then he raised his head and smiled at her.

☀ ☀ ☀ ☀

Jake, feeling uncharacteristically edgy, waited in the chief's office for their Friday morning status meeting, tugging at his ice blue tie. The chief had just stepped out for a moment, and impatient, Jake rose and began to pace. He was *not* looking forward to this meeting with Natalie, yet he knew his impatience was also related to his desire to see her again. He felt like he was being ripped in two.

Since the scene at her house Wednesday night—which had played over and over in his head like a broken record—Jake had done his best to steer clear of Natalie, arranging for a couple of seasoned FBI officers to be stationed at her house Thursday night in addition to the cruiser Bill had provided. Jake wanted to be sure. But he had barely slept Thursday night, still worrying in spite of the extra coverage.

Jake had done all this despite the chief calling him yesterday to ask him to personally stay with Natalie, since she had adamantly refused to go to a safe house after the incident. It was the only way the chief would agree to let her stay in her own home, he'd said. Jake had reluctantly agreed, but after he'd hung up, he had almost instantly realized he could not trust himself, so he had arranged for his two cohorts to take his place.

Jake admired Natalie's nerve to stick it out even while he thought it was a damn fool decision. She was putting herself at greater risk. Not to mention that she was placing Jake in the no-win situation of wanting to be the only one to protect her but knowing that he couldn't because of the ferocity of the desire he felt for her. Every time he thought about that scene on the couch, he got hard. It was insane how much he wanted her. It was even more insane that he wanted her so much in spite of the fact that she thought she talked to dead people.

"Come on in, Natalie. Jake's already here." The chief entered the room, Natalie following close behind in a pale yellow tank and tan slacks. Her russet hair was pulled back in a neat braid revealing her guarded, shadowy brown eyes.

Jesus, seeing her again was like a blow to his solar plexus. He had to force himself to breathe. He stood as she walked to the chair next to him and sat down. Her soft "Hi, Jake" and strained smile was almost painful. He sat down again.

"Thanks, both of you, for coming," the chief said. "I think it's important that we continue to have these weekly meetings. Not only do they provide me with an update, they force you to reassess the case on a regular basis." He smiled at them both. "Okay, enough lecturing. Let's talk about the case. Jake?"

Jake tried to focus. "We got the results back from the lab—the DNA from the blood on the front seat of the truck matched Whitney's, so it's conclusive that this was the vehicle used by the perp. Also, though it's somewhat superfluous, the paint chips from the bumper of the truck were consistent with the type of paint the manufacturer used on Whitney's type of bike. The bike still hasn't been recovered, though." He tugged at his tie again. "A profile has also just been generated that I'd like Natalie to look at—" he glanced at her "—when she has the time."

As the chief listened, he glanced at Natalie and then back at Jake. Natalie was unusually quiet, and the tension in the room was as thick as a meatball sub. The chief frowned slightly as he spoke.

"Thanks, Jake. Do you have anything, Natalie?"

"No, Bill, I don't. I haven't been contacted by Whitney in almost a week, and quite frankly, I'm still a bit … shook up from Wednesday night."

"I understand, Natalie," Bill said. "Thank you for providing blood and hair samples yesterday. They've been sent to the FBI lab, and we should have the results soon." He tried one more time. "Are you positive we can't talk you into relocating temporarily? At least until we get some kind of break in the case?"

Natalie shook her head. "No. I'm sure." She glanced at Jake— and quickly looked away again. "Are we done here, Bill? I have to get to the office and take care of a few things."

Hearing the strain in her voice, Jake was at a complete loss. He had no idea what he could do to fix this. Natalie was so clearly uncomfortable around him now that it was likely they would not be able to work together anymore. It was a double-edged sword. He was better off staying away, yet all he really wanted was to be near her. To touch her.

The chief rose. "Yes, done enough, Natalie. Thanks for coming. And please be careful. You know I worry about you."

After she left, the chief walked over and shut his door, and then he turned to Jake. "What the hell is going on here, Jake?"

❦ ❦ ❦ ❦

On the way to Natalie's house that evening, Jake was calling himself every kind of fool in the book. But the chief had simply refused to take no for an answer when they'd discussed it that morning after Natalie had left.

The chief simply didn't care that Jake had already arranged for two other seasoned agents to stay; he didn't care that Jake and Natalie didn't see eye to eye on the paranormal aspects of the investigation; he didn't care about any reason that Jake had tried to throw at him, except the real reason—that Jake didn't trust himself to be alone with Natalie.

He suspected the chief knew it anyway, but once again, just

didn't care. He'd explained to Jake that Natalie had come to mean a great deal to him, professionally and personally, and her safety was paramount. Said he'd looked into Jake's background—which he didn't apologize for—and had decided that Jake was the only one who could do the job properly. Nor did he care *what* kind of tension might exist between the two of them—Jake was to stick to her like glue, and that was that.

Now here he was. He got out of his car, nodding to the officer sitting in the cruiser across the street, and walked slowly to Natalie's front door, talking to himself the whole time. You can do this. You can simply stay in a different room than Natalie. Don't let her near you. Don't let her hands slide over your chest …

"What can I help you with, young man?"

Jake looked up to see an elderly lady with short, white hair holding the front door open, eyes squinting at him as though she was having trouble seeing him. In polyester stretch pants and a flowered blouse, what he could only term as old lady clothes, she was slightly stooped over and hanging on to the doorknob with her hand.

He cleared his throat to respond when Natalie came to the door, quickly stepping in front. Her slender legs looked a mile long in the white shorts she wore, her royal blue tank outlining the delicate curves of her breasts. Jesus, he was a sick bastard. All he could think about was having those long, smooth legs wrapped around him, his hands and mouth on her breasts, on her …

"What do you want, Jake?" Natalie abruptly turned. "Bernie, please go back inside. I'll take care of this."

The lady named Bernie clearly did not take kindly to being relegated to the background or being told what to do and instead hobbled around Natalie, sticking her hand out to Jake as he reluctantly made his way up the steps.

"I'm Bernice Morgan, Natalie's guardian, surrogate mother, voice of reason. Please call me Bernie—and don't pay any mind to her. She's just miffed right now because I'm beating her at Scrabble." She grinned at him.

Charmed in spite of himself, Jake smiled back, shaking her hand. "Agent Riggs, ma'am. FBI." He felt the gnarled knuckles and slightly crooked fingers before releasing her hand, and then he watched her survey him critically in his navy sport jacket and tan slacks.

"I guess you are kind of cute, aren't you?" Bernie said after a moment.

"*Bernie!*" Natalie hissed at her. She turned to Jake, sighing. "Why are you here, Jake?"

He paused, hearing the wariness in her voice, noting the heightened pink blooming in her cheeks, and her cautious, dark eyes. He just stood for a moment, unable to prevent the sheer pleasure washing over him from simply looking at her.

"Well?" Natalie crossed her arms defensively. Bernie just stood there smiling.

Here goes nothing, Jake thought. "I'm here at Chief Garrett's insistence. To provide overnight protection." He watched Natalie's eyes widen at the statement, and then he saw Bernie's eyes narrow at Natalie's reaction—and knew immediately that Bernie was one shrewd old woman.

"But I … I thought that the other two agents were assigned for that duty."

"According to the chief, I've been reassigned to it. He wouldn't take no for an answer."

Bernie chose that moment to jump in. "Well, then, come right in, Agent Riggs. Do you play Scrabble? How about some raspberry iced tea? And Natalie made some chocolate chip cookies, too." Bernie winked at Jake as she grabbed his hand and led him into the living room, where it was clear their game had been interrupted by his arrival. She went to grab another fold-up chair from the closet until Jake realized what she was doing and politely took it from her, placing it at the card table. Bernie smiled tellingly and patted his hand in thanks.

"Tea sounds great," he said. "And I'm a sucker for good cookies. My mom used to make the best ginger snaps in North Carolina, or so she always told me." Jake sat down and glanced at the Scrabble board. His eyes immediately landed on *j-e-r-k*. Hopefully, it had been one of Bernie's plays.

"Oh, so you're a southern boy, Agent Riggs."

"Yes, ma'am. But please—call me Jake. If I'm going to beat you at a board game, we should at least be on a first name basis." He smiled innocently.

Bernie hooted. "I guess we'll just see about that, won't we? But it's really going to depend on the game, now, isn't it? I'll give you Twister, sure, but I'm nearly unbeatable at Scrabble. And card games—you don't want to mess with me on those. Especially strip poker." She cackled at her own joke and Jake joined in, her laugh infectious.

Listening to their exchange, Natalie closed her eyes for a moment and prayed for the night to end uneventfully. No, scratch that—she just wanted it to end, period.

❧ ❧ ❧ ❧

"Oh, Jake, you are the devil incarnate! How in the world did you manage to pull that one out of thin air?" Bernie grumbled good-naturedly as he tallied his final score after earning a triple word score for *q-u-i-z*.

"Looks like I just snuck past you with that word, Bernie. I guess you owe me a batch of gingersnaps after all." He sat back in his chair, grinning, slightly surprised at how much he had enjoyed himself playing Scrabble with a sharp-tongued and still sharp-minded seventy-nine-year-old *flirt*.

Natalie had played as well but had been quiet and distracted, letting Bernie keep the conversation lively and flowing. Jake had tried to ignore her as much as possible without being rude and was pretty proud of himself for what he considered a successful beginning to the evening. Maybe if Bernie could just stay …

"Well, that's my cue to leave." Bernie pushed herself up from the table and started to gather the letter blocks and put away the game.

"I didn't mean to run you off by winning, Bernie. Give me another chance—I can lose with the best of them." *Don't go.*

"Oh, phooey—don't you go doing me any favors, young man. When I beat you, it will be fair and square, and you won't know what hit you." She folded the board and placed it in the box, and then she looked at Jake. "I do need another kind of favor, though. Natalie picked me up earlier this evening, so someone will have to drive me home."

Jake knew he needed to stay at the house with Natalie, so he'd have to have another agent come and get Bernie. "I'll take care of it right now. Agent Jorgenson should be able to hold his own with you on the drive to your house." He winked at Bernie as he pulled out his cell phone on the way to the kitchen to make the call.

Natalie rose from the table. "I'm going to take a bath." She walked over and hugged Bernie. "Thank you for being here tonight. I think Jake had fun. You took his mind off the case for a while."

"Are you all right, dear? You were awfully quiet during the game." Even though Bernie knew exactly why, she wanted to hear Natalie admit it. If she could admit her feelings for Jake, she could then deal with them.

"I think I'm just tired. I'm going to soak in the tub and then hit the sack." She glanced toward the kitchen. "Would you tell Jake that … that I'll see him in the morning?"

"Why don't you wait and tell him yourself?" Bernie wasn't sure how much she should interfere. Oh, fiddlesticks. This was Natalie. *Her* Natalie. She'd interfere as much as she needed to. "Does he know how you feel, sweetie?"

Natalie jerked her head sharply to stare at Bernie. "I …" She closed her eyes. "No."

Bernie raised an eyebrow. "Aren't you the one who's always telling me how important it is to be honest in relationships?"

"We don't *have* a relationship, Bernie."

"Then start one, Natalie. It's as simple as that." Bernie turned as Jake walked back into the living room.

"Agent Jorgenson will be here in ten minutes to take you home, Bernie."

"Thank you, Jake. Why don't we go outside and wait for him? I think a little fresh air and a talk would do us good." She smiled at him and shuffled toward the door.

Jake looked back at Natalie to find her staring at him speculatively.

"I'll be upstairs," she said softly and left.

As he watched Natalie go, Jake uttered a quick prayer for strength and followed Bernie outside to Natalie's front porch. He helped her slowly lower herself into one of the two green Adirondack chairs and then pulled the chain on the fan hanging from the porch ceiling above them. The steady whir of the blades underlying the random chirping of the sand field crickets was almost peaceful, he realized. He sat down next to Bernie and scanned the darkness of the yard and beyond from sheer force of habit, and then he glanced up at the night sky. It looked like it might rain again.

Bernie suddenly interrupted his thoughts and got right to the point.

"Let me tell you a story, Jake. It's about an old woman who'd lost all faith in life until a brave, determined young girl showed up on her doorstep one evening, asking about the room for rent. The girl lied about her age and looked like she hadn't eaten properly in months, but this old woman saw something in her eyes that night. Something that reached out and grabbed the old woman by the heart and seemed to say, *I'll help you if you'll help me.*"

Bernie rolled her head toward Jake as she rested it against the back of the chair. "And that's exactly what Natalie did. She gave me a reason to live again, Jake. I'd lost Holman, my husband, the year before to a sudden heart attack. He was only sixty-two. And just before Holman died, we had been trying to recover from the shock of losing Will, our only son, and his pregnant wife in an auto accident. We'd had him late in life and were looking so forward to that grandbaby. I was a bitter shell of a woman railing at God for taking away every person that I ever loved or could love. Then it was as though he dropped Natalie on my doorstep and said, 'I'm giving you Natalie to love instead. She needs it, and you need her.'"

Jake listened quietly to Bernie's words, heard the depth of emotion in her voice. It was clear she had suffered greatly and that Natalie had pulled her back from the brink.

"But I didn't know just how brave Natalie was until she finally told me her story one night on my front porch, much like you and I are sitting here now. She told me of a life with a woman who had no right to be called mother, who physically and verbally abused that sweet girl every chance she got. Told her she was worthless and stupid, then would neglect and ignore her for weeks on end to party and do her drugs, leaving Natalie, just a child, to fend for herself. How her mother's boyfriend almost raped her, then basically killed her, until God saw fit to send her back to me to help heal her—and for her to help heal me."

Bernie looked back out into the darkness as light drops of rain began to fall. "So I accepted God's peace offering and vowed to do my best. I know it sounds silly, Jake, but she was like a flower in the empty, forsaken desert that my life had become. She was sweet, funny, and she was a hard worker. Honest as the day was long and amazingly innocent for all she had suffered. But she cursed like a sailor when she first showed up. We had to work on that quite a bit." She chuckled at the memories.

"When Natalie told me that she was beginning to hear voices, I never questioned it. I knew if she said it was so, it was so. I like to think I helped her accept the gift she was given, which I believe is part of the reason she *was* given a second chance."

Jake didn't want to hear this part. He stopped her. "Bernie—I appreciate the information, and I have no doubt that Natalie is an amazing woman, was an amazing girl. But I don't believe that she hears or talks to the dead. I'm sorry. I just don't."

Bernie watched the nondescript gray sedan pull up to the house, its windshield wipers stopping as the agent parked. "You will, Jake. You will." She took his offered hand when she started to pull herself out of the low chair. "In the meantime, just know that if you hurt her, you'll have to deal with me." Then she smiled, patted his arm, and hobbled out into the now-steady rain as her driver came to escort her to her glorified cab.

⚓ ⚓ ⚓ ⚓

Natalie finished rubbing the cucumber melon lotion onto her skin, donned her pink chenille robe, and knotted it loosely at her waist. She removed the clip that held her hair on top of her head and brushed out the thick brown tresses, contemplating her decision and the risk she was taking. The risk of rejection.

Bernie had made it sound so simple. Only it wasn't simple at all. *And* she realized she was nervous. She had never tried to seduce a man before.

She knew Jake desired her, knew it in her bones. But could she convince him that desire was enough? And *was* it enough? In the long run—no. But it was a start, and she had made up her mind. She wanted to start a relationship with Jake, despite the risks.

Her heart fluttering in her chest, hoping she was doing the right thing, she shut off the light in her bathroom and padded barefoot down the hardwood steps, hearing the steady sound of the downpour outside as she entered the kitchen, where Jake was making coffee. *Here goes nothing*, she thought.

He was instantly still when he saw her, the carafe of water in his hands forgotten. She looked just fresh from a bath, rosy and glistening, like a sweet, ripe peach that he could sink his teeth into. Holy Mother of God. It was almost a physical pain not to be able to reach out and just touch her.

He closed his eyes and let out a slow, silent breath. Be strong, Jake. You cannot let her distract you. Coffee. You were making coffee. He suddenly smelled something fruity and opened his eyes to find Natalie standing right next to him. She was so goddamned beautiful, he didn't know if he *had* the strength to resist her.

"Jake." The whisper slid over him like a caress, and he barely stopped the groan before it escaped his lips. He looked away, cursing his body as his pulse started to pound and his blood thicken.

"*Natalie*, I told you. I'm here for one reason, one reason only. To protect you. I can't do that when you're ..." *So damn close. So damn desirable.* He focused on pouring the water into the coffee maker as distant thunder echoed outside.

"Jake, you're good at what you do, aren't you?" He turned at the question and wished he hadn't. Her deep brown eyes were staring at him, pulling him in, sucking the free will from him. Coffee grounds. Did he already put them in the machine? Turning back to check, he saw that he had and pushed the ON button. Now, what had she asked? His job. Yes, he could focus on that.

"Without sounding arrogant, I suppose I like to think I am good at what I do. Why do you ask?" He finally risked another look at her.

Directly ignoring his question, Natalie asked another. "Do you have your gun with you?" As he wondered at that question, she started tugging at the knot on the belt of her robe. It was pink and fluffy, and he couldn't help but speculate about what kind of wispy thing she might be wearing underneath. He narrowed his eyes, watching her hands.

"Yes," he said slowly. His gun was on him, in his shoulder holster under his jacket.

"Are all the doors and windows locked?" One end of the now-loose knot came free as Natalie inched closer to him.

Jake swallowed. "Yes." He had checked everything when he'd come back in after Bernie had left. But all his blood had just left his brain, and hell if he could be any more articulate than the one-syllable responses he was giving her.

"Is your sedan parked out front, the cruiser across the street?" Her voice had lowered, and she now had the two ends of the strap in each hand, and her robe started to slip open just as lightning flashed outside the kitchen window.

Shit. He quickly reached out and grabbed the material at her stomach, crossing one side back over the other to cover her up.

"*Stop it*, Natalie." He'd never be able to withstand even the tiniest glimpse of her bare flesh underneath. He grabbed the belt from her hands as thunder rumbled, and retied it before he could give himself a reason not to.

"Jake."

Damn it, why tonight, of all nights, was the sound of his name on her lips like a quiet subliminal coaxing, as steady and hypnotic as the rain? He was afraid if she said it one more time, he'd be on his knees begging. She reached out and touched him lightly on the arm, and the expected jolt ran straight through him.

"You've done everything you can to keep me safe. The only way I'll feel any safer is if I'm in your arms." She moved her hand to the front of his shirt, tugging it free from the waistband of his slacks, keeping her eyes on him as she began unbuttoning it.

"Although tonight," she continued, "I'm not really interested in safe—but I am interested in being in your arms." She moistened her lips with her tongue. "*Very* interested."

He did groan this time, stopping her hands with his own as they worked the buttons of his shirt. "I told myself a thousand times this wouldn't happen."

A secretive smile curved her lips; her dark eyes at once turned mysterious and knowing. Jake could not look away this time.

"Sounds like you had a difficult time convincing yourself," she murmured. "Maybe I can help."

She gently pulled her hands free from his grasp, slid them up his chest to curl around his neck, and gently pulled his head toward hers. "Kiss me, Jake." Her voice dropped to a whisper. "Like you did before. I can't stop thinking about that night on the couch … and what almost happened …"

He surrendered to the seductive cadence of her voice, the irresistible allure in her heavy-lidded eyes, allowing her to eliminate the remaining distance between them as the storm intensified outside.

And God help him, he knew there was no turning back now.

Chapter Nine

The moment Jake's lips touched hers, all Natalie's reservations dissolved. The kiss was instantly addictive; like a drug to her senses. She was incapable of stopping the long, low moan that rose from her throat, powerless to stop her mouth from opening beneath his or her tongue from seeking and finding his.

His mouth and his hands were equally demanding, insistent, relentless. He hastily worked the knot of her robe loose again, to reach inside and graze her hips on his way around to grab her butt and pull her against him.

Groaning, he suddenly released her mouth. "Jesus, Natalie, you're *totally* naked under that thing."

His hands, so warm and sure on the bare skin of her backside, were like heaven. "Is that a problem?" she whispered, amazed she could speak at all, the delicious sensations assailing her as she moved against the ridge of his erection pressed firmly against her. She reached up on her toes and bit his neck, licking him there, breathing in his heady, masculine scent, the spicy taste of him.

"No problem," he muttered, his hands continuing to move restlessly over her skin as she found again and started working feverishly on his buttons, finishing the last one to spread open his shirt and finally, *finally*, touch his gloriously warm, bare chest. She pulled back, her breath coming in short little bursts as the lightning flashed again, followed almost immediately by a loud clap of thunder.

God, he was so magnificently male. So strong and hard and beautiful. Just looking at him had her trembling all over. Staggered by the intensity of her reaction to him, only him, she looked up into his eyes and they were glittering again, locking with hers as his hand reached up to capture her breast inside her robe, to stroke it while his thumb brushed her sensitized nipple. He watched her eyes darken to midnight at his touch and then helplessly close, her head falling back as she whimpered, and he bent down to replace his thumb with his mouth.

Her legs threatening to give out on her, she gripped his shoulders and then the back of his head, sure she was going to die from the sheer pleasure of his warm, wet mouth on her breast. "Jake … I …"

But he gave her no mercy, his hand simultaneously seeking and finding her moist center, his finger slickly gliding into her and back out again, then sliding over her most sensitive spot, and she was suddenly mindless and crying out as the orgasm ripped through her without warning, her legs buckling until Jake caught her against him, holding her while the rhythmic contractions pulsated through her.

"Where's your bedroom? Upstairs?"

She nodded almost drunkenly, her eyes still closed, and he covered her mouth with his, the kiss fierce and thorough, and then he scooped her up and carried her from the kitchen up the stairs, the sound of the storm merciless as it pounded the house.

Natalie could only hang on and meet him kiss for kiss until he found her room and lowered her to her bed. Breath ragged, Jake stood and quickly discarded his jacket, and then he removed his gun from the holster, only to momentarily pause. "Natalie …"

Sensing his sudden indecision, Natalie stood back up and pressed two fingers to his lips, shaking her head. "No second thoughts, Jake." *But was that really fair?* she wondered. What if he *was* having second thoughts? Natalie tried to clarify her meaning.

"At least not because you're worried about me. But if you're not … if you don't want …"

Jake laid his gun and holster on the side table and was back before Natalie could finish. He pulled her to him, pressing her firmly once again against his rock-hard arousal.

"I *want*, Natalie. There's no question about that. There never has been."

Liquid heat curled in Natalie's belly at his words, at the evidence of his desire. She reached up and nipped at his lower lip with her teeth. "Then what are you waiting for?" she whispered. "Make love with me, *right now* …"

He didn't wait for a second invitation, just captured her mouth again, and pushed her robe off her shoulders so that it fell to the floor behind her. Impatiently discarding the remainder of his own clothes, he pressed her back onto the bed.

Natalie sucked in her breath at the full skin-on-skin contact—it was intoxicating, with legs entangling, hands seeking. Just his warm thigh pressing between hers was incredibly erotic, while his hands touched her everywhere, skilled hands that were sliding, gripping … driving her insane with wanting him.

She couldn't get close enough and was consumed with the incredible feel of his smooth skin over firm muscles, with all of his solid, unyielding contours. She reached for and found the velvety warmth of his powerful erection, encircling him with her hand, and was rewarded with an answering groan. Pure lust licked at her insides at his response, and she became bolder, thrilled at the knowledge that she could bring him pleasure with just a touch.

His warm, wet mouth once again closed over the tightened bud of her nipple, and Natalie lost all ability to think rationally. Arching her back in mindless pleasure, she couldn't stop the sounds that spilled in abandon from her mouth. When his clever fingers moved into her, her gasps were uncontrollable. "Jake, Jake, *please* …"

His breathing harsh, he was suddenly still. "Natalie, wait." He took several deep breaths. "Christ, I just realized I didn't bring anything with me."

Natalie struggled to get her own choppy breathing under control, to try to slow her racing heart. She lay for a moment, chest rising and falling, absorbing the impact of what he had just said. What kind of man would refuse his own imminent pleasure to ensure a woman's protection? A responsible, wonderful, *beautiful* man, she realized.

Her breath still coming in short little pants, she laid her hands on his cheeks and pressed her lips to his, deepening the kiss for just a moment, and then she pulled back.

"I have something." She reached over for the drawer on her bedside table, and his mouth resumed its attentiveness to her breast. She paused, eyes closing, head momentarily dropping back. "*Jake*, I can't even think when you do that."

"Good," he growled, and he started nuzzling her neck, his other hand simultaneously reaching underneath her to cup and knead her bottom.

Letting out a shaky breath, she finally opened the drawer, grabbed a foil wrapper, and handed it to him. "It's fairly old, and I … I don't know how long these things last."

He took it and covered her mouth with a quick, hard kiss. "Good." Then he grinned. "I mean the part about it being old." When he was finished, Jake became still, staring long and hard at her. His hand slowly slid up her leg, over hip and waist, to come to rest on her cheek, his thumb rubbing her lower lip.

"You have no idea how beautiful you are, do you?"

Natalie was unable to move or look away, mesmerized by the deep, rich timbre of his voice, with its ever-so-subtle trace of the South, and sound of the rain relentlessly pounding the roof. Without conscious thought, she reached up and grabbed his hand and held it there, her teeth nipping, her tongue laving at his thumb until she took it fully into her mouth.

Jake's eyes darkened to emeralds as thunder and lightning suddenly cracked and boomed, and he lost control, roughly pulling his hand away and imprisoning her mouth with his own. His hands impatiently moved over her body, from breast to hip to thigh, only to land on the dark curls at the juncture there, his fingers once again sinking deeply into her moist heat. Inhaling sharply, Natalie's hips unconsciously raised to meet the firm pressure of his hands, silently urging him to assuage this sudden, immediate *ferocious* need.

"Jake, oh God, Jake, I need you … inside me … now, *now* …"

At her urgent plea, he simply grabbed her hips and plunged into her wet, slick center, groaning deeply as he began to move within her. "Christ, Natalie …"

As the storm continued to rage outside, Natalie could not respond coherently, overcome with the *rightness* of him filling her, completing her, uttering only an inarticulate "yes, *yes*" as the intensity built; an intensity that said this was Jake, he was here, inside her, loving her, until she was shattering into a million pieces, his name leaving her lips over and over, and only vaguely aware of her own name tumbling from his as he found his own release.

❧ ❧ ❧ ❧

Jake's face was buried in Natalie's neck as he lay on top of her, resting his weight upon his arms, his breathing finally slowing to a manageable pace. *Jesus.* When he had ever lost total control like that? He inhaled deeply to try to calm his racing heart and caught again that subtle scent she wore.

"What's that fruity smell? It makes me want to take a big bite out of you." To prove his point, he lightly bit her neck and then soothed the spot with his mouth and tongue.

"Just lotion," she murmured, leisurely arching her neck to give him better access.

But Jake slowly rolled to the side, pulling her with him as he did, so they were facing though still touching. Suddenly he noticed that the bed did not spring back when he pushed down on it.

"What the hell kind of mattress is this?"

Natalie's responsive giggle made him smile. "It's a memory

foam mattress. It molds to your shape. It's *good* for you; for your back, your alignment."

"You're kidding." He pushed on another spot, watched the indentation linger. "I'll be damned." He grinned again. "Two comments come to mind." His eyebrows rose leeringly as he glanced down at her curves and back up. "One: you have a very fine shape for it to mold to." He leaned in and kissed her. "And two: it was, *indeed*, good for me."

She grinned back at him, clearly delighted at his words.

Running his hand over the delicate curve of her hip, he was a bit amazed at how stirred he was even now by the lovely, long lines of her, at how much she affected him just lying there. "You know, I was a bit apprehensive about this."

Natalie's brow wrinkled slightly, her eyes suddenly wary. "What do you mean?"

He smiled, remembering. "When I first shook your hand in the chief's office, you shocked me. Literally. I felt the jolt go right up my arm. Then you did it again. And when we first kissed in the car, and again on the couch, it was nothing short of … electric." He brushed her lips with his. "I was worried that you might really put me out of commission, possibly stop my heart completely, if we ever did this." He grinned again. "Which I thought about quite a lot—but decided I was willing to risk it."

Natalie's luminous smile returned, her eyes sparkling as she leaned in and kissed him back. "I thought about it, too, you know," she said, running her thumb over the faint cleft in his chin, and then down to his chest, watching her fingers burrow into the smattering of hair in the center. She raised her eyes to his. "Though I tried not to."

He covered her hand with his own. "Apparently no more successful than I was?"

"Apparently not." Then she grinned impudently at him. "Though I must admit, the reality was far better than I ever anticipated."

"Hey, now—that sounds like some sort of backhanded compliment to me. Were your expectations that low to begin with?" He nipped at her mouth in mock punishment and then settled in for a long, slow kiss. She returned the kiss, deepening it, and he felt that fist of desire in his belly again. Amazing.

He pulled back suddenly. "Natalie, wait." He rested his forehead against hers. "Before you make me lose my mind again, I need to go check things out. With the weather as it is, I doubt there's anything to be concerned about, but I still need to check it out. Okay?"

"Okay." She touched his cheek. "Be careful."

"Always." He dropped another quick kiss on her lips and then slid off the bed, grabbing his pants off the floor and his gun from the side table on his way to the bathroom.

Natalie unashamedly admired the taut, lean lines of his muscled backside as he left the room, and then she dropped her head against back the pillow. Lord, Natalie, *you* need to be careful. You could easily fall hard and fast for this guy. She rolled her head to stare at the door he had just walked through. Maybe you already have.

❦ ❦ ❦ ❦

As she stirred the pancake batter to smoothness the following morning, Natalie said a quick thank-you that it had been an uneventful night. Well, not *uneventful*. The storm had certainly been a doozy. She smiled softly, feeling oddly lighthearted in spite of the underlying reason why Jake was there. As Jake had suspected, Daryl hadn't shown up last night to throw a wrench in things, and it had allowed Jake to relax a bit and for them to ... get to know each other better.

Oh, who did she think she was she kidding? Last night had been, quite simply, the most amazing sex of her life. Jake had made her feel things she had never felt before. Lust with a capital L. Thank God she didn't live in an apartment with thin walls or the neighbors surely would have been talking.

Yet she knew she had also felt a different kind of connection to him, an emotional one, which had only served to intensify the experience. She acknowledged that she was drawn to Jake, physically *and* emotionally, as she had been to no other man in her life.

They had alternately talked and made love the entire night, only sleeping for short bursts of time before Jake would rouse her again with this overwhelming need that seemed to consume them both. Then this morning, waking up to the sight of his sinfully masculine visage endearingly rumpled from sleep, the feel of his stubble-roughened chin and cheeks pressing into her neck, had touched some place deep inside of her, and she had simply been stunned at how good, how right, it felt.

She recalled patches of their conversation as she turned on the griddle, pulled the syrup from the cupboard, and got out plates and utensils. When Jake had told her what Bernie had said to him on the porch the night before, Natalie had opened up a bit about her younger years and how she had learned to survive, then serendipitously landing on Bernie's doorstep, and how Bernie had slowly become the only real mother she had ever known. Jake had listened quietly, simply holding her as she had talked, and it had felt almost cathartic. She understood very clearly that the restorative feeling stemmed from her underlying need for Jake to understand, *accept*, who she was and where she came from, even if there was still a small part of her he didn't.

She had, in turn, asked Jake about his family, and he had briefly mentioned a sister who had died at a young age, and then he had talked mostly about his parents, Phillip and Anne, who still lived in Raleigh, and whom he only got to see a couple of times a year due to the demands of his career.

Natalie had given him the same courtesy of simply listening while he talked, but she had sensed there was much more to the story of his sister's death than his casual words had conveyed. She only hoped that they would eventually reach a point in their relationship where he could, and would, open up to her. If they even had a relationship. Natalie had no idea how Jake felt about that.

"I was half-kidding about the pancakes the other night," Jake said as he came into the kitchen, having just visited with the on-duty officer parked across the street and performing a quick, routine check around the exterior of the house.

Natalie turned at his comment, noting the competent image he projected in his navy slacks, crisp white shirt, and tweed sport jacket. Then she turned to hide the secret little smile she couldn't stop at the unbidden thought that she *knew* what was under those clothes, knew it *intimately*. Oh boy, she was in trouble. She flipped the first bubbling pancake.

"I just thought you might be hungry … I mean … you've probably worked up an appetite …" She closed her eyes. "I'm just digging a deeper and deeper hole for myself, aren't I?" Her cheeks heated as Jake laughed, approaching her from behind and wrapping his arms around her middle.

"I can't deny those pancakes smell great, but somehow, I prefer the smell of this spot right here," he said, bending his head and kissing the hollow between her neck and shoulder. "And I can probably eat a whole stack of them, but I'd much rather feast—" he lightly bit her neck "—on you." Sucking gently where his teeth had been, his hands slid under the material of her pink cotton T-shirt and came up to cup her breasts through her lacy bra.

"Jake …" Her head fell back against his shoulder. "You're going to make me burn these pancakes …" He flipped her around and kissed her thoroughly, moving her over and away from the griddle and then pressing her back against the counter. Spatula in hand, she curved her arms around his neck and forgot about the pancakes altogether.

He released her mouth, groaning. "Jesus, Natalie, you're like crystal meth. Now that I've had a taste of you, I can't get enough."

She laughed outright at that, coming back to her senses and turning slightly in his arms to expertly flip the remaining pancakes while he held her, watching. "I'm not entirely sure I like being compared to that drug." She turned back. "But I know what you mean." She reached up and kissed him. "Now let me go so you can eat and get going to wherever it is you need to get going to."

He grinned, releasing her, and Natalie noticed a spring in his step as he walked to the coffee pot, poured two cups, and then carried them over to the table she'd set for breakfast. A moment later, she followed him with two plates heaping with golden brown hotcakes and sat down next to him.

He looked at the plates and then at her, and said with a smile, "I feel like the luckiest guy on the planet. Can we do this again tomorrow morning?" Natalie smiled back, her heart full, as he gestured for her to use the syrup first.

"What do you have scheduled today?" he asked as he finally dug in.

"Actually, I've been meaning to tell you—I've rescheduled things a bit at work for the next couple of weeks." She took a bite of her own pancake. "I decided I wouldn't be much use to my patients if I was constantly looking over my shoulder, so I thought I'd take a two-week hiatus until we get this case solved."

His chewing slowed as he thoughtfully considered her statement.

"Is two weeks not enough?" she questioned with a slight frown.

"No, no, that's not it." His eyes turned glinty. "I'll get this bastard in less time than that. I'll just need to know your schedule so we can make sure we've got all your days covered."

At his response, Natalie realized how *glad* she would be when all this was over and done. How she could go back to her normal life, and maybe Jake would want to be a part of it without feeling obligated to protect her from a maniac.

"Okay, I can do that." She took a sip of coffee. "I do know I have to go in this morning to the police station to see Detective Rawlings. I was working on a case with him a couple of months ago, and he left a message yesterday that he needed me to come in and go over the file one more time and to review my notes from the victim. They haven't had a break in the case, and he was hoping I might be able to … help out a bit more."

She glanced away, trying to ignore the strange little ache in the middle of her chest from talking about what they had somehow, subconsciously at least, been able to avoid last night. The big blue elephant in the room.

Jake laid his fork down and took a drink of his own coffee. "What kind of case?"

Natalie turned back to him, surprised at the question. Was he really interested in hearing this? How much should she disclose without risking a shift in the atmosphere, a break in this idyllic connection they had made last night and this morning? As her gaze wandered over his carefully neutral face, Natalie knew she had no choice but to tell him the truth. It was the only way this thing between them would—could—ever work out.

"A college student disappeared about three months ago. Tara Jameson. She was walking home one night from an evening class on campus at FSU, and that's the last time anyone saw her." Natalie wrapped her hands around the warmth of her coffee mug.

"She was only twenty; shy, not many friends. Originally from Sarasota. She contacted me one night shortly after it happened and told me *how* it had happened." Natalie's eyes closed.

"He came at her from behind, so she never saw him, but she smelled him. Like motor oil or car grease. She saw his hands, saw the black under his fingernails before he covered her mouth and dragged her away … and …"

"Natalie, if you don't want to …" Jake stopped, clearly struggling for words.

She opened her eyes. "It's okay." She just wished … no matter. "It's not really important that you know all those details anyway. I gave Detective Rawlings everything I had, everything Tara told me, they just haven't been able to find the guy yet. He wants me to go over everything one more time just in case I missed something."

She paused, her eyes troubled. "I'm not sure you can understand how frustrating it can be for me, Jake, how helpless it makes me feel, to get *some* information but not *enough*. Not enough to help the innocent victim, not enough to get some sick person off the street."

Jake didn't respond, but Natalie could all but see his internal conflict and knew that this would always come between them until he learned to believe that there was more to life and death than met the eye. *If* he learned to believe. Her heart constricted in her chest.

Jake stared back at Natalie across the table, feeling as helpless as he ever had. He could clearly see, clearly feel, that the words she spoke represented the truth as she saw it; but his mind, his intellect, wouldn't let him accept the words *as* truth.

Troubled by the sudden change in mood, not knowing how to fix it, Jake scooted back his chair. "I really should get going. I have some things I'd like go back over on the case." He picked up their plates from the table.

"Jake, just leave those; I can take care of them." He ignored her and walked to the sink anyway, placing them in there, the clinking of the dishes sounding unnaturally loud in the suddenly taut atmosphere.

He turned to her again, rubbed a hand over the back of his neck. "Natalie …"

She stopped him. "Jake—it's okay. I know that you still don't … accept that part of me. I just have to figure out if *I* can accept that."

He paused, wanting to say something, wanting to take her into his arms and forget this conversation, go back to the way it had been earlier this morning, last night.

"Look, I …" He sighed, frustrated. Christ, why did this have to be so complicated? "I'll just see you later," he said, and turned and left.

❧ ❧ ❧ ❧

"'Lo?"

Natalie smiled, despite her heavy heart. "Hi, is this Kendall?"

"Uh-huh."

"Hi, sweetie, it's your mommy's friend, Natalie. Is your mommy there?"

"Uh-huh."

Silence.

"Can you go get her for me?"

"Uh-huh."

Silence.

Natalie's smile widened. Hope had to be around somewhere. She'd never let two-year-old Kendall run around by herself.

"Can I talk to your mommy, Kendall? Can you give her the phone?"

"Uh-huh. *Mommy!*"

Natalie pulled the phone away from her ear. The girl had lungs.

"Hello?" Hope came on, sounding out of breath and a bit frazzled.

"Hi, Hope, it's Natalie."

"Oh, thank goodness. I've been expecting a call from a potential donor. My little stinker of a daughter has figured out how to answer the phone, and she's been racing to get it first whenever somebody calls. If I don't hear it, there's no telling what kind of conversation she might have."

Natalie laughed. "I'm sure most people would be understanding, even enjoy it. She's a charmer."

"Well, she can be if she wants to, but she can also be a little stinker." Hope laughed. "Anyway, what's up?"

"Just wondering if you're free tonight. I need to get out of the house and take a break from this case I'm working on. Hang with the girls for a while. I was thinking it's been a while since we had a Girls Night Out, and we could go get a glass of wine at Pamona's. Maybe Jackie and Sara would want to join us."

Hope's coworkers at the center, Jackie Renfro and Sara Kensington, were hilarious—Hope had affectionately dubbed them Abbott and Costello—and they joined in on Girls Night Out whenever they could. They would definitely help Natalie get some perspective.

"That sounds like fun! Let me make sure Charlie doesn't have anything scheduled that I don't know about, and then he can have a Daddy's night with Kendall and we girls can talk about men and sex and all that good stuff. I'll call you back in just a bit, okay?"

"Okay, thanks."

Hope paused. "Are you okay, Natalie?"

"I'm fine. Just dealing with some stuff. We can talk about it tonight, and you can provide some of that fabulous insight you always seem to have."

"Deal. Talk to you in a bit."

Natalie hung up, afraid it would take more than perspective and insight to make whatever she had with Jake work.

❧ ❧ ❧ ❧

"She's *what?*" Jake barked at Agent Hansen over the phone.

"Sir, she's at a wine bar called Pamona's on North Orange Avenue in downtown Sarasota. With three friends. Female. Agent Larson has been with her the whole time, sir. I got pulled aside by Stollmeyer to work on something else, so I arranged for Larson to stay with her until I could reach you."

Agent Hansen spoke quickly. He was secretly half-afraid of Agent Riggs, as Riggs had a reputation in the agency. They called him Poker Face. No one ever really knew what he was thinking, though everyone always assumed it was the worst because he was usually scowling. Which was why Agent Hansen did not tell Agent Riggs that he'd gotten sidetracked on the new assignment and had forgotten to call him until now.

"Shit. All right, Hansen, thanks for the heads up." Jake disconnected. Jesus H. Christ, did the woman have no sense?

Going out to a bar when it was clear that someone was watching, waiting for his chance to … *God damn it*. She was going to get an earful from him.

But he was kicking himself at the same time. He'd been so wrapped up in trying to make some headway in the case today that he had lost track of time and had only just now gotten back to his condo to pick up some things before heading back to Natalie's for the night. He was kicking himself for not following up on Natalie's schedule for the day like they'd talked about that morning. Instead, he'd just focused on the case file, trusting that the other agents who'd been assigned to her for the day would take care of her.

If he was totally honest with himself, he had worked like the devil today because he wanted this case behind him, behind *them*, so he could figure out a way to just be with Natalie. To be able to all but remove this damnable psychic issue that hung like a black cloud over them.

He shook off his thoughts and punched in Larson's cell number that Agent Hansen had provided.

"Agent Larson."

"Larson, Jake Riggs. Hansen just informed me that you were assigned this evening to provide surveillance and protection for Natalie Morgan in his absence."

"Yeah, Riggs, that's right. I'm at Pamona's right now. Not a bad duty, too—she's a real looker."

"You're not there to drool, Larson; you're there to do a job. Make sure you do it."

"Now don't get your panties in a wad, Riggs. I'm watching, I'm watching. Four subjects of the female persuasion. Right now, they're having a ball. If I wasn't on duty, I'd be joining them." He snickered.

Jake's blood began to boil. "You listen to me, Larson. It's eight thirty now. I want you to walk over there and politely tell Dr. Morgan it's time to go home. My orders. Then escort her and her friends back to Dr. Morgan's house. Do you think you can do that?"

"Jesus, Riggs, what's up your butt? You can relax; I got it covered."

"You'd better hope to hell you do. I'll expect you at Dr. Morgan's house in thirty minutes." Jake hung up and tried to ignore the fear that licked at his insides.

※ ※ ※ ※

Natalie was on her third glass of wine and feeling pleasantly buzzed. They'd just listened to Jackie crack them all up with a story, her sleek, dark ponytail swinging and wide smile flashing as she'd animatedly described how her sister had come home from work one day and had seen the lower half of a man, from waist to feet, sticking out from under the crawl space of their house. Apparently thinking it was her husband working on the house *and* being in a playful mood, she had reached down and unzipped his pants and then had gone inside the house—only to find her husband standing at the kitchen sink. The guy under the house had turned out to be a contractor hired by her husband, and he had abruptly jerked upright when somebody started to unzip his pants, hitting his head on a floor joist and knocking himself unconscious. Of course, Jackie's sister had then been forced to call the ambulance and explain to the paramedics what had happened—and *they* had been so amused they had accidentally dropped the guy while carrying him on the stretcher to the ambulance.

The girls had all laughed uncontrollably, trying to imagine what had gone through the poor guy's head when he'd felt the hand on his zipper. Truth be told, Natalie had wiped tears of laughter from her eyes several times this evening, talking about all the things women talked about when men weren't around and giggling like they were back in high school. Of course, the alcohol hadn't hurt.

Natalie had also been forced—after much pleading and cajoling—to disclose the fact that she had recently had sex. Good sex. No, great sex. No, *phenomenal* sex. When she had first admitted to it, she tried to act like it wasn't that big of a deal, but Hope knew her too well. As they pried for details—which she *wouldn't* give them, other than to provide a deliberately vague, overall positive rating of the experience—Natalie couldn't stop her cheeks from heating nor hide the foolish grin that split her face. Seeing her reaction, Hope had been the first one to start whooping and hollering.

But when Hope asked if it was the FBI agent she was working with on the case, Natalie quickly fell back to earth. Just the mention of the case brought back all the unsettled feelings she'd been trying to ignore since that morning.

Sarah's whisper interrupted Natalie's train of thought. "Take a look at the Suit coming our way. You think he's going to hit on one of us? Or maybe he's full of himself and is going to attempt a quadruple?" They all dissolved into giggles again as the guy slowly approached their table in the back section of the bar.

He was not a bad-looking man, Natalie thought. But he just looked like every other man in a suit. Except Jake. Dang it, Natalie, knock it off.

"Evening, ladies."

A chorus of hi's greeted Larson. He grinned. Too bad he was working. "I'm Agent Larson, FBI. You may not have been aware, but I was assigned to provide Dr. Morgan some protection tonight. I've been nursing an orange juice across the room for the past two hours."

Oh, *crap*. Natalie hadn't even thought about that. She'd been so consumed by the issue between her and Jake that when she'd decided to call Hope on a whim, it hadn't even crossed her mind to let him know her plans. Maybe Agent Larson was just one of the agents generally assigned to her today, and Jake would never know about this little escapade. If she could just get home first …

"Unfortunately, I'm going to have to break up your little party. At the request of Agent Riggs, I've been instructed to follow all of you back to Dr. Morgan's house immediately."

Uh-oh … busted. Natalie could hazard a pretty good guess at

Jake's reaction to her going out to a bar given the circumstances. Then she looked up at Agent Larson, considering. He'd been there all night, right? She was also in a *public* place, for crying out loud. She hadn't been in any real danger. She tossed down the last of her wine. She didn't have to slink away in fear just because some wacko was on the loose. The FBI had her back, right? Even if Jake wasn't always there to see it.

She stood, swaying slightly, and Hope quickly grabbed her arm to steady her. "Are you okay, Nat? How much did you drink? I wasn't paying attention."

"Only three glasses of wine. I'm fine."

Hope laughed. "Right. You rarely do this, you know, so you have no idea what your limit is. Plus, you didn't eat any of the appetizers the rest of us pigged out on. We'll just ride home with the windows open, and I'll make some coffee when we get there."

"Sure. Whatever." Natalie was more worried about what Jake was going to do when they got there.

❧ ❧ ❧ ❧

Hope, designated driver for the evening, pulled into Natalie's driveway as Jackie and Sarah continued to chat nonstop in the backseat, Natalie in the front with her head back, eyes closed. Hope shut off the car and immediately noticed the scowling man in faded jeans and a black T-shirt leaning casually against the door jam on the front porch, arms crossed.

"Natalie," Hope whispered as she tapped her arm. "Is that your FBI agent?"

Her eyes still closed, Natalie sighed. "He's not *my* FBI agent, Hope." She opened one eye and glanced toward the house. "But yes, that's Jake." Natalie wondered if anyone else noticed his clenched jaw. Damn. She *was* going to be in trouble.

"Holy cow, Natalie, he's hot!" Jackie piped up from the backseat.

"Shhh! He'll hear you!" Natalie whispered fiercely as Jake

pushed his shoulder off the door and started toward them. Agent Larson pulled in behind Hope as Jake walked to the car.

"He doesn't look pleased, Nat," Hope mused. "Why would he be so upset?"

Natalie reached for the car door handle, intending on getting this confrontation out of the way so she could escape to the safety of her room. "Who knows? But I'm sure we'll find out soon enough." She got out of the car, doing her best to act unconcerned, not wanting to let Jake know she was just the teeniest bit worried about his reaction.

Hope followed, coming around the front of the car to make sure Natalie had support. Which it looked like she would need, Hope thought, if the look on this guy's face was any indication. Even up close, Hope saw Jackie was right—Mr. FBI was one serious hottie. No wonder Natalie was all in a dither over him.

Hope watched as Jake stared hard at Natalie for a moment. Natalie's chin lifted a notch.

"What were you *thinking?*" His voice was low, the words clipped.

Natalie inspected her nails. "About what?"

"You know damn well about what! Going out without telling me when or where, in the middle of a murder investigation in which you're a potential target, for Christ's sake! Or are you so unconcerned with your own life that you think everyone else should be, too?"

Agent Larson approached and tried to intercede. "Now, Riggs, hang on just a minute. I was on duty the entire time, and Dr. Morgan never left my sight for even a second. She was perfectly safe."

"Obviously, you missed training that week at Quantico, Larson," Jake responded, never taking his eyes off Natalie. "A witness is never 'perfectly' safe no matter how much protection we give them."

Hope watched in interest as Natalie withstood his fierce gaze calmly and silently, and after a moment, Jake appeared to try to rein in his frustration, inhaling slowly and deeply. He turned to the other agent. "You can go now, Larson. I'll take over." He paused and took another breath. "Thanks for the assistance."

Larson just shrugged. "No problem. Glad I could be of service tonight." He turned to Natalie. "You just call if you need anything else." He winked at her and walked off.

When Hope saw Jake's jaw clench at Agent Larson's actions, she realized Mr. FBI had a serious thing for Natalie. He probably didn't even know it yet. Hope was thrilled. Natalie lived her life constantly giving to others; it was high time that she found someone to give her what *she* needed.

"Natalie, aren't you going to introduce us?" Hope gave Jake her best smile.

Natalie groaned and glared at Hope. Hope just continued smiling. Natalie quickly waved her hand toward Jake and said, "Hope, this is Jake Riggs, FBI Agent Extraordinaire." She then flipped her hand back to Hope. "Jake, this is my *friend* Hope Saunders. Jackie Renfro and Sarah Kensington are in the car." Natalie briskly pointed at them still in the backseat and watching everything with interest.

"Now"—she turned back to Hope—"I'm going to go inside. Thanks, and tell Jackie and Sarah thanks for tonight. It was fun. At least up until now." Natalie raised a hand in farewell and turned to walk up the steps, weaving slightly as she went.

Jake's eyes narrowed as he watched Natalie walk gingerly to the front door. "How much has she had to drink?"

"She said three glasses of wine," Hope replied as she saw Natalie carefully shut the door behind her. Hope turned back to him. "Agent Riggs. You should know that Natalie rarely, if ever, drinks. Said her biological mother was an alcoholic so she avoids it like the plague. But something apparently happened just recently that bothered Natalie deeply. I'm pretty sure it has to do with you. So go easy on her tonight. I think she's feeling pretty unsteady, in more ways than one."

He didn't respond to Hope's unsolicited advice as he continued to stare at the closed front door. "Are you ladies all right to get home on your own?"

"Yes, thanks. I haven't been drinking, so I'll drive everyone home."

"Okay, I'll take my leave then." He glanced briefly at her and then walked to the house.

As she got in the car with Jackie and Sarah, Hope prayed that Agent Riggs had heard her.

Chapter Ten

Natalie was in the kitchen waiting for the coffee to finish percolating when Jake came in. She didn't turn around. "Natalie."

"Hmmm?" She reached for a mug in the cupboard.

"You have to understand why you can't just up and do something like this without telling me." Especially looking like that. She probably had no clue how insanely gorgeous she was in her heels, glittery purple tank top, and short black skirt emphasizing her long, slender legs, her hair wavy tonight and pulled back from her unforgettable face. Jake recognized she was simply a magnet for men, sane or crazy. Him included.

Natalie apparently decided she was done waiting for the coffee and pulled out the carafe, quickly pouring a cup, but not quickly enough.

Jake came over and grabbed a paper towel for her, wiping up the excess liquid as he spoke. "Natalie, please. Just tell me you're not going to do this again." He threw the wet paper towel into the garbage can nearby and leaned back against the counter next to her, waiting for her response.

"I can't tell you that, Jake."

"Why the hell not?"

"Because I may very well go out again with my friends for a glass of wine."

He growled. "That's not what I mean, and you know it." Frustrated, he rubbed a hand over his eyes. "Why didn't you tell me where you were going, or what you were planning on doing?"

Natalie took a sip of the coffee, grimacing at its strength. "I didn't think about it."

"How could you not have thought about it? We'd just talked about it this morning." When she had been so relaxed, so at ease with him. Which seemed light years away from where they were now.

"Why didn't you ask me for my schedule for the day when you left this morning?" she countered as she stared out the window above the kitchen sink.

Touché. Hadn't he already lectured himself for that very thing? But he refused to acknowledge that out loud to her. "Answer my question, Natalie."

"Why don't you answer mine, Jake?" She abruptly put her coffee down and walked away from him toward the table. "You want to know why I didn't think about it?" She turned, facing him. "Because I didn't *want* to. I wanted to forget you. I wanted to forget about this … this thing between us, because I don't know if it's ever going to work, Jake. I don't know if you're ever going to …" She trailed off, closing her eyes, and whispering, "I just wanted to forget."

But she started to sway when she closed her eyes and lost her balance. Trying to catch herself, her ankle buckled and her heel gave way. Jake was there before she could fall, scooping her up into his arms and holding her to him. She wrapped her arms around his neck as if she would never let go.

"How much did you *really* have to drink tonight, Natalie?" he asked as he started up the stairs to put her to bed and let her sleep it off.

Natalie didn't immediately answer and instead stared silently at his profile as he carried her up to her room. At his dark brows still scowling over his intense, mossy green eyes, his almost patrician nose, his firm, beautifully sculptured lips—clever, *magical* lips, which she admitted, knew in her heart, she wanted pressed against her own, pressed against her body. Now. Tonight. Forever. It was like an ache, an unfulfilled need deep within her. And only he could assuage it.

And she didn't want to fight it anymore tonight. "Jake." Her voice was a whisper as she leaned in and pressed an open-mouthed kiss just below his ear. "I had three glasses of wine. I'm not inebriated. I'm just ... loose-limbed." She lightly bit his neck.

Jake half laughed, half groaned as he reached her bedroom. "Loose-limbed, my ass." But he very gently laid her on her bed, disentangling her arms from around his neck, and then stood, just staring at her.

"Jake." Her heart in her throat, she could barely get the words out. "I ... I don't really want to forget. Please. Stay. *With me.*"

He could no more resist the mesmerizing sound of her voice than he could her solemn, guileless brown eyes. He knelt on the bed, his hands on either side of her, and placed a soft, quiet kiss on her waiting lips. That lightest of touches was all it took.

Natalie's mouth parted instantly, willingly, and she reached up and pulled his head closer, deepening the kiss to become instantly primal. Basic. A human need that could not be denied.

Jake groaned, returning her kiss, and then reached under her, grabbing her and rolling them both over so she was on top of him on the bed. He immediately reached underneath her skirt to grab firmly onto her sexy-as-hell ass and press her against his instantly rigid erection. Jesus, he really was *addicted* to her and knew he would be for a long time.

Natalie pulled her mouth free from his and sat up to straddle him, her skirt riding up as she moved against him in the most excruciatingly pleasurable way, and quickly reached to grab the hem of her top and pull it over her head. The sight of her sitting there astride him, her chest rising and falling in excitement, her incredibly lovely breasts filling her wispy black bra, did something to Jake. It hit him straight in the gut. It was more than sexual, he realized with a start. It was because this was Natalie. *She* was what he wanted. More than anything he had *ever* wanted.

He grabbed her under the arms, flipping her again to lay her back on the bed. When she gasped at the sudden move, he kissed her, devouring her mouth with his own. God, her mouth—he craved it.

But not just her mouth. Every single part of her. And he intended to show her. Releasing her lips, he trailed quick, moist kisses down her neck, over her collarbone, to detour at the curve of her breast. Her nipples were tightened nubs, straining against the delicate fabric of her bra, and he encircled one with his mouth, laving it, suckling it, moistening the material.

"You're so beautiful. Every single part of you." Her back arched in response to his mouth and his words, and Jake was overcome with the need to give her pleasure, intense pleasure that she had never known, that only *he* could give her. He released the clasp of her bra and freed her breasts, worshiping them with his mouth and tongue. The uncontrollable moans escaping Natalie's mouth told him she was indeed feeling pleasure, but it was not enough.

He moved down to her flat, creamy stomach, the same stomach that she had revealed to him that very first day and had haunted his dreams since. He placed open-mouthed kisses across the broad expanse of smooth skin, stopping to dip his tongue into her belly button, only to hear her quick intake of breath again. Not *nearly* enough. Venturing farther down, he placed a kiss upon the faded marking, a battle scar to him of her toughness, her resiliency. He pushed up her skirt, not bothering to unsnap or remove it, and placed another kiss on the soft skin of her inner thigh next to her black satin panties, breathing in the intoxicating scent that was uniquely her.

Natalie moaned, Jake's name leaving her lips again and again as she moved restlessly beneath his persistent hands and seeking mouth. He slid a finger beneath the material and slipped into her moistness. Writhing against his hand, Jake knew Natalie's pleasure was increasing and *still*, it was not enough.

Removing her panties in one swift motion, he kissed the essence of her, using his mouth and tongue until she was mindless and abandoned and crying out his name as she climaxed. Even *then*, he knew it would never be enough.

Quickly removing his own clothes as Natalie lay there, eyes closed, breathing heavily, Jake was suddenly acutely aware of his own need. He slid up her body and entered her in one slick, smooth thrust.

Holy mother of God. He buried his face in her neck, remaining motionless for a moment, kissing her, nipping at the delicate skin of her neck, trying to calm his own racing heart and spiking pleasure. He began to move slowly, and Natalie wrapped her legs around him, urging him on with her own murmured words, moving her hips back and forth against him, increasing his pleasure tenfold. He pulled back, breathing harshly.

"Christ, Natalie, you'd better stop that if you want this to last."

She smiled at him, slowly, that damnable secretive smile, like she knew something he didn't. Then she suddenly pushed at his shoulders, rolling him over and underneath her, and doing it so expertly that he never left her warmth.

Jake groaned. "Where the *hell* did you learn to do that?"

She smiled again under slumberous eyes as she sat astride him a second time, this time skin upon skin, biting her bottom lip as she did so, and Jake had to grit his teeth to avoid losing all control. When she began slowly moving her hips, he acknowledged it was inevitable.

"Jesus, Natalie, you're killing me." He gripped the curve of her hips to slow her movements.

She leaned down and kissed him, her tongue teasing, and then she pulled back slightly, the intensity of her gaze all but scorching him. "I want you to lose control," she whispered. "I want to *make* you lose control."

"You do," he muttered through a tightened jaw, her whispered words shooting a blistering flare of heat straight to his loins. He forcefully rocked her hips against his, again and again, until the exquisite friction became devastating, and they both lost control and fell over the edge together.

❧ ❧ ❧ ❧

The shrill ring of the telephone interrupted the lovely dream Natalie was having. She was lying on her stomach on the warm sandy beach, her head resting on her arms, the heat of the sun beating down upon her back. Jake was slowly walking toward her, his gorgeous body on full display, his eyes glittering at her, telling her without words what he was going to do to her when he reached her. Delicious thrills ran up and down her spine, until a black crow flew in front of Jake and started cawing. The cawing did not stop until Natalie slowly woke and realized it was the telephone.

Reaching groggily for the receiver, she became aware of Jake, warm and curled against her back. Smiling sleepily, she brought the phone to her ear and answered quietly. "Hello?"

For a moment she heard nothing. "Hello?" she asked again. Then she heard the breathing just moments before she heard the whispered, evil words. "Are you dying for me to fuck you, Natalie? Or are you just dying?" The sick laughter lasted only a moment before he disconnected.

Jake instantly became aware of the change in Natalie, of her shocked stillness, and he quickly grabbed the phone from her, only to hear the dial tone.

"*Shit.*" He reached over her and hung up the receiver, and then he gently touched her arm. "What did he say?" When she just lay there unmoving, staring unseeingly at the wall across the room, Jake grabbed her shoulders and turned her into his arms, holding on tightly. "Natalie, sweetheart, you have to tell me what he said. I know you're scared, but I'm here. *Tell me.* Then we can catch him and put him away for good."

He pulled back and was thankful to see that she was blinking again, but she still looked at him with wide, shocked eyes. She swallowed convulsively, her breath now coming in short, choppy bursts.

He placed a hand on her cheek, rubbing the smooth skin with his thumb as he tried to encourage her. "He did say something, didn't he?"

She nodded jerkily then, her eyes never leaving his. Jake swore he was going kill this bastard if it was the last thing he ever did.

"Jake." Her eyes closed briefly, and she swallowed again. She took a deep, shuddering breath as she opened her eyes again. Then repeated to Jake the vile words.

"Christ Almighty." Jake gathered her close again to try and stop her sudden trembling. He had to put a call in, get a tap on the phone. But he didn't want to let her go. "We're going to get him, I *swear* to you, Natalie." He felt helpless, impotent. "Tell me what I can do. Tell me how I can help."

She held on tighter. "Just you being here is all I need, Jake. Thank you for being here." She started to cry.

"Aw, hell, sweetheart. Don't cry. This asshole isn't worth it."

"I'm sorry." Her voice was muffled against his neck. "I never cry." She sniffled and made a concerted effort to stop. Pulling back, she wiped at her eyes and blew out a breath, letting her hands fall to his warm chest. "Jake, I have to tell you something."

"Okay. Anything. You can tell me anything." He covered her hands, felt how cold they were, and started gently rubbing them as she spoke.

"What he said tonight … it … it's the same thing he said to me all those years ago. When he tried to kill me."

She drew another shuddering breath and then doggedly continued.

"You know how I told you before that I became separated from my body and watched him carve the symbol on my stomach?" Jake just nodded. "Well, I heard him say the same thing then, while I watched him use his knife on me. He just said it a little differently, like 'I guess you were just dying for me to … '"—well, you know.

Then he laughed at the joke he'd made. It's so clear in my mind, like it happened just yesterday." She closed her eyes again, her head leaning forward to rest on his shoulder.

What could he say? While he may not believe she had heard it as she was remembering it, he knew she believed with all her heart that she *had* heard it. He just didn't want her to be scared anymore.

"Natalie, look at me." He eased her back to look into her eyes. "I've got to make a call. We're going to have to place a tap on your phone. We want him to call again. But next time we'll be ready for him, so that when he does, we'll trace it and get him." He bent forward and gently kissed her. "Are you okay to wait here while I make this call? I need to use my cell, and ... well, you know." He smiled lopsidedly at her.

Natalie saw his sweet, goofy smile and knew in that instant that she loved him. She *loved* him. Incredible. It was like a million bursts of light suddenly warming and filling her heart. Without warning, her eyes threatened to spill. She quickly squeezed them shut. Get a grip, Natalie. Now was clearly not the time to reveal such a momentous discovery. Opening her eyes, she gave him a wobbly smile and just nodded.

"Good girl. I'll be right outside the door." Jake got up, grabbed his cell from the pocket of his jeans, and walked quickly into the hall to report the incident and arrange for the wiretap.

Natalie lay back, feeling almost exhausted from the tension and the revelation she had just had. It was at once freeing and terrifying. It wasn't as if she had never loved before. But it *felt* as if she had never loved before. It was amazing. Miraculous.

But she loved *Jake*. Jake didn't believe in her. What was she going to do?

Hope's words suddenly came back to her again. *The heart has a mind of its own.* Maybe there was nothing she *could* do. She knew she couldn't simply tell herself to stop loving him. That was impossible. Nor could she make him love her, or believe in her. So maybe she just had to accept it for what it was for now and just keep these new, wondrous, *scary* feelings to herself.

"It's all set. They'll be here at oh-six hundred to install the bug." He sat down on the bed next to her, taking her hand, totally unconcerned that he was still fully nude. Natalie could only drink in the sight of him, almost overwhelmed with the secret she held.

"You okay?" He cocked his head slightly, as if sensing something had changed.

Natalie nodded. "I'm just glad you're here."

His thumb moved slowly over the back of her hand, and she was amazed at the response of her body over such a simple action. When he brought her hand to his lips, kissing her knuckles tenderly, she felt like weeping again. Was this what love did to you, made you cry at every sweet, simple gesture? If so, how long did such an emotional maelstrom last?

He climbed in next to her, gathering her close, murmuring that he wouldn't leave her again. Oh, how Natalie wished that could be true.

Kissing her neck, his hands slowly began to rediscover all her curves and secret, sensitive places, and Natalie felt like she was right where she was supposed to be, like she had come home. He continued to murmur to her, making love to her as much with his words as with his mouth and hands. This time, Natalie couldn't stop the silent tears that rolled down her cheeks at Jake's tenderness while he held her until she forgot everything but him.

※　※　※　※

"That should do it, Riggs." Agent Hansen entered the living room where Jake was standing at the window, staring sightlessly out at the street. Jake was both relieved and on edge at Hansen's comment. The bug was a step in the right direction, but it meant Natalie had to go through more of the same shit. They were still just way too far from where they needed to be. Jake didn't think he'd ever wanted a case closed more than this one.

"Everything's in place; we're just packing up," Hansen continued. "The only remaining item is to advise the subject on what to do and say when the call comes in. I assume you'll be handling that." He waited for Riggs to acknowledge, and when he remained silent, Hansen's navy polo shirt suddenly stuck to his skin and beads of moisture popped out on his forehead, moistening his hairline.

Finally Jake turned. "Yeah, I'll be handling that." Jake knew he needed to sit down with Natalie and go over it. But he wanted to give her a break, knew she *needed* a break. She was in the kitchen talking to Bernie on the phone, though he imagined she would not be relaying the details from last night's call.

Jake shook the other agent's hand and thanked him, and then he headed into the kitchen where he heard Natalie working hard to convince Bernie that nothing was wrong. Cagey old woman. Jake decided then and there that Natalie was going to get that break. Today.

Walking over, he took the phone from Natalie midsentence. She sputtered, and he just smiled and shook his head, placing a finger over her lips as he spoke to Bernie. "Hi, Bernie, it's Jake. How's my favorite Scrabble player this morning?"

He waited for the expected response. Bernie did not disappoint and promptly grilled him about what might be bothering Natalie.

"Besides me, you mean?" When she chuckled, he hoped his subtle avoidance of her question was enough to initially sidetrack her. He immediately followed with one of his own to totally redirect her attention. "I wanted to ask you, Bernie, if you'd mind if I took Natalie on a Sunday drive, maybe down the coast to this quaint little place I know." Out of the corner of his eye, he saw Natalie's mouth open in surprise and mentally crossed his fingers that it was the good kind of surprise.

"That sounds like just what Natalie needs, young man. Maybe there's hope for you yet. Go—go and have some fun."

"We will, Bernie. I'll make sure of it." And he would.

As he hung up, he turned to see Natalie staring at him with something that looked like begrudging respect.

"I have never met anyone, I mean *anyone*, who could pull one over on Bernie. But you just sidestepped that whole conversation so neatly that I almost missed it." She shook her head. "She wasn't going to let me off the hook until I told her what was wrong. Said she knew something was going on, and she could outwait or outtalk me any day of the week." Natalie laughed. "But you just waltz in, take the phone, and sweet talk her into forgetting all about it and letting me off the hook in record time. Amazing."

Jake grinned. "My talents are varied and unique. Stick around, kid. Maybe I'll teach you a few of them."

Natalie smiled back. "Did you really mean that we would take a drive?"

Jake feigned an insulted look. "You wound me. Of course I meant it. You think I could get away with what I just did with Bernie if I didn't really mean it? That woman could spot a fib a mile away." He glanced into the dining room to make sure the rest of the crew had gone. Then he took her in his arms and kissed her slowly and thoroughly.

When he finally released her, her eyes remained closed for several more moments. A good sign, he thought. Maybe they should just stay in bed all day. As much as he wanted to, Jake knew that what Natalie really needed was a change of venue. He rested his forehead against hers.

"I *meant* it. I planned on taking the day off, and I thought you might want to join me. Maybe we could have a nice meal along the way."

"It sounds wonderful. Heavenly." She pulled back and reached up and placed a hand against his cheek. "I know what you're doing, Jake." Her eyes were intent on his. "It's incredibly sweet of you. So thank you."

"Hell, I'm not sweet. Just ask my coworkers."

She just smiled knowingly as he grabbed her hand to leave.

※　※　※　※

Natalie stared at her reflection in the mirror as she washed her hands in the restroom at Morretti's Seafood Restaurant in Matlacha. Her cheeks were still rosy from the drive down, her hair tangled and wild from being whipped about by the warm wind as they had sped along Interstate 75 in Jake's beautifully restored 66 Mustang convertible.

They had stopped at his condo that morning and swapped the sedan for the Mustang, Jake enthusiastically describing to her all the work he had done over the past two years to bring it back to its former glory. Natalie had been suitably impressed with the craftsmanship and detailing, telling him so again and again and generally ooh-ing and ahh-ing over everything until he had stopped her with a grin and said, "Okay, now you're laying it on a bit thick." But Natalie could see that he was pleased at her comments. Secretly, she had been encouraged, because the car showed her that when Jake was passionate about something, he was extraordinarily committed. She could only hope that she would fare as well as the Mustang.

She pulled her brush out of her purse to repair the damage to her hair and shed the just-survived-a-hurricane look she saw in the mirror. Despite the mess, she smiled happily at her reflection. She just felt too wonderful to worry overly much about her hair. There was an underlying sense of freedom, a lightness of spirit, permeating her that she didn't think anything could affect today. Last night's call seemed a world away. Jake had done that for her.

When they'd finally taken off, he had asked if she had any special requests for activities or destinations, and she'd just smiled and said no. She didn't tell him that going anywhere or doing anything with him was simply perfect. So he had brought her down the coast to Matlacha, a tiny little town that seemed to have escaped the notice of modern society.

It was the gateway to Pine Island off the coast near Cape Coral, about an hour and a half south of Sarasota. Jake told her Matlacha meant "water to the chin" and that because of zoning restrictions, it couldn't be commercially overdeveloped and thus was one of his favorite little hideaways, especially with its nearby aquatic preserves. After their meal at Moretti's, Jake wanted to take her wandering through the streets of Matlacha and explore its quaint little shops and galleries and show her all the telephone poles he told her were painted by local artists.

But right now he was waiting for her at their table out on the deck of the restaurant overlooking the water. As gorgeous as any man had a right to be in his khaki pants and olive drab polo shirt complimenting his dark hair and intense green eyes. Butterflies suddenly flitted in her stomach at the thought that this sit-down meal would really be their first formal date. She imagined Jake didn't see it that way, however; he probably thought of it as just another way to keep her mind off the case for a bit longer. So she'd probably be wise not to think of it as a date either. She could do that. She dabbed on a little lip gloss and returned it and her brush to her purse, and then she smoothed the fabric of her coral sundress and exited the bathroom.

Jake was lost in thought as he waited for Natalie at their table on the far corner of the deck, the light breeze off the water and island music in the background wonderful complements to the atmosphere of the place. He was surprised at how much he had already enjoyed himself today, even just driving and talking. He couldn't remember the last time he had totally forgotten about work and had been able to fully relax. Natalie had done that for him.

Since Jess's murder, he had been so focused on work and everything that went along with it that his personal life has dwindled down to next to nothing. The few relationships with women that he had pursued had not lasted because he was not able to give them the attention they deserved, and they had eventually gotten fed up with him and his stock response that his job and his commitment to it came first. He never blamed them. He simply didn't have the emotional investment to blame anybody.

As he thought about today and this entire past week with Natalie, he recognized he had just been going through the motions of life, not really living it. He acknowledged to himself that he had essentially shut down emotionally after Jess had died and had never really come back into the land of the living. That he had subconsciously refused to allow himself to get emotionally invested in anyone. Until Natalie.

"You look like you're chewing over one very serious issue." Natalie smiled at him as she sat down before he could get up. "Anything I can help with?"

Jake appeared to think it over. "Well, Doc, I'm think I'm suffering from something called acute enjoyment. I've never really experienced it before, but the symptoms seem to include smiling at will, lack of stress, and general contentment with life." He grinned. "And I'm pretty sure you're the cause of my ailment."

Natalie giggled. "I'm not sure if I should say I'm sorry or I'm glad."

"Well, all I can say is that if there's a cure, I don't want it."

Natalie shook her head, still smiling. "You're such a goofball. Who would have guessed? But that can't have been what you were thinking about, because you had a much more serious look on your face."

Jake sobered and stared at Natalie for a moment. "Actually, I was thinking about my sister, and how I've been living—or actually, not really living—since she died."

Natalie reached across the table and slipped her hand into his. "Do you want to talk about her?"

He looked down at Natalie's hand in his, so small and yet such a perfect fit, and was once again surprised at his feelings on this day. At the realization he *wanted* to talk to her about it. That it was finally time to stop avoiding the subject of Jess.

"Oddly enough, I think I do."

A waiter approached, interrupting them. "What can I get for each of you? Our specials today are a delicious shrimp scampi with garlic butter or our mouth-watering filet mignon." They both ordered the beef, and Jake smiled at her as the waiter left.

"You know, I never even asked, but I guess you're not a vegetarian. I'd have pegged you as a vegetarian."

"Really?" Natalie shook her head, smiling. "Not even close. Give me a good steak or burger over a tofu salad any day of the week."

A meat-loving woman. Jake knew he was in trouble. "Then you'll have to sample my famous grilled onion burger sometime." He reached for Natalie's hand again across the table, thinking that he could get used to this, just talking like they were doing, for a long time to come.

"Jake, look," Natalie whispered. Her eyes were trained out on the water.

He turned and saw the dolphins, two of them, slicing through the water side by side, jumping and frolicking as they swam and played.

"Pretty amazing, huh?" he said, looking back at Natalie and her enchanted smile. Funny how he felt a little bit like the dolphins today. Carefree. Almost buoyant. Without thinking, he took out his cell phone and snapped a picture of her with the dolphins in the background. Then realized that his phone hadn't acted up. Interesting.

But she had asked about Jess, and he knew it was time.

"I want to tell you about Jess, Natalie."

She squeezed his hand. "Okay."

He squeezed back and looked out over the water again. "She was your typical teenager. Thirteen that summer and wanting to grow up way too fast." His eyes took on a faraway look. "Mom and Dad were planning on taking a short, much-needed vacation and asked if I'd come home from summer session at UNC for the weekend, since she was still too young to stay alone—though she didn't think so." The corners of his mouth tipped up slightly at the memory.

"Dad was a captain at the time on the Raleigh police force, and his job consumed their lives, so Mom finally put her foot down and insisted they get away that weekend." Jake affectionately recalled his mom's subtle but skillful ability to maneuver things until they worked out the way she wanted them.

"When I got there on that Friday afternoon, Jess was already mad at me. She didn't think she needed a 'glorified babysitter' and told me I could just go back to school and that she'd go stay with her friend, Annalisa. I just laughed at her, and she stormed off even angrier at me."

He continued to rub the back of Natalie's hand as he spoke, as if to subconsciously reassure himself that she was still there. "Jess refused to talk to me for a while, then eventually calmed down and made some soup and sandwiches, I guess as a peace offering because she didn't really cook. Anyway, we were back to normal and started watching television that evening, and I ... I got tired and fell asleep on the couch." He swallowed convulsively as he continued to stare out at the water.

"I slept like a rock on that couch until the next morning, and when I woke, Jess was gone. Nowhere to be found." His jaw clenched, unclenched. He continued, but his voice had gone flat.

"I called every friend that I knew or could think of, and when no one had seen her, I called the local force, then Dad. So they came home, and Mom never got her vacation."

His head shook imperceptibly.

"The police investigated, but because there were no signs of forced entry or a struggle, they concluded she had left of her own free will. After twenty-four hours, we filed a missing persons report, but ... a city maintenance worker found her body in a Dumpster that Sunday morning. She had been sexually assaulted and badly beaten, and the coroner ruled she had died of a combination of internal injuries and blood loss from several knife wounds." He squeezed his eyes shut, pinching the bridge of his nose with his free hand.

"Jake, I'm so sorry." Natalie leaned toward him, brought his hand to her mouth, and kissed it, wishing she could comfort him, ease his pain. "Did they find and prosecute the person responsible?"

He took a deep breath. "No. It's still an unsolved case. I try to work on it when I can."

Natalie could only guess how hard that was on him. "Jake, why do you blame yourself?"

When he opened his eyes again, they were full of torment. "How can I not? She was in my charge, and if I hadn't been so tired ... the bottom line is that I failed to protect her. It's that simple."

"No, Jake, it's *not* that simple. You had to sleep sometime, right? She could very easily have snuck out in the early hours of the morning."

"But why didn't I hear her? How could she have left the house without me hearing anything?"

"So now you're supposed to be the Bionic Woman?"

"Who?"

"You know, the character from that seventies show who had bionic hearing? It doesn't matter." She gripped his hands tightly. "Listen to me, Jake. I know from personal experience that teenagers can be as sneaky as the devil. It's just not reasonable to place the responsibility for her death entirely on your shoulders. Your sister apparently made some choices that night, choices you had no control over."

It wasn't his fault.

Natalie was abruptly still as Jake replied.

"No matter how many conversations I've had with myself, or with my parents—who never blamed me, by the way—I still can't get past the fact that I was supposed to watch over her that weekend, and I didn't."

Please, tell him it wasn't his fault.

Natalie closed her eyes for just a moment. Jess, is that you?

Yes. Tell Jake he couldn't have prevented what happened that night.

"Natalie, is something wrong?" Jake had finally noticed her

silence. She knew immediately that he wasn't ready to hear from his sister, despite Jess's apparent ability to ease his guilt. She quickly opened her eyes.

"No. I just wish there was something I could do. Something I could say to help you see it differently." I'm sorry, Jess, I can't tell him right now. I don't think he's ready. But I know it's something he needs to hear, so I will soon, I promise. Please come back and talk to me again. I'll be here.

But Natalie heard nothing. She only hoped Jess had heard her.

Jake interrupted her thoughts. "You remember early this morning when you told me that you were just glad I was there?" Natalie nodded. "Well, it's kind of funny, isn't it, that that's exactly how I feel right now. How you just being here and listening has helped. So thanks." He brought her hand to his lips.

"You're welcome." Natalie's answering smile was luminous. Jake had just unknowingly given her the compliment that meant more to her than anything else, telling her that she was still fulfilling her destiny, the one that had been set for her eighteen years earlier. Her heart overflowed.

Natalie knew she could get sappy at any second, so she decided it was time to lighten things up. Without warning, she spoke with a bad Russian accent.

"Just seet back and reelax, Jacob Riggs. I am going to dazzle and amaze you veeth vun of my many parlor tricks." She waved her hands and fingers dramatically.

Jake grinned and leaned back in his chair, playing along. "Does this trick involve fire or any other dangerous elements? Should I notify the management?"

"No, dah-ling, the only danger is that you vill be even more fascinated by my … magnetic prezence." Natalie smiled mysteriously.

He laughed outright at that. "Then please proceed, *dah-ling*."

Giggling, she continued, "If you would, take your knife and

your fork and place them next to each other in the center of the table."

Jake complied.

"Now, take the knife by the handle and touch it to the fork and raise the fork off the table."

His brow wrinkled. "That's not possible." But he tried anyway. The fork remained stubbornly inert on the table.

"Here, dah-ling, let me show you how." Natalie grabbed the knife from him and held it for a few seconds in her right hand while waving her left hand in front of it. Then she touched the knife to the fork and raised the fork off the table. "Viola!"

Jake's eyes widened. "How the hell did you do that?"

Natalie grinned. "A magician never reveals her secrets." She grabbed the fork and separated it from the knife and laid them both back in front of Jake. "Actually, I just magnetized the knife. With all that electrostatic energy that flows through my body."

Jake lifted an eyebrow and smiled roguishly. "Honey, you can magnetize me anytime."

The waiter chose that moment to approach their table and place their plates of steaming filet mignon in front of them. Natalie blushed as the waiter grinned, clearly having heard Jake's remark, though he was professional enough not to comment on it.

"Can I get you anything else?" The grin remained.

Jake looked at Natalie, suddenly serious. "I think we have just what we need."

Natalie's heart overflowed again.

Chapter Eleven

Natalie saw it first: the yellow iris lying by the front door on Bernie's porch with its edges blackened as if it had been burned.

They had just called Bernie to tell her they were going to stop by and check on her after getting back into town. Natalie had just been thinking that this day would go down as one of the most perfect days of her life. Until she saw the flower.

Her heart thumped heavily in her chest. "Jake."

"I see it, Natalie. Wait here."

"Like hell I will." If this freak had decided to threaten Bernie, Natalie would certainly have something to say about that. No doubt about it.

He turned to her. "Natalie, it's not a good idea. You're too emotionally involved."

"Damn *right* I am. This is Bernie, Jake. She's my rock. If he's been here … if he's even thinking …" Natalie trailed off. Jake was right. She was too emotionally involved. Only her emotion was based on pure, unadulterated fury, not fear. She was royally pissed.

"I don't think that's what he's thinking, Natalie. I don't think he's interested in Bernie—it doesn't fit his MO. His intent with this is simply to yank your chain."

She spoke in a clipped tone, her jaw tight. "Okay. But we need to nail this bastard. Soon. If he does hurt Bernie, there's no telling what I might do. You may end up having to pursue a murder case against me."

Jake grabbed her chin, smiling slightly at her vehemence. "I had no idea you had such violent tendencies, Doc." He kissed her quickly. "Let's go see what's up."

They walked to the porch and examined the flower without touching it. It had definitely been charred at the edges. Jake was convinced it was a message intended solely for Natalie's benefit. What the killer didn't realize is that he may have tipped his hand somewhat. To make even a veiled threat against Bernie said that he knew how close Natalie was to her. That he knew that it would be the one thing that would really get to her.

Which told Jake this asshole had been watching from a distance for some time now, maybe even before the case had officially started, or had some other nexus to Natalie to know the extent of her relationship with Bernie. He could very well be watching them right now. Only Jake didn't want Natalie to worry about that.

"Natalie, I want you to go inside and check on Bernie, keep her distracted. I don't think she's seen this, and I don't want her to. I'll call it in and get somebody over here to quickly process the scene. Maybe we can get it done without Bernie being aware."

Natalie shook her head. "Good luck with *that*. But I'll do my best. I need to go in the back way, right?"

Jake kissed her again, couldn't help himself. "We just might just make a fed out you yet."

❧ ❧ ❧ ❧

Natalie did her best. But even Cary Grant couldn't have distracted Bernie well enough that night, and Bernie was *gaga* over Cary Grant.

Natalie had decided she would keep Bernie talking with elaborate stories of how much fun she and Jake had had on their day out and just throw in a comment here and there to get Bernie wondering if there was really something going on between the two of them. Natalie knew Bernie wouldn't be able to resist that subject.

So she had kept Bernie in the kitchen with a pot of coffee and conversation, and Bernie *had* asked her pointed questions about how she felt about Jake. Which Natalie thought she had neatly sidestepped with vague responses like, "He's a good guy, Bernie," or "He makes me laugh, that's for sure."

After forty-five minutes had passed, Natalie thought Jake surely would have been done by now and that she might actually succeed at this assignment, until Bernie looked at her slyly and said, "It's so nice to hear that you enjoyed yourself today, dear, and that you really like Jake. I do, too. But my real question is, why are you stalling?"

Natalie shook her head in resignation. Would she never learn?

"What makes you think I'm stalling?"

Bernie took a sip of her coffee as she sat at the table. "Oh, maybe the fact that you keep pacing and sneaking glances into the dining room as though someone might walk through at any minute. Or maybe that you told me *three times* how relaxed Jake seemed to be today. Or possibly that I peeked out the window without you knowing when I went to the bathroom and saw the men out there on the front porch."

"Bernie! You shyster! Why did you let me go on and on?"

"I just wanted to see how far you'd go." She chuckled. "But now it's time to pay the piper. What's really going on? What are those men doing?"

Natalie knew she couldn't very well fib now. "When Jake and I got here, there was … a flower on your front porch."

Bernie squinted her eyes, as if looking for any signs of deceit. "A flower?"

"Yes, one of your yellow irises. Only it was … it was burned at the edges and laid at your front door as a message to me, I think. Those men are FBI. They're processing the scene for evidence."

"Now who would do some crazy fool thing like leave a burnt flower on my front porch as a message to you?" Bernie's eyes bored into Natalie's. "Unless ..." She got up and hobbled over to Natalie, grabbing her arm. "Unless it's Daryl."

"That's what we're thinking."

Bernie's hand flew to her chest. "Natalie Rae Morgan! Why didn't you tell me this?" Then she started scowling at her fiercely.

"Because I knew you'd react just this way. I didn't want to worry you."

Exasperated, Bernie threw her hands up in the air. "You think by *not* telling me you're going to protect me? I don't need that kind of protection, child." Now she started pacing, as fast as her arthritis would allow her. "I knew you were working on this case with Jake about those poor teenage girls. But it never occurred to me that you were also dealing with Daryl after all these years."

"We think Daryl is tied to this case, Bernie, that he's actually responsible for the murder of those two girls."

At Bernie's shocked look, Natalie walked over to her and directed her back to the chair. "Sit down, and I'll tell you everything."

Bernie gave her the squinty-eyed stare. "You promise?"

Natalie sighed. "Yes, I promise."

Jake walked in on them several minutes later and knew immediately the cat was out of the bag from the look on Bernie's face. When she looked up at him from the table with that steely-eyed stare of hers, he felt like he was ten years old again and had just been sent to the principal.

"Jacob Riggs, I'm ashamed of you, and I'm not even your mother. You of all people should have told me what was going on. Especially when it's my Natalie who's in danger. Isn't knowledge power? Maybe I could have actually helped if I had known what was going on."

She had him there.

"Bernie, I understand your frustration, I do," Jake said in an attempt to pacify her. "I'd probably feel the same way if I were in your shoes. But we made a decision, Natalie made a decision, to try to keep you out of it to the extent we could. We arranged for extra protection for you but felt it wasn't critical that you know the details of the case." When she only continued to stare at him, he cleared his throat. "I can see now that we might have been wrong."

"At least you're man enough to admit that, Jake. Maybe saying I was ashamed was a bit harsh. But this is Natalie. If anything happened to her ..." Bernie's chin started to quiver.

"Nothing's going to happen to her, Bernie," Jake said firmly. "I've made that my personal mission."

Natalie reached for Bernie's hand on the table. "Jake *is* going to get this guy, Bernie. I'm sure of it. Then my past will truly be my past." She looked over at Jake.

Jake returned Natalie's gaze, praying she was right. "We're putting an agent on you twenty-four/seven until we do, Bernie. Bill Reardon, who's as good as they get, has been assigned for tonight and most of tomorrow, so just try to ignore him. But don't try anything else. He's married."

He smiled and winked as he said it, trying to charm her into forgiving him for not trusting her with the truth.

"Oh, quit pulling that crap on me. You young whippersnappers are all alike, thinking you can smile your way out of trouble. You won't get off so easily, Jacob. I'll have to think about how you might be able to redeem yourself. Rest assured, it will probably involve begging."

Jake grinned at her. What a treasure she was. Her husband had been one lucky guy.

❧ ❧ ❧ ❧

After confirming that Agent Reardon was briefed and in place, Jake and Natalie took off. He asked Natalie if she'd mind if they stayed at his place tonight, so he could work from his home office more easily. He didn't tell her it was really because he felt she'd be more out of harm's way. Though Natalie said fine, she probably saw right through him just like Bernie did. As long as it kept her safe, he didn't care.

They quickly stopped at her house to grab a change of clothes, and then they dropped by the agency to get the files from his office. When they finally arrived at his condo at One Hundred Central, Natalie was trying to clamp down on her sudden nervousness.

His place. Did that mean they were taking another step in their relationship? Did they *have* a relationship? It seemed she kept coming right back to that question. She'd just have to try to put it out of her mind for now. There was really nothing they could resolve until the case itself was resolved.

"Pretty nice place, Jake," Natalie commented as they got to his unit on the third floor.

"Yeah, it is. I got in early and cheap." Grinning, he unlocked the door, and Natalie had to stifle a sudden giggle.

"What?" Jake turned, smiling as he pulled his key free and opened the door.

"Should I let you go in first and clean things up? I just had this vision of women's underwear draped all over the exercise equipment." She bit her bottom lip to keep from grinning.

"Oh, you think that's funny, do you? What do you take me for, some kind of Lothario?"

Natalie laughed outright. "*Lothario?*"

He feigned insult as he ushered her in before him and shut the door. "What? You don't think I could have read that play? I did go to college, you know."

She continued to laugh at his indignation as she followed him down a short hall until it opened to his living room. He set the files on the low coffee table in front of his brown leather couch and turned back to her.

"I've read Shakespeare. Voltaire. If you still doubt, I can quote Aristotle. 'At his best, man is the noblest of all animals; separated from law and justice, he is the worst.'"

Natalie cocked her head at him, considering. "'No one knows

whether death, which people fear to be the greatest evil, may not be the greatest good.'"

He raised his eyebrow. "Plato. I'm impressed."

She laughed again. "Don't be—it was something I used in my doctoral thesis about near-death experiences." She set her bag down and walked toward him. "You know, Jake, your expansive knowledge is starting to turn me on."

He grabbed her unexpectedly, causing her to squeal. "Really? Maybe something else of mine that's … expansive would work a little better." He nipped her bottom lip as he pressed her back against the wall to prove his point, and then he sank into a kiss that stopped her laughter altogether.

When he finally raised his head, she was no longer breathing normally. "Your kisses work pretty well, too, you know. But don't get a big head about it." When Jake grinned, she realized the implication of her words and swiftly placed a hand over his mouth as he started to speak. "Just keep it to yourself," she said, smiling back.

"But you're so much fun to tease." He began nibbling on her neck and pulled the strap of her sundress and bra off her shoulder, his mouth following to explore the newly bared area.

Natalie tipped her head to the side as she reached for and found the hem of his shirt, sliding her hands underneath and up to his hard, warm chest, her thumbs brushing his nipples. When he sucked in his breath, she was suddenly overcome with the need to seduce *him*, to make him lose his breath over and over as he did her.

"You can have as much fun as you want, Riggs," she whispered as she leaned in and captured his earlobe between her teeth, "as long as I get to join in." Then she grabbed his shirt and pulled it over his head, proceeding to make him forget all about the case. *And* lose his breath.

❧ ❧ ❧ ❧

"Jake, have you thought about using me as bait?" Natalie asked as she munched on a carrot stick much later that night. She was in her sleep shirt on the couch, looking at her old file from Tennessee, he in a pair of sweats at his dining table, jotting notes as he went back through the current files yet again.

He stopped writing for a moment and then resumed. "No."

"No, you haven't thought about it?"

"No, it's not going to happen."

"Why not? It makes sense. We could draw him out by—"

"I said no, Natalie. It's not up for discussion."

She sat up a little straighter. "What you do mean, it's not up for discussion? Don't I have a say in this?"

"Not in that, you don't." Didn't she know the very thought of it filled his gut with fear?

"Now wait just a minute, Jake. Just because we're sleeping together doesn't mean you can tell me what I can and can't do. I think I'll talk to Bill about it."

"And you think he'd have a different response?" Jake stopped writing altogether and turned in his chair to face her.

"I don't know. But at least he'd listen. Instead of just dismissing the idea without so much as an 'I'll think about it.'"

She laid the old file on the coffee table and stood up impatiently.

"Jake, you know my history. You know I've seen a lot in my life. Yes, maybe this case has shaken me up a bit, but I'm not by nature some swooning damsel in distress." She began to pace. "He's involved Bernie now. I can't let anything happen to Bernie." She rubbed her arms as she walked over to the window, only to come back again. "I'm just tired of *waiting* for something to happen."

Jake watched her frustrated movements, her ponytail swinging as she turned back and forth. She looked like she was about sixteen, damn it. In that short sleep shirt with her legs bare and her face scrubbed clean of make-up. Jake knew he couldn't let anything happen to *her*.

"Natalie, come here."

She stopped pacing. "Why?"

"Because I need you to come here. Please."

She walked over to the table slowly. When she stopped in front of him, he just scooted his chair back and patted his lap. She narrowed her eyes at him but complied, sitting down and placing her arms around his neck.

He wrapped his arms around her waist, just drinking in the sight of her, absorbing the feel of her body against his, drowning in her deep chocolate eyes as they penetrated into his soul.

Natalie finally raised an eyebrow. "Are you going to tell me what you're thinking, or are you just going to look at me all night?"

"I like looking at you."

She smiled, shaking her head in resignation.

"In fact," he continued, "I like looking at you so much that I've decided I want to keep doing it. Indefinitely. And I'm just selfish enough to want you safe so I can."

"Jake, I …" He kissed her quickly to silence her words.

"Natalie, please listen to me. I can't let you take the risk. No matter how much we might try to control any situation we set up, there's still a risk, and any risk is too much." *For your safety and my sanity*, he added silently.

But a thought suddenly popped into his head.

"Natalie, do you have a Facebook page?"

She looked at him curiously. "Yes, but I can't always access it, as you can probably imagine. It took me three tries just to get it set up, and Hope had to help. Why?"

He smiled at her. He couldn't have said why he found that unique quality about her so appealing, but he did. "A couple of reasons. Do you have pictures of Bernie, information about her on it?" Natalie nodded. "Depending on the permissions you've set, or how tech-savvy our perp is, it's possible he found out about your relationship with her through that.

"The other thought that occurred to me is that if he is accessing your page, we might be able to use it to draw him out. Plant some subtle information that might lure him to a particular location on a particular date where we would be waiting. Which wouldn't require you to be personally involved or compromise your safety in any way." And he could live with that.

Natalie leaned in and kissed him softly. "See? You thought about it after all and came up with a compromise that we can both agree on." She kissed him again. "Thank you."

"Don't get too optimistic. It's still a long shot. But it's better than, as you say, waiting for something to happen." He lifted her off his lap. "Let's take a look at your Facebook page, see what we've got to work with."

Sitting on the couch together, Jake held his laptop and navigated to her page after Natalie gave him her e-mail and password. Her profile came up, and Jake quickly scanned the comments, postings, and pictures. Sure enough, Bernie was featured heavily in them.

Watching Jake, Natalie could almost see the wheels turn in his head and fervently hoped this idea would work. She glanced at a favorite picture of Bernie, and then her eyes were suddenly drawn to an ad for jewelry on the far right of the page.

Go to the website.

Natalie stilled. Whitney, is that you?

Silence.

Lauren? Maybe after all this time, the first victim was finally coming through. But Natalie heard nothing further. Nevertheless, she had learned over the years how critical it was to follow her instincts, so she didn't hesitate.

"Jake, wait." She scooted forward on the couch and started to reach in and point to the ad on the monitor. He grabbed her hand quickly and pulled it away.

"Hey now, don't get too close. I like this laptop." He smiled and kissed her knuckles as he placed her hand back in her lap.

"Sorry. But would you click on that ad on the right? The third one down, for *Jewelry By Design*? Something's telling me we need to go to that website."

Jake decided it was better not to ask about the "something" and just humor her. Using the touch pad, he clicked on the link and the company's home page came up.

Scanning the contents, he saw a category entitled "One of a Kind Designs" and moved the cursor toward it. Natalie saw it at the same time and glanced at him. "You think?"

Nodding, he clicked on the link, opened that page, and there it was. Just that easy. A thumbnail picture of the very same gold necklace they had found at Whitney's crime scene—the very same design that matched the scar on her stomach.

Natalie sucked in her breath.

Jake sat silent, absorbing the implications of this find. Ignoring for a moment how Natalie had known to go to this site, he knew it was a huge break. They could contact the company, find out where or who the design had come from. Then figure out how the perp was tied to it. Employed by the company? Knew the designer? Lived close to where it had been made? However it turned out, this was the break they needed to find the asshole and lock him up once and for all.

He turned to Natalie. "I don't know how you knew. I don't think I want to know." He tried to convey both the puzzlement and appreciation that conflicted him. "But I'm *glad* you knew."

Then he grinned widely. "We're finally getting somewhere, Natalie," he said, the elation he felt clearly evident in his voice. He turned back to the laptop and copied the link, sending it to his office, Chief Garrett, and Special Agent in Charge Stollmeyer.

Natalie was stunned as she watched him quickly and efficiently send out the information. This was the first time Jake hadn't retreated after being directly confronted with her psychic abilities. She could only look at him, her eyes wide, her heart hopeful.

"Yes, we are," she finally said quietly.

※ ※ ※ ※

Natalie called on Jake's landline to check in on Bernie the next morning after a decidedly delicious shower with him, which was after an even more decidedly delicious awakening by him. If not for the case, Natalie would be floating on top of the world.

Despite the fact that Jake hadn't said he loved her, she knew he cared about her. They were close to catching Daryl. Last night's break was huge. *And* Jake was close to believing in her. She could feel it. Things were looking *way* up.

"Natalie … are you there?"

"Oh, sorry, Bernie, I was just thinking."

"Yes, I could hear it."

Natalie laughed. "Okay, okay, so I'm a little distracted. We're getting ready to go in to Jake's office to follow up on a lead we got last night. It's really encouraging, Bernie. We're getting close. Then we can get back to our regular lives." Only she hoped hers would not be quite so regular anymore.

"That's wonderful news, dear. You tell that man of yours I'm still thinking about his lack of trust and how he's going to fix it for me."

Natalie didn't feel like correcting Bernie's comment. Jake was no more "hers" than she was "his." But it was still secretly thrilling to think that maybe, soon, they'd be …

"*Natalie …*"

Natalie started. "Here. Sorry. I just can't seem to concentrate this morning. You know, the case and everything."

"Oh believe me, I know, sweetie. I was young once and madly in love with Holman. So don't try to fool me—I have no doubt it's not the case but the 'and everything' part that's got you all worked up."

Madly in love. Natalie supposed she was. She should have known that Bernie would see it; would see right through her words. That thought prompted her to immediately issue a warning. She dropped her voice to a whisper.

"Bernie. Please don't say anything to Jake. He … he doesn't really know yet how I feel. He's still working through his own feelings, I think." She glanced furtively over her shoulder and saw Jake was still on his cell phone.

Bernie was silent a moment. "All right, dear, I won't say anything. But trust is a two-way street, you know. If Jake has to learn, you should, too."

Natalie glanced over again and saw Jake punch a button and place his cell phone in his pocket. "I have to go, Bernie. I'll talk to you later today, okay? And please be careful. Make sure you stay within sight of the agent."

"Don't you worry about me, dear. I'm way too ornery for Daryl to try anything."

Natalie prayed she was right. "Love you."

She hung up as Jake walked over and flipped off the light switch. "Ready to roll?"

She took a deep breath. "Ready."

An hour later, they were at his desk at the FBI agency office, Jake making contact with the jewelry company and working his way through the myriad of corporate officers to try to find someone who could tell him how they came by this particular piece of jewelry. Finally, he was transferred to the marketing department and someone named Julia Reeves.

"Ms. Reeves, this Agent Jake Riggs, FBI. I'm calling to get some information about a particular necklace that you advertise for sale on your website under the 'One of a Kind Designs' category. It's an oval-shaped pendant with a series of lines crisscrossing back and forth within. You've titled it 'The Legacy.'"

"Oh, yes, the Legacy. That's a handcrafted piece. We only have about seven or eight left from the original purchase we made from another company—I can't recall the name of it off the top of my head. I'll have to pull my files. But you should know our original order was placed several years ago, so I'm not sure that this company is still around. If you'll hold, I'll see what I can find and be right back."

"Thank you." Jake covered the mouthpiece and told Natalie he was on hold, and they were looking for the information. "Fingers crossed," he mouthed.

When Ms. Reeves came back on the line, she indicated the

jewelry had been purchased from a company called Barker's Jewels out of Marion, Virginia. She recalled now after reviewing her records that this company had been looking for an existing online distribution system for their unique pieces that were individually fabricated by hand, and Jewelry by Design had been interested in pursuing a relationship with them. But after several orders they'd placed with Barker's had been late or shipped incorrectly, Jewelry by Design had severed the relationship, though they had continued to market the pieces that they had already purchased from the company.

Jake asked for the business address and any contact names for Barker's, and she indicated she didn't know who the actual owners were but identified the individual that Jewelry by Design had originally negotiated with, a guy named Marty Reynolds. Jake thanked her and hung up, quickly going back over the notes he'd taken as she'd talked. He looked up at Natalie across the desk.

"One step closer. Now we just have to do some digging on this company called Barker's out of Virginia, which originally sold the pieces to the online company. We need to know where it was founded, who the owners and employees are, and whether we might be able connect any of them to the Smyrna, Tennessee, area around the time Daryl was there."

Natalie was hopeful. They really were getting somewhere. She smiled at Jake as his desk phone rang and he picked up to answer.

"Agent Riggs." He winked at Natalie, feeling upbeat about the progress they'd already made this morning. "Hansen. What's up?" He listened a moment and glanced at Natalie. "Okay."

Natalie watched and waited as Jake quietly absorbed whatever the other agent was telling him.

"Okay, thanks, I appreciate the call."

He hung up and was silent for a moment, his eyes on the phone. Then he looked up at Natalie. "The lab has some results. They were able to get some DNA from the cigarette butt we found behind your house, but there are no matches in the system. Which doesn't really surprise me, given that we haven't had a match on fingerprints either."

Natalie nodded in agreement.

Jake got up and came around to the front of his desk, sitting on the edge of it next to her in the visitor chair, never losing eye contact with her. "The lab also confirmed a DNA match between the lock of hair we found in the box on your front steps and the hair sample you recently submitted."

He stared intently at her. "It's your hair, Natalie. Which tells me we have to solve this case, and damn soon."

Chapter Twelve

Munching on a ham and Swiss after a quick run to Subway, Jake continued working his way through the information, or lack thereof, on Barker's Jewels. The business itself was no longer an active business in the state of Virginia and hadn't filed an annual report for three years. The registered agent that had been listed on the secretary of state's website was MIA. Marty Reynolds was also nowhere to be found.

On a hunch, Jake accessed the bankruptcy records for the District of Virginia and did a quick search. Bingo. He noted Barker's had initially filed for reorganization under Chapter Eleven and then converted to a Chapter Seven and dissolved. Jake pulled up their schedules and looked at the contact information entered. Marty Reynolds was listed again as principal owner. But at the same address and phone number that Jake already had. Damn.

"Making any headway?" Natalie sat back down next to Jake's desk after a quick trip to the restroom and a call to check on Bernie, and then she picked up her own turkey and cheddar and took a bite.

Jake rubbed the back of his neck in frustration. "So far, not much. I did find that Barker's filed for bankruptcy two years ago. I'm just checking out their bankruptcy schedules now to see if there's any other information that might be useful." He continued to scroll through them as they ate.

"I guess that time period would be consistent with what we found out this morning," Natalie mused as she munched on a tart pickle. "But how is Daryl tied to this company? I just have a difficult time believing he was involved in the jewelry business, or any business for that matter." A long ago memory of seeing him steal some of her mother's cash while she was passed out suddenly flashed through Natalie's mind.

"Wait." Jake abruptly paused in his review of the bankruptcy documents. "They listed in their asset schedule an exclusive license agreement with a Zoe Valdez." He clicked on a few links and brought up a scanned copy of the document and took a moment to peruse it. "The agreement is old, effective about twenty years ago, but it looks like Zoe Valdez issued a perpetual license to Marty Reynolds for use of her original design." He scrolled down the document and suddenly hissed a quick *yes*!

Natalie leaned forward in her chair. "What is it, Jake?"

"This says Zoe Valdez was the original creator of the Legacy—and if you can believe our good fortune, the agreement even has an exhibit that contains an illustration of the design." He turned his laptop toward Natalie.

She saw the picture of the necklace. It *was* a perfect match. Natalie looked back up at Jake with eagerness.

"So this Zoe Valdez must be the connection to Daryl." Natalie took another quick bite of her sandwich.

Jake couldn't stop the grin that split his face. "Appears so. And we're going to find out how, starting with the address she listed in this agreement twenty years ago." He brought his laptop back around and began his search on Zoe Valdez, his own sandwich forgotten.

Natalie watched his fingers for a moment as they almost frantically worked the keyboard and mouse. Jake wouldn't rest until he had something, she knew. Her thoughts turned back to the necklace as she reconsidered its design. A design by a woman named Zoe Valdez.

Natalie picked up a pen and drew the pattern once again on a piece of paper. Then stared at it in complete surprise. How could they have been so blind? She now clearly saw the "V" slicing through the "Z" within the intricate markings. And if she eliminated those lines—letters, she acknowledged now—from the design, it appeared that what remained was a simple peace sign. Amazing how a tiny piece of information could snowball into something so much bigger. This Zoe Valdez must have grown up in the sixties or seventies. Did she grow up in the South? Natalie remembered that Daryl had had a strong southern accent.

That thought had Natalie sucking in her breath.

"What's wrong?" Jake had stopped his search and was staring at her, frowning.

"I just realized something, Jake." Natalie frowned herself, looking off in the distance, remembering. "I don't know if it's significant, but … it just occurred to me."

After a moment's silence, she turned back to Jake. "You know how I described what Daryl said to me the night he tried to kill me and then again on the phone on Saturday night?" Jake nodded. "Well, I just realized what was different about it. Daryl was from the South. He had a southern accent. So when he said the word 'dying' to me when I was fourteen, it came out as 'dyin'.' No G closing it off. Yet on the call on Saturday night, there was no accent. He said 'dying' *with* a G."

Jake considered her statement for a moment. "People lose their accent all the time, especially if they move around. You and I both grew up in the South—and I can't hear yours at all, and you can barely hear mine. I imagine Daryl left the area for a time and just eventually lost that southern drawl."

Natalie's instincts told her it was more than that. She closed her eyes and opened her mind, trying to re-create the voices again in her mind, trying to hear the exact sound of the words as they had been said to her, eighteen years apart.

Natalie. It's time to tell him.

She quickly opened her eyes. Who is this?

It's Jess.

Jess. Natalie blew out a slow, silent breath. Jess. Are you sure? I still don't know if it's the right time. We're trying to figure out who might have killed Whitney and Lauren …

It's time. It's the only way.

Natalie saw that Jake had gone back to his computer, once again totally focused on his efforts to locate Zoe Valdez. As Natalie's gaze journeyed over his beloved features compressed fiercely in concentration, she prayed he would be receptive.

Okay, Jess. Tell me what you want him to know.

I was getting involved with the wrong crowd. I think my father suspected it. I was just tired of being told I couldn't do what I wanted to do, and these kids had so much freedom. I wanted it too. When Mom and Dad planned their vacation, I knew it was the perfect opportunity to make some plans of my own and grab that freedom with both hands. Only Jake messed it all up by coming home. So I took matters into my own hands that night and took Jake out of the equation. I drugged him, with some of Mom's sleeping pills. He needs to know that nothing was his fault. Only things didn't turn out like I'd planned …

"Natalie, I think we've hit pay dirt." Natalie was jerked from her telepathic conversation with Jess. Jake's eyes were gleaming as he stared at the computer screen.

"Zoe Valdez had a son. Sonny D. Valdez. Born 1971. I think we've found Daryl. Now I can run the name through NCIC …" He looked up at her as he spoke and then narrowed his eyes. "What is it?"

Natalie's heart began to thump harder. Please, *please* let him hear me.

"Jake, I … I need to tell you something." She took a deep breath. "Jess just spoke to me. She's insisting that I tell you what happened the night she disappeared, that it wasn't your fault."

Jake went instantly still. His eyes never left Natalie's. She could see his chest suddenly rising and falling as he struggled to get his breathing under control.

"Jake, *please*. You have to listen. Jess needs you to know this. It's very important to her that—"

"Why are you doing this, Natalie? Why Jess?" he said in a low, pained voice. "Especially now?"

Natalie's heart took a blow. But she determinedly continued. For Jess as much as for her and Jake's future. "Jake, I'm not *doing* anything. I'm just relaying what Jess is telling me. Information she wants you to have. That night she disappeared, she said she drugged you—"

"*WHAT?*" He shoved his chair back, raked a hand over his hair. "Just stop it. Right now. I don't want to hear any of this." He was angry. "When I told you about Jess, I thought …" He turned away. As if he couldn't look at her anymore. Natalie's heart took another direct hit.

Jake continued in that same low voice, still staring across the room. "I thought you understood how I felt about her. About her murder." He finally turned back to Natalie. The look in his eyes was the final knife to her heart. "But I can see now that you didn't understand anything."

Natalie told herself she would not cry. She would *not*. But it was suddenly and unmistakably evident to her from the look on his face, from his response, that Jake would *never* fully accept her. Would never *believe* in her. Would never *love* her for who she really was. She had simply been living in a fantasy world these past few days.

As Jake watched, she wrapped up her leftover sandwich and tossed it in the garbage, and then she grabbed her purse and stood, staring at him for one long, immeasurable moment. All the love and hope she had felt just this morning was being crushed beneath the weight of his stare. The pressure on her chest made it almost impossible to speak, yet she forced the words to come.

"You're right, Jake. I didn't understand." The first tear slipped unnoticed from her lashes. "I was a fool to think for even one second that you might …" She swallowed convulsively. "That you might … trust. Believe."

The second tear fell. She needed to get out of here before she made an even bigger fool of herself.

"I'll contact Bill and ask him to release me from the case. Immediately." She angrily swiped at the tears that now wouldn't seem to stop. "I think it's best if I … if we don't see each other anymore."

Jake didn't respond. He just stood there, frozen, watching her. She turned to leave, and then she stopped and looked back at him, struggling with what she wanted to say. Then she just whispered, "Be happy, Jake." He continued to watch as she quickly crossed the room and disappeared out the door.

❖ ❖ ❖ ❖

Jake sat down in stunned silence. What the hell had just happened? He felt shell-shocked. They were *this* close to finding out the identity of Daryl, his whereabouts, and she hits him with the whole spiel about Jess. He rubbed a hand over his face. What in God's name had possessed her to bring that shit up now? He simply couldn't fathom it.

He couldn't believe she had done it deliberately to hurt him. She just wasn't a cruel person. It didn't have anything to do with the case. So why? She'd said Jess had contacted her. *Insisting* he be told. Maybe Natalie really did hear something in her head. Maybe she really was just a bit crazy. Christ if he knew.

But when she had said she wanted to be released from the case, that they shouldn't see each other again, Jake had felt like he had been sucker punched in the gut. Had just lost his breath and been unable to speak. As he'd watched Natalie walk out that door, the fear in him had taken hold.

What if she wasn't coming back? What if she was true to her word, and he never saw her again? He suddenly knew that the only way he could get her back was to get this goddamned case solved and behind them. He went back to his computer and started searching for Sonny D. Valdez with a vengeance.

❖ ❖ ❖ ❖

Natalie continued to swipe at the tears that refused to stop as she drove to her house. She was just as angry with herself for crying as she was for ever believing that she and Jake might have had a future. Would she never learn that it just wasn't in the cards for her? Hadn't her history with men told her anything?

She pulled into her driveway, intent only on putting on her swimsuit, packing a bag, and heading over to the spectacular white sand beach and cerulean blue waters of Siesta Key to try and find that sense of peace, that certainty she always felt when she was there—that she was right where she was meant to be; that she was *who* she was supposed to be. She certainly didn't want to stay in the house and bawl her eyes out. She wasn't that pathetic. She sniffed and grabbed a tissue from the kitchen counter as she climbed the stairs to her bedroom. She'd rather be surrounded by a crowd of unfamiliar people laughing and having fun, with the warm sun beating down upon her cold heart.

But she had to make a couple of calls first.

She picked up the phone by her bed and left a voice message for the chief when he didn't answer, asking to be released from the case effective immediately. She didn't go into details. She knew Bill would call her back with questions as soon as he heard her request.

She then quickly called Bernie, also expecting to get her voice mail, as Bernie had already told Natalie when she'd checked on her earlier that she was going over to a neighbor's house for some tea.

"Hello?"

Natalie started. "Bernie, I didn't expect you to answer."

Bernie chuckled. "Well then, why'd you call, dear?"

"I …" Natalie didn't want Bernie to worry. "I just wanted you to know that I'm going to take the afternoon off and head to the beach. I'm feeling a bit stressed and thought an afternoon in the warm sun would be just the thing." Natalie closed her eyes, praying Bernie bought it.

There was a moment's hesitation on the other end. "All right, dear. That sounds nice. But would you stop by here for just a second before you go? I have something for you."

"Bernie, I don't think …"

"Humor me, dear. I'm old, and I think I've earned the right to get my way once in a while."

Natalie sighed. "Fine. I'll stop by in just a couple of minutes, but I can't stay. Okay?" If she stayed, Natalie would probably break down and tell her everything.

"That's fine, dear. See you in a few minutes."

Natalie hung up and grabbed her two-piece from the drawer and hastily pulled it on. She threw on a T-shirt and a pair of shorts over it, and then she took an oversized bag from the shelf above the closet, grabbed some sunscreen and a towel from the bathroom, and headed back downstairs. A couple of water bottles from the fridge and some magazines from the coffee table, and she was ready. She looked around her living room and took another deep breath to try to stop the melancholy from taking over again.

You can get through this, Natalie.

❧ ❧ ❧ ❧

Damn it. Jake was thoroughly frustrated. It seemed that all his efforts kept leading him back to the inescapable conclusion that Sonny D. Valdez, a.k.a. Daryl, disappeared from the face of the earth seventeen years earlier. Oddly enough, right around the time his mother Zoe had been killed. A murder that had never been solved.

Jake had to admit it looked as though Daryl may have killed his mother and then effectively disappeared, changing his identity and starting a new life, which could explain the lack of information on him since that time. But … it didn't explain the lack of fingerprints. Even if he'd changed his identity, Daryl's fingerprints should have eventually shown up again. Getting fingerprinted for a job, for example. Or if he'd messed up and gotten arrested. It just didn't make sense to Jake that Daryl would have been careless enough to leave his prints at Natalie's house all those years ago, yet be slick enough to never leave another print anywhere. Assuming Daryl wasn't, in fact, that careful, his prints would have been in AIFIS to match up against when Hansen had recently reran the old prints from the original crime scene.

Natalie's concern about the difference in accents between the recent phone call and Daryl's statement all those years ago suddenly came back to Jake, bringing another troubling possibility to mind—that Daryl may have been killed right along with his mother by someone else. Someone who may have known Daryl and what he'd done. Someone who was smart enough to make it look like Daryl after all these years.

Shit. If that was true, and Daryl was long dead, Natalie was at a distinct disadvantage now. She had no idea what this perp looked like. She was out there right now, without this knowledge. Without his protection.

He frantically grabbed his keys and his cell phone, dialing her home number as he exited the office and ran down the hall to the ninth floor elevators.

❧ ❧ ❧ ❧

As Natalie made the short drive to Bernie's house, she suddenly realized she hadn't told the officer on duty what her plans were. Come to think of it, she didn't recall seeing him, just his car. He must have been in back, doing a quick check of the perimeter. She'd have to make sure Bernie would let him know where she was going. She just didn't feel like dealing with it right now.

She pulled into Bernie's drive and quickly parked behind the Ford. This was the moment of truth. Or untruth. The real test of Natalie's ability to fool Bernie. If ever she needed to deceive her, Natalie knew it was now. She was barely hanging on by a thread as it was. If she had to tell Bernie anything about what had just happened with Jake, she knew she'd break down and fall into a million pieces.

"Bernie, I'm here." Natalie called out as she opened the front door.

"We're in the kitchen, Natalie."

We? Bernie's neighbor, Dorothy Masterson, must have stopped by, Natalie thought as she walked into the kitchen—and saw the man in dark sunglasses sitting with Bernie at the table.

Bernie turned and smiled. "Hello, dear. This undercover police officer said he saw something suspicious in the backyard and came in to check on me, to make sure everything was all right."

She stared at the man in confusion. He somehow looked familiar but she knew he was not one of the officers assigned to Bernie. She looked more closely—and her eyes suddenly widened. Ronald Julian? Her newer client who'd been blinded in the accident at work? What was he doing here?

"Mr. Julian?"

He slowly took his glasses off and stared directly at her with eyes that looked hauntingly familiar. Her heart stopped. They were Daryl's eyes. Only they weren't because this man wasn't Daryl. But she knew, without a doubt, she was looking into the eyes of the man who had killed Whitney and Lauren.

Her heart immediately started up again and hammered triple time in her chest. She knew she would have to keep all her wits about her if they were going to survive this.

Without taking her eyes from his, she said, "Bernie, I just remembered that Dorothy wanted you to come over and play some pinochle. Why don't you go on over there and—"

Ronald Julian stood up. "No one's leaving now."

Bernie looked up at him in surprise. "What's the matter with you, young man? Didn't anyone ever teach you any manners?"

Natalie could see his eyes start to change in response to the admonition, and she quickly moved to stand between him and Bernie. She spoke to him in a quiet, easy voice. "Your issue, whatever it is, Ronald, is with me, not her. You need to let her go."

"Natalie, what's going on?" Bernie's voice sounded scared.

"It's all right, Bernie. We're just talking." Natalie continued to keep her eyes on Ronald. She repeated herself in slow, measured tones. "You need to let her go." She was starting to sweat. *Steady, Natalie, steady. Don't let him see.*

Ronald narrowed his eyes at her. "I don't *need* to do anything, bitch. Other than finish this." Then he laughed, and the sound crawled up her spine. It was the same laugh she had heard on the phone Saturday night. *Oh God, Jake, please come.* She had to keep Ronald talking, keep his focus off Bernie and on her. Stall for time so Jake could get there. Jake would figure it out and come. She had to believe that.

"How are you related to Daryl?" Natalie asked, still standing between him and Bernie. When she'd heard Bernie's intake of breath at her question, she tried to silently communicate to her with a hand behind her back just to sit tight.

Ronald laughed the same creepy laugh. "Don't you know? I'd have thought a smart lady like you would have figured it all out by now." He cocked his head and considered her, his eyes slowly dropping to take in her casual attire, pausing on her lean, bare legs. When he raised his eyes to hers again, Natalie knew she should be very afraid.

"But I guess you're not as smart as you like to think." He smiled again and spoke in a sing-song voice. "Help me, Doctor, I'm blind and can't deal with my life." His sick laughter rang out. "I even impressed myself. But I'll take pity on you—Daryl was my piece of shit half-brother. We shared the same lovely, fucked-up mother."

Was. Daryl must be dead, Natalie realized. She wondered if Jake had figured this out yet. "Zoe Valdez was your mother?"

He raised an eyebrow at her. "Well, now, I guess maybe you're not as clueless as I thought."

"Is Ronald Julian your real name?"

He laughed again. "I take that back. But please, continue to feel free to call me Ronald." His smile was pure evil.

Natalie was quickly running out of questions. "Did you harm the police officer at my house?"

"He was an idiot, easy to take out." Ronald bragged. "I almost took you in your own house, you know. But when I started to come in, I heard you on the phone with Granny here. I knew she'd throw a wrench in things if you didn't show up on time, so I decided to come here first. But I had to take care of one little problem before I did." He laughed. "That agent never knew what hit him. And now Granny gets to join the party."

Bernie had been sitting quietly listening to their entire exchange, inching her chair ever so slowly toward the phone on the wall. If Natalie could just keep him talking, she might be able to grab it and dial 911 before he noticed …

Ronald chose that moment to look at Bernie and saw that she had moved, and then he glanced over in the direction she was headed, seeing the phone on the wall. "You sneaky little shit." He pushed Natalie aside and grabbed Bernie by the arm. "It's time to tie you up, Granny."

Oh God, Natalie couldn't stand it. If he hurt Bernie … "Please, she's not a part of this. Let her go. I'll do anything you want."

"Shut up, bitch." Ronald pulled a small nylon rope from the pocket of his pants and began to roughly bind Bernie's hands behind her to the back of the chair. Natalie glanced at Bernie and knew she was deathly afraid.

"Ronald, please. She doesn't fit into your plans. She means nothing to you. You have to let her go."

"I said *shut up, bitch*!" He took the gun shoved into the back of his pants, the one he'd pilfered from the cop, and swung it quickly, pistol-whipping Natalie without warning. She went down with a sharp cry.

Bernie was instantly incensed and screamed at him, "You leave her alone, do you hear me? What did she ever do to you?" He quickly slugged Bernie in the face and knocked her out cold.

Natalie was kneeling on the floor in a daze, her head throbbing a painful beat, but when she heard the sick thunk of his hand connecting with Bernie and the resulting silence, a fury so great surged through her body and gave her the energy to stand. She determinedly raised her hands to the table, pulled herself to her feet, and swayed as she faced him, her eyes flashing fire. The mouth that Bernie had worked so hard to curb over the years came back in full force.

"Keep your *fucking* hands off her, you son of a *bitch*! You'll have to kill me first before I let you touch her again." She staggered over to stand in front of Bernie, slumped unconscious and still tied to the chair.

Impressed at her defense of the old lady, despite the rivulets of blood running into her eye and down the side of her face, Ronald smiled maliciously. "Daryl said you were a tough little bitch the first time, and it looks like things haven't changed much, have they?"

Still smiling, he walked over to her while reaching into his pocket. Natalie took advantage of the fact that his hand was out of commission for a moment and suddenly kicked with all her might directly at his crotch.

Taken by surprise, he sucked in a breath and doubled over. Natalie watched as he slowly raised his head to stare at her. His eyes were enraged, his lips curled back in a snarl. She had known her kick would not totally disable him, but it would at least direct his anger toward Natalie and away from Bernie. And it had felt damn good to hit him where it counted.

A growl rose in his throat and without warning, he swung the gun again and hit Natalie on the other side of the head, knocking her down once more. Quickly pulling the soaked rag free from his pocket, he held it over her mouth and nose as she struggled in vain to pull his hands and the cloth away from her face, and then she abruptly went limp.

Placing the rag back in his pocket, he raised the gun to Bernie's temple. A loud knock suddenly sounded on the front door and he jerked the gun up without firing. He quickly stuffed it in his pants and bent down. Grunting, he hefted Natalie's lifeless body over his shoulder and quickly but silently snuck out the back door.

Chapter Thirteen

ick up, Natalie, damn it, pick up. The single blue light Jake had placed on the roof of the sedan continued to flash as he drove like a maniac down Procter. He dialed her home number yet again. *Natalie, please pick up. I need to talk to you. I need to tell you that Daryl is probably dead. That the killer isn't likely someone you know or will recognize. I need to tell you that I'm sorry about all that stuff about Jess. That I love you.*

Jake was instantly shocked at the direction of his thoughts. But as he took a screeching left onto Sawyer, he realized with a sudden clarity that it was true. He *loved* Natalie. Loved her with all that he had in him. He suddenly knew that he didn't care that she thought she could communicate with the dead. He just loved her—and he had to tell her.

Natalie's line went to voice mail again. *Shit.* Punching in Bernie's number and squealing the tires again as he turned the final corner a bit too fast, he listened in frustration as Bernie's line also rang and rang, and then it, too, switched to voice mail.

Reaching Natalie's house, he hit the brakes hard and skidded to a stop in her driveway. He jumped out and sprinted to the front door, throwing it open and running through the house, yelling her name. The silence in response was almost eerie.

Sprinting up the stairs to her bedroom, he immediately saw the disarray. It looked as though she had changed quickly, the clothes he recalled she had been wearing earlier thrown haphazardly across the bed or dropped carelessly on the floor. The closet door was wide open. She must have been planning to go somewhere.

He checked the bathroom and the second bedroom upstairs, saw nothing out of order, and then he quickly ran back down the stairs to check the backyard—and saw the officer down. Jake was suddenly more scared than he'd ever been in his life.

He ran out and checked for a pulse. God *damn* it. He called it in as quickly and dispassionately as he could. Then he contacted the chief to advise him of the situation and that he was on his way to Bernie's. Dreading what he might find there, praying he wasn't too late.

※ ※ ※ ※

A low humming sound slowly penetrated Natalie's consciousness. Focusing on the sound, she mentally tried to clear the cobwebs from her brain. She became acutely aware of a dull, throbbing ache in her head. She gingerly opened her eyelids to a narrow slit—which caused the pain in her head to go from dull to sharp and searing—and quickly closed them again. Intense nausea rose up without warning. But the sudden thought of Bernie lying unconscious, maybe dead, had Natalie trying again.

She fought through the pain, blinking several times before she was finally able to open her eyes. After the dizziness and nausea subsided a bit, she concentrated on her surroundings and saw above her some exposed metal I-beams and rafters in an open, high ceiling. Realizing she was lying on her back, she slowly moved her fingers and felt a cold, hard floor beneath her. Concrete. She turned her head slightly and felt another wave of nausea roll over her. She closed her eyes for a brief moment, and then she opened them again and saw rows of stacked boxes against a far wall. Though groggy, Natalie knew she must be in some commercial building or warehouse.

"Good, you're awake."

Natalie sucked in a sudden breath. Ronald was here. Her heart immediately slammed like a sledgehammer in her chest as she watched him come toward her out of the corner of her eye, still talking.

"You might have a headache and want to puke from the chloroform. Well, and from me smacking you in the head with the gun—" he laughed at that "—but it was necessary." Natalie knew she would hear that sick laugh in her head for a long time to come. "I almost didn't get you out in time, you know. But lucky for you, I parked in the driveway of the house right behind Granny's after I watched for a couple of days to find out their schedule. Let me tell you, throwing you over that back fence wasn't as easy as I thought it would be—though you might not look like it, you weigh a ton as dead weight." He laughed out loud at that. "Get it? *Dead* weight?" His eyes gleamed with sick humor as he stared down at her.

"You know, you put up quite a fight for the old biddy." Then he sobered. "Too bad my mother never did that for me. She might still be alive today."

Natalie wanted so badly to ask about Bernie, if she was still alive. But she also understood that she mustn't anger him and that maybe, if she got him talking, even about his mother, she might buy some time for Jake to get there. Jake *would* get there, she told herself. Despite what had just happened between them, Natalie had no doubt that he would come. She clung to that thought.

"What happened to your mother, Ronald?" As she asked the question, she continued to furtively glance around for clues, for anything that might tell her exactly where she was.

"Oh, she's definitely dead. Daryl killed her—just like I told him to." He dropped a duffel bag next to Natalie, crouched down next to her, and reached into the bag.

"Why did you want her killed?" Natalie was afraid of what he might pull from that bag, but even more terrified that she wouldn't be able to move or fight back. She had just tried to innocuously move her legs and they felt sluggish, like molasses moving through ice.

"Because she was a whore—and because she made a fatal error in judgment. She kept that worthless piece-of-shit brother of mine and gave me up to live with the wolves." He pulled a nylon rope out of the bag and proceeded to roll Natalie on her side and bind her wrists behind her.

Think, Natalie, think. Should she fight now, or keep him talking a while longer? Instinctively, she knew she needed some more time to recover from the effects of the chloroform. She'd read somewhere that directly inhaling it caused the central nervous system to become depressed. She didn't know how long she'd already been out. But based on how her legs felt, she knew she wouldn't be successful if she tried to fight or escape now. Instead, she tried to keep her right wrist turned at an angle while he wrapped the rope around them, not enough that he would notice while he was talking, but maybe enough to give her some wiggle room so she could slip free when he wasn't looking. It was all she could think of.

She also knew she had to keep the dialogue going. "Maybe it wasn't a mistake, Ronald. Maybe it was the ultimate sacrifice, that she thought you could have a life better than the one she could give you."

He laughed harshly in response. "That's just a big load of bullshit, *Dr.* Morgan. But I understand, it's what you shrinks are paid for, to try and put a positive spin on a situation that just ain't positive no matter how you look at it."

He tied a knot in the rope and then allowed her to roll onto her back again, her hands tucked beneath her. He paused as he sat on his heels. "But you know, I feel like I can talk to you about it—being a client and all." That sick grin flashed as he continued.

"I found out about Daryl when I was sixteen. I broke into the files at that shit-hole group home where I was living at the time and looked at my records. My mother hadn't requested they be sealed, so it was all there. She hadn't even listed any father. Like I'd been conceived in a fucking lab or something." His eyes narrowed as he looked off in the distance.

"So I did some checking on my own and found out that she'd

been married before I was born and had another kid—a son—she'd kept. As you can imagine, I was furious. She had no idea of the life she'd sentenced me to." He stopped. "Or maybe she did." Shaking his head, he turned back to Natalie, the look in his eyes as evil as anything she'd ever seen.

"So I decided that she had to die, as did the son she chose to keep. When I turned eighteen, I went to Tennessee and found them. Daryl's father had long since left. When I met my shit-for-brains half-brother, it was easy to see why."

He rummaged around in the duffel bag again and pulled out another rope. Natalie knew her feet were next. Her options were quickly disappearing, and she knew she had to do something soon. But *what?*

"That's where you came in, my dear. Daryl bragged about you right away. Bragged about the whole thing. How he'd killed you and then choked your old lady to death when she tried to stop him. How he'd left his *mark* on you and taken a lock of your hair as a souvenir. He even told me what he'd said to you as you laid there, like he'd made some kind of cosmic joke or something. He had no clue that *he* was the joke."

Ronald wrapped the rope around Natalie's ankles multiple times and started to tie the knot. "When he said what a high it had been to kill you and that he intended to keep doing it—you were his first, by the way—I knew he was eventually going to dig his own grave. He'd even kept a little box with his trophy in it—your hair—and said he planned to add to it."

"So I couldn't decide if I should just let him go ahead and do that, if I should stick to my original plan of killing them both, or if I should come up with a new plan. Then I realized that having Daryl kill our mother while I watched was so much better. Then I could also get rid of him and make it look like he'd just up and left after killing her. So he'd go down in history as the depraved man who murdered his own mother without a second thought. Kind of like a male Lizzie Borden." He laughed at that. "Then I'd be free of them both once and for all."

He tugged at the knot at her ankles, pulling it tight, and then he sat back and smiled malevolently at Natalie. "Are you enjoying this little story yet?"

Natalie swallowed, but she had no saliva in her mouth. It was bone dry. *Just keep him talking, Natalie, keep him talking. Jake will be here soon.* "I don't understand how you convinced Daryl to kill his own mother. Why would he do that?"

Ronald unexpectedly stood up and started pacing, leaving her bound and lying on the floor. "You know, Doc, it was pathetically easy. When I first told him how much I hated her for throwing me away like a piece of garbage when she'd kept him around, he got this weird look on his face and said, 'Yeah, right, like I lived in fucking Mayberry RFD.'"

Ronald stopped pacing and shook his head. "She'd kept him, yeah, but she'd also fucked him up, in more ways than one. Hit him *and* played with him, if you know what I mean. Don't that just beat all? Said he couldn't get the image out of his brain of her above him with that damn necklace of hers hanging down in his face. So maybe I did come out on the better end of the deal after all."

He laughed callously and then came back to stand over her. "That's where your little *mark* came from. The necklace our whore of a mother designed and, according to Daryl, wore every day of her life. Right up until the day she died. Did you figure that out yet, Doc?"

His lips curled.

"Anyway, so I just played up on that little detail of his life, and Daryl fell right into my hands. Just like you did. Just like the police did. Lucky for me, Daryl's little box of trinkets held a couple of those necklaces too, huh?"

Then his smile grew as he picked up the duffel bag once again, never taking his eyes off of her.

❧ ❧ ❧ ❧

"Holy mother of God." Jake ran into Bernie's kitchen and dropped before her, still slumped and unconscious in the chair. He lifted her chin, felt and found her steady pulse, and immediately saw that her right eye was swollen and starting to bruise. She was going to have a doozey of a shiner.

Not seeing any other major injuries, he made a quick call for emergency response and then hurriedly checked the rest of the house and backyard, once again yelling for Natalie, his heart in his throat. Then he saw the agent who'd been assigned to Bernie lying in a pool of blood near the back corner of the house. *Shit.* Jake quickly ran over and once again checked for a pulse. Faint, but this time still there.

This asshole was going down, Jake vowed. He must have taken Natalie. Jake ran back into the kitchen and knelt behind Bernie, working frantically to untie her bound hands, the only thing that had kept her upright in the chair. "Bernie, wake up. I need you to talk to me. I need you to tell me where Natalie is."

He removed the ropes, moved around to the side of the chair, and lifted her into his arms, carrying her into the living room and laying her gently upon the couch. He lightly patted her cheek. "Bernie, wake up. You can do it. Come on, honey, please wake up. Natalie needs you." *And I need Natalie,* Jake added silently. Please, God, let Bernie know something.

Bernie's eyelids fluttered and a low moan escaped. "That's it, Bernie," Jake encouraged. "Come on, fight through it and open your eyes. Talk to me."

Bernie blinked several times before fully opening her eyes and focusing on Jake's face. "Jacob." Her eyes immediately welled with tears as she reached blindly for his hand. "Jake, he was here. Where's Natalie? Is Natalie okay?" She lifted her head to look around and fell back in sudden pain. "Oh God, Jake, he tied me up, then he hit Natalie, hard, with his gun, and she went down. Then he hit me, and I don't remember anything after that." The tears flowed freely now. "Jake, please, is Natalie okay?"

Jake temporarily sidestepped her question. "What did he look like, Bernie? Did he say anything, give you any information that would tell us who he is or where he went?"

The Bernie he knew started to come through as she frowned at him through her tears. "Jacob Riggs, stop avoiding my question right now, and tell me truth about Natalie. I deserve the truth."

She was right. But the truth sucked. "It's looking like he took Natalie with him."

"Oh, dear God, he took my Natalie?" She gripped his hand hard. "You have to find her, Jake. She's all I've got."

"I will, Bernie, but you have to tell me everything you do remember. Right now, it's all *we've* got."

Bernie wiped at the tears. "He ... he said he was a client of Natalie's, but I think that was just a ruse. I think Natalie called him ... I think ... Lord, my head hurts." She closed her eyes for a moment.

"A name, Bernie—did she use a name?" For the first time, Jake felt hopeful.

Sirens blared as he waited for a response. "Bernie, if you can give me the name, some details of what he looked like, how long ago he was here, we can find him." *And* Natalie.

Bernie opened her eyes again and then furrowed her brow as she tried to concentrate. "He came to the back door claiming to be an undercover police officer and said he needed to check the house, that he saw someone prowling around. I didn't even question it. It was about one o'clock because I was just getting ready to make some lunch." She took a deep, dragging breath.

"That's good, Bernie, that gives us a timeline. Can you describe what he looked like?"

"He was only a couple of inches taller than Natalie, I think. Average build, probably in his late thirties or early forties, and he had slicked-back hair and bad skin, like he'd had acne as a child ... Mr. Julian! That's it, Natalie called him Mr. Julian when she came in." Her eyes narrowed as she thought. "Ronald. Ronald Julian. Yes, that was the name she used. But I don't think it was his real name. I remember Natalie asking him that question, and he just laughed."

"That's great, Bernie, that really helps. You did good." He patted her hand as an EMT knelt beside the couch. "Just rest for a minute, Bernie, and let this lady take care of you. I'll be right over there."

He quickly rose and pulled out his cell phone, calling the chief to relay the information and to request that he coordinate with the FBI in issuing an APB. They could also get a quick search warrant approved and send someone to Natalie's office to pull any records she had on the guy if he had, indeed, posed as a client. Analyzing the timeline based on Bernie's information, the guy couldn't have gotten very far yet, and they could establish some roadblocks on all the major arterial roads within a certain periphery. He'd let the chief coordinate that. In the meantime, his only option was to talk to Bernie again to see if she could remember any other details, details that might give them a clue as to where Natalie might have been taken. Before it was too late.

❧ ❧ ❧ ❧

Natalie *almost* had her right hand free. Ronald was rambling about how stupid she'd been not to suspect he wasn't a real client, so she continued to pretend she was listening while twisting and wiggling her hands in an effort to get free from the ropes. It was proving to be a lot more difficult than she had originally thought, but she was slowly, painstakingly making headway. At the same time, it was taking all her skills as a psychologist to keep him talking without angering him.

Her thoughts turned once again to Bernie. Please don't let her be hurt badly, please don't let her be dead. Natalie didn't know what she'd do if she got out of this only to find Bernie didn't make it. She could feel her throat constrict and knew she had to stay focused on the moment or those kinds of thoughts would take her under.

Ronald was up and pacing again. He had temporarily abandoned the duffel bag after she had asked him some subtly leading questions about his own childhood, and he had taken off on his response, apparently forgetting, at least temporarily, what he had originally reached for in the bag.

Though the rope continued to chafe her skin, Natalie worked her right hand back and forth, back and forth, as she tried to tug free. She casually glanced around again, knowing time was running out, looking for a sign of anything familiar. Damn, if only she could use a cell phone and carried one with her. Then they could have simply used the signal to pinpoint her location.

Her eyes landed on a row of high windows above the boxes along the far wall of the warehouse. She saw trees and then stopped suddenly. Just beyond the line of trees, she could make out a building, with letters on the side. She glanced back at Ronald to see if he was paying attention.

"Do you know how I found you? It was pure luck. No, on second thought, let's call it fate—I like the sound of that better."

He laughed and walked back toward her. Damn, she couldn't risk a glance out the window right now. But she knew she'd be one step closer to freedom if she could figure out those letters and determine where she was.

"I was passing through Sarasota some months back, eating breakfast at Denny's one morning. Gotta love those Grand Slams, you know? So I glanced at a copy of the *Herald Tribune* someone had left behind and saw this picture of a pretty little lady and just had to read about her." He stopped and cocked his head as he stared at her. "You know, that picture didn't do you justice." A smile slowly spread across his face.

Get your hand free, Natalie, get your hand free. She pulled and tugged as hard as she dared without alerting him to the movement. "What article was that? I don't recall it." She was lying, but it would keep him talking.

"Oh come on now, Doc, surely you remember the interview? The one where they spotlighted your business and talked about how you'd come from a background similar to the messed-up kids you try to help? How you'd survived a brutal attack by a man back in Smyrna, Tennessee, when you were only fourteen, and how it had changed your life and made you what you are today, blah, blah, blah?"

Almost loose now. She could feel the warm trickle of blood on her hand from the chafing of the rope and the constant friction she'd been creating. But if she could just get her hand through … "Okay, I remember now. You saw the article?"

"Didn't I just say I did? Pay attention, Doc, or I might get pissed. You don't want me to get pissed."

"Sorry, I'm still a bit groggy." Which was also a lie, since the effects of the chemical appeared to have finally worn off. But Ronald didn't need to know that just yet.

He knelt back down beside her and reached once again into the duffel bag. "Anyway, I read that article and got to thinking that maybe my dumb-ass brother had committed the biggest screw-up of all—that it was possible that the girl he'd said he'd killed had survived after all. Then I suddenly realized this was an *opportunity*. For me to enhance my brother's already stellar reputation. But I had to find out if it was really you, so I became one of your pathetic little clients. You never even suspected."

He laughed again, clearly relishing this part of the story. Then he laughed harder when her eyes widened as he pulled a shiny scalpel out of the duffel bag.

"This get your attention, Doc?"

Natalie swallowed hard as she stared at it, her heart suddenly thudding in her chest. "Why do you need that, Ronald?" Her hand was almost free, damn it! Just a few more seconds …

"Well, clearly, Daryl has to finish what he started. So I hand-picked those two lovely young girls to set the final stage for this. Because Daryl not only hates his mother, he's a serial killer." He smiled as he took the scalpel and ran his tongue against its length while he watched her. "Since Daryl never finished the scar—or you—I'll do it for him."

I'm so sorry he dragged you into this, Natalie silently apologized to Whitney and Lauren as she continued to pull and tug as Ronald lifted her shirt to expose her stomach just as Natalie's right hand finally jerked free. *Yes!* Before Ronald could even assimilate the thought that she might have escaped the confines of the rope, she pulled her arms from beneath her and grabbed his wrist with one hand, while at the same time stiffening her other wrist, flattening her palm and slamming it up and into his nose as she'd been taught in self-defense class all those years ago.

He howled in pain as the blood spurted from his nostrils. When he doubled over in reaction, Natalie used both hands and wrenched the scalpel from his grasp, slicing the thin skin of her right hand between the thumb and forefinger in the process. Her feet still bound, she rolled away from him, holding on to the scalpel, but he recovered quickly and came after her. She knew she might not have had enough time, but she had to take the chance—she flung the scalpel up as high and as hard as she could, hoping against hope that it was now magnetized and would hit one of the metal I-beams.

When he saw what she had done, he watched the scalpel's flight, expecting to see it land back down on the concrete floor. They both heard the sound of the instrument hitting a beam above them and saw it stick firmly to the beam's bottom lip, the sharp point sticking out slightly over the edge as it lay lodged far above them.

"NOOOOO!" Ronald was incensed; swiping at the blood still dripping from his nose, he turned and marched back to the duffel bag, pulling out the gun he had used at Bernie's house. "You bitch, you've just signed your death warrant!" He pointed the gun and shot her in the stomach.

The force of the bullet hitting Natalie had her gasping and staring at her stomach in shock. Blood began to seep through her clothes as she looked back up at Ronald in disbelief. Had she really made it this far only to die now? She heard him laughing as she tried to crawl away and found that she had lost the power to move her limbs. She collapsed, breath heaving; the pain was now intense. She rolled her head to the side and saw the building through the windows again—and suddenly realized where she was. Her last thought was of Jake as the blackness overtook her.

❧ ❧ ❧ ❧

"Jake, I need to know why I got a message from Natalie earlier today asking to be released from the case." The chief had arrived at Bernie's house and was finally getting around to the troubling voice message. He didn't know what had happened between Jake and Natalie but knew it had to be significant for her to take that step.

Jake ran a frustrated hand through his hair and looked at Bill, his expression troubled. "She told me this morning that my long-dead sister had communicated with her and that she needed to tell me the details of what had happened on the night Jess had died."

Looking back on that conversation now, Jake suddenly understood that Natalie had put herself on the line to tell him what she thought she was supposed to be telling him. Especially when she knew how he felt about his sister *and* Natalie's paranormal abilities. For her to do that with him was a huge risk for her. He saw that now. Only he had responded with more of the same—skepticism, anger, denial. Not with the love and acceptance that Natalie had needed but had never demanded from him. Christ, he was such an idiot.

The chief's blue eyes were bright with his own fear. "Jake, I hope to God that someday you'll understand how special Natalie is. If we can find her and bring her home."

Jake looked the chief straight in the eye. "I do understand how special Natalie is. It may have taken me awhile, but I understand. When I find her—and I *will* find her—I'm going to tell her that."

Bernie heard Jake's words from the couch and closed her eyes, the tears seeping through.

Chapter Fourteen

Natalie slowly became aware of a sensation of warmth enveloping her. She savored it for a moment, knowing instinctively that something had changed. She opened her eyes, expecting to see the sun, and saw a brilliant white Light instead.

At once, Natalie realized what had changed—she had crossed over for the second time in her life. The Light was just as she remembered it: magnificent and pure, satiated with complete and utter love. And she felt just as she had the first time: peaceful, safe, *understood*. Yet in spite of all that, Natalie grieved. For the life she was beginning to understand she could never have with Jake.

Why now? she wondered. Why had everything come full circle now? Despite the absolute love and acceptance she felt here, she was overcome with sadness at the thought of never seeing Jake or Bernie again.

Natalie. Welcome home, child.

Natalie turned at the words permeating her thoughts, sudden gladness pushing aside the sorrow as she saw the older man who had guided her eighteen years earlier. Her angel. He looked just the same, his hair and neat beard a soft gray, his eyes kind.

Smiling in recognition, she responded in kind. *Hello.* But her smile faltered as the sadness once again reasserted itself. *I don't understand why I am here again.*

You are here because of the choices you have made in your life, he responded. *Now you will be given one final choice to make.*

What choice? Natalie asked.

This time, you may choose to stay here or you may choose to return to the life you know. You were not given that choice before because we had other plans for you. You have not disappointed us, child. We are pleased.

Natalie's heart overflowed.

Yet you are here again because of those choices you have made. Choices based on love, based on trust, and your inability to believe in them. You must decide now if you can open your heart and choose to love and trust without reservation in spite of the unknown. In spite of the obstacles or risks. Just as we have loved you.

Natalie knew with a sudden, blinding clarity that despite everything, she loved Jake unconditionally and would no matter what he said or did, in spite of the fact that he didn't accept her or believe in her.

I want to go back—I must go back, Natalie responded with unqualified conviction. *I love Jake with every part of me. I know this in my heart without any doubts. Please tell me what I need to do.*

Natalie was abruptly aware of activity beneath her and realized that once again, she was somehow suspended above her body as it lay immobile upon the concrete floor below her. She saw that her feet were still bound, her shorts and shirt soaked in her own blood. She saw Ronald's frustrated movements, felt his anger, as he paced back and forth, clearly trying to think of a way to retrieve the scalpel that was still stuck to the beam twenty feet above him.

Her own feelings of frustration quickly surfaced. *There isn't much time left, is there?* she asked. *Jake will have to come soon. Please help me. Please tell me what I need to do.*

Do you remember Jenny's love for you as a child?

Yes, I remember.

Did you believe in that love?

Yes. You know I did.

Then that is your answer.

Natalie at once understood. Jenny had heard her in that most critical hour because Jenny had loved her and believed without question. Natalie was certain Jake loved her even though he had never told her so. She could only hope—*trust*—that he would believe.

✵ ✵ ✵ ✵

"Damn it, Bill, there has to be something more we can do!" Jake felt utterly helpless and more and more desperate that they might not get Natalie out of this alive. All he wanted was the chance to hold her and tell her that he loved her; he didn't care about anything else. But it looked like his chances were quickly fading with each passing minute. It was déjà vu all over again, just like the morning after Jess disappeared. Was he simply destined to be unable to save the ones he loved the most?

"Jake, I understand your frustration. Don't you think I feel it, too? Natalie is like a daughter to me." The chief paced back and forth in the confines of Bernie's living room, smoothing his mustache time and again, while the forensics team continued to work on the kitchen. "But we've done everything we can. We've scoured the neighborhood for signs of which direction he might have gone. For evidence of any kind. We've set up roadblocks and issued the APB, but we've got damn little information on him and nothing on the vehicle he may have been driving. We're waiting on the judge to approve the warrant for Natalie's work files, and we've got men right now searching all available records for another son of Zoe Valdez to see if that might lead us to any useful information. Hell, the only thing more we could do is to bring in a psychic."

Jake ran a restless hand through his hair. At this point he was open to anything, but he really didn't know how much good a psychic would do; it might even lead them in the *wrong* direction. He also knew he was taking this out on the chief, when they all were on the same team. "I'm sorry, Bill. I just … I just need to find Natalie and tell her …"

His cell phone rang once in his pocket and then was silent. He pulled it out and the display was going haywire, just like the time Natalie had been standing near him at her house. Suddenly her picture came up on the screen, the one that he had taken only yesterday at Moretti's—God, it seemed so long ago—right after they had seen the dolphins. What the hell?

He stared at her picture and was immediately overcome by emotions so strong he could barely restrain himself. God, he loved her. More than anything or anyone. Please, *please*, let them find her soon so he could tell her.

Jake.

His head jerked up, and he glanced frantically around. Had anyone else heard that? He could have sworn it was Natalie's voice.

Jake, please come and get me. I need you now more than I ever have.

Was he going crazy? Did he want so badly to find her that he was imagining her talking to him now?

I know this will be difficult for you, Jake, but you have to trust me. Just this once. I'm in a warehouse next to the city transit building on Ashton and Macintosh. You have to come now. There's not much time left.

Jake heard the urgency of the words as clearly as if Natalie was standing right next to him. Only she wasn't. He looked around and saw Bernie staring at him strangely from the couch. Had she heard it?

He quickly walked over to her. "Bernie, did you hear that?"

"Hear what, Jake?"

He paused. God, he was going to sound nuts.

"Jesus, I might be going crazy, but did you hear ... Natalie's voice?"

Bernie continued to stare at him for a moment and then grabbed his hand. "No, Jake, I didn't, but I have no doubt that you did."

Had he? Had he really heard it? Holy Christ. What was he supposed to do now?

Bernie slowly sat up and rose from the couch, holding the compress to her swollen eye as she looked up at him intently with her good eye. "Jake, I don't know how Natalie has communicated with you, but I *believe* that she has. It's time, Jake. For *you* to finally believe. There's no other way, Jake."

He looked at Bernie, could see that she was utterly and completely convinced in what she was saying, that Natalie had somehow contacted him, yet Bernie hadn't heard a single word. And he had, yet was still having trouble believing.

Jake, I love you. Please come.

He suddenly knew this *was* the only choice. If he ever had a chance of saving Natalie, he knew he had to listen to what he was hearing. He turned back to the chief.

"Bill, I know this is going to sound crazy, but I think Natalie is somehow trying to communicate with me. I just heard what sounded like her voice telling me she's in a warehouse in that industrial section where the Sarasota City Transit offices are located, near Ashton and Macintosh. If I recall, there's some kind of supply warehouse next door that's used solely for storage. It's about five minutes from here, and I'm headed there now. I'd appreciate if you'd arrange for some backup and emergency medical personnel to follow me."

Jake didn't wait for a response; he ran out the front door and jumped into his car. *Hang on, Doc, I'm on my way.* And he prayed that this time, she could hear *him*.

❧ ❧ ❧ ❧

Ronald's triumphant shout brought Natalie's awareness back to the activity below her. She saw why he was exultant: his toss of the rope had finally gone over the rafter where the scalpel was stuck. She watched as he fed the rope over the beam until he could reach the other end where he'd tied a roll of duct tape for weight. Grabbing both ends, he slid the rope back and forth until it dislodged the scalpel and it fell at his feet with a clang.

"Yes!" He picked it up and held it almost reverently. "Now I can finish this once and for all." Natalie continued to watch as he walked back over to her body and knelt down beside her once again. He moved her shirt and shorts out of the way and exposed her stomach for the final carving, but there was so much blood, it was clear that he would not be able to complete the task until he cleaned it up.

She saw him pull more cloth out of his duffel bag and begin to wipe her stomach clean so he could locate her existing scar. He took the cloth he was using and placed it against her bullet wound, and then he pulled two long strips of duct take and secured the cloth in place over her wound.

Natalie knew instantly that he had no idea he had just prolonged her chance of survival, possibly just enough to allow Jake to reach her in time. That is, if Jake had, in fact, heard her words, and if he had, in fact, chosen to believe them and come. Two very big ifs. Especially since she saw now that Ronald had just started to score the final, remaining lines of the symbol upon her exposed stomach.

⚜ ⚜ ⚜ ⚜

Jake arrived at the warehouse quickly but without fanfare. He had turned off his siren several blocks earlier, simply allowing his single flashing light to keep traffic out of the way as he sped to Ashton and Macintosh.

He scanned the large parking lot outside the warehouse and saw a lone vehicle parked at the very end of the building. Driving to it, he kept his eyes and ears trained for the sight of anything out of the ordinary. Parking and exiting in one swift, silent motion, he made his way to the vehicle, gun drawn.

A glance inside revealed blood spatters on the seat, and Jake knew he was close. Damn close. I'm almost there, Doc, hang on, just one minute more.

He turned from the car toward the warehouse. In front of him was a single door. Natalie was behind that door. He knew it. His only fear was that he would jeopardize her safety by his actions—or that he was already too late.

He had to trust. He had to. He grabbed the knob, turned the handle, and threw open the door.

"FBI! *Freeze!*" All at once, he saw Natalie lying motionless on the floor covered in blood, and a man kneeling over her with a knife in his hand; the man's head jerked up at Jake's words, and then he suddenly raised his arm in order to bring the knife violently down and into Natalie.

His heart in his throat, Jake fired once, twice, three times, until the man finally crumpled over on the floor next to Natalie, the bloody knife falling from his fingers to clatter upon the concrete beside him.

Knees shaking, heart pounding, Jake ran to Natalie, praying as he had never prayed in his life that she was still alive. He dropped to the floor beside her and touched his fingers to her carotid artery. He couldn't feel a pulse. He cried out in helplessness.

"Damn it, Doc, don't die on me now, I just found you!" He could not stop the silent tears that slid down his cheeks as he probed for injuries. He saw the blood-soaked cloth taped to her skin and knew that her primary injury was underneath that cloth. He gently picked her up and applied pressure to the cloth as he held her close, pleading with her, begging her, not to give up now.

Sirens suddenly sounded in the background.

❧ ❧ ❧ ❧

Jake had come. Jake had *come*. She had watched as he'd shot Ronald and ran to her, and now she felt all the love and anguish that was pouring from him as he held her lifeless body. She turned back, knowing it was time to go. And then she saw Whitney Robertson.

Whitney called to her. *Natalie. I wanted to tell you thank you. For everything you did for my family.*

Natalie heard this beautiful, incredible young girl's words and thought that it was she who should be thanking Whitney. Whitney had been instrumental in opening Natalie's eyes to what it truly meant to love.

Then Whitney smiled, her face the expression of pure love. *I talked to my mom, Natalie, and she heard me. It's all going to be okay. Don't grieve for me. This is a wonderful place. But it's almost time for you to go back.*

Natalie smiled back at Whitney, so pleased at her words, and then she saw another young girl appear beside her. She knew without hesitation that this was Jess. She was slender and so pretty, and she looked just like Jake must have looked at that age. Natalie's heart swelled, and she wanted to reach out and hold her. It would be like holding Jake.

But it was Jess's turn to communicate with Natalie.

Natalie, before you go, you must know the story of what happened the night of my death, so Jake can finally be at peace. You must promise me that you will tell him.

I will, Natalie promised.

Jess glided toward Natalie, her entire body glowing with the Light, and she reached out and touched Natalie's temples with her fingers. In the space of a heartbeat, Natalie's mind was flooded with words and images from that fateful night. Then Jess lowered her hands.

Go to him, Natalie. Love him with everything you have, and tell him I will always love him. And one more thing …

Natalie heard Jess's final words just as she felt her spirit being pulled back down to her body. This time, the pain that hit her as she rejoined her physical self was welcome, and the fleeting feel of Jake's hand holding tightly to her own as the paramedics worked on her was a miracle. Then she knew no more.

Chapter Fifteen

Natalie woke to an insistent beeping sound. She opened her eyes and adjusted to the dim light in the room. Moving her hands, she felt the stiff, cool sheets beneath them and knew immediately she was in a hospital room. The memories of what had happened came rushing back, and she closed her eyes again briefly, relieved. She had survived.

Rolling her head to the left, she saw Bernie asleep on a chair, her feet propped up on a second chair. Her hair was mussed, her head tipped back, her mouth slightly open—and she had a bright purple shiner. Natalie thought she had never looked so dear. *Thank you for giving me more time with Bernie. I swear I won't take it for granted.*

Natalie rolled her head to the right. Slumped in what had to be an incredibly uncomfortable position in yet another chair next to her bed was Jake, in all his stubbled, rumpled glory. His eyes suddenly opened, and he stared at her intently. Then a slow smile softened his features. The force of her love for him slammed into her like a Mack truck, and the tears immediately started to fall as she realized how close she had come to losing him.

"Hey now, Doc, don't do that." He sat up and reached for her bandaged right hand, gently bringing it to his mouth and looking at her with those glittering green eyes that she so loved.

"Jake," she whispered hoarsely, curling her exposed fingers around his hand despite the pain.

He leaned forward, softly kissed her lips, and then shushed her. "Natalie, my love. It's all right. Don't talk for a minute, just listen."

"But I …"

His fingers covered her lips.

"I've been waiting for two long days and nights for you to wake up so I can tell you this." He smiled crookedly. "So I'm sorry, but I can't wait a second longer."

She gave him a wobbly smile in return and nodded, hearing the underlying urgency in his words.

He continued to hold her hand as he spoke. "When I couldn't reach you after you'd left my office on Monday, I was frantic. I had discovered some things that told me Daryl had possibly been dead for many years, which meant you wouldn't recognize your killer. Only I couldn't find you to tell you that. When I realized the danger you were in and that I really could lose you, it all became clear to me."

He paused and brought her hand to his lips again, clearly struggling with his emotions.

"I realized right then and there that I love you. More than anything. That without you, my life is empty, meaningless."

Natalie's eyes brimmed with tears once again as she absorbed the power of his words and the incredible healing effect they had on her heart.

Jake gently cupped her cheek and brushed away a stray tear with his thumb. "So when you were somehow able to communicate with me that day and tell me where you were … well, let's just say that I don't think I would have believed it, much less acted on it, if I hadn't admitted those feelings to myself. I still don't understand how you did it, but I know that you did it."

Natalie reached up and covered his hand with her own and turned her head to kiss his palm. Oh, how she loved him.

"So what I learned that day," Jake said as he gazed into the beloved brown eyes he had feared he would never see again, "is that love gives you the ability to do things you didn't think were possible. Like putting aside your skepticism and trusting in something, or someone. Like the woman you love."

He couldn't help himself and leaned in for another kiss, lingering for a bit longer this time.

When he pulled back, his eyes were once again intense on hers. "I'm sorry it took me so long to understand what you were trying to tell me. What I'm trying to tell you now is that I believe you, but in the end, none of that really matters. What matters is that I can't live without you. So don't die on me again. I don't think I could survive it."

The last came out in a hoarse whisper as his head dropped to the bed and he was overcome by the intensity of his emotions.

Tenderness surged up in Natalie as she stroked his hair. "Jake, I love you, too, more than I ever thought possible. I knew it the first time you smiled at me." She smiled herself, as she gazed down at him so overcome with feeling.

Natalie heard a cough to her left and turned to see Bernie awake and grinning. Natalie grinned back.

"I guess this is my cue to leave, child." Bernie stood up, stretched out the kinks, and then leaned down to give Natalie a hug, careful of her injuries. "I love you, sweetie. So much. It's so good to see you alive and kicking again. But you and I can talk later. Right now you need to be alone with that man of yours."

She winked at Natalie as Jake lifted his head and smiled at her.

Hobbling around the bed to go, Bernie issued a parting shot at Jake. "I'm watching you, Jacob Riggs, so you'd better take good care of her. And you should know I've got eyes in the back of my head." She chortled as she walked slowly out the door. "Just ask Natalie."

Jake watched her leave, his eyes still glistening but now alive with laughter. "That woman is definitely one in a million."

"Yes, she is." Natalie smiled in response as she laid her head back against the pillow, and then she immediately raised it up again when she heard whispering outside the door.

"Do you think she's awake?"

"Probably not, but the nurse said we could go in for just a second so you can see for yourself that she's going to be okay."

Natalie saw Danny's dark head peek around the door and then watched his eyes light up and a big grin split his face when he realized she was, indeed, awake. Melinda Talbot followed, her smile apologetic. "We don't want to intrude, Dr. Morgan, but Danny insisted—actually, demanded—that we come and see you when he saw the news on television."

Natalie waved them in with a smile. "Please come in." She looked at Danny and patted the side of the bed in invitation. "I'm so glad you came to see me, Danny." He scurried over and awkwardly climbed up, his arm still in a cast, and then looked at Jake suspiciously.

"Hi." Jake smiled at him. "I'm Jake Riggs." He stuck out his hand.

Danny reluctantly placed his good hand in Jake's as Natalie clarified. "Jake is with the FBI, Danny. I've been working with him on a case."

Danny let go and turned back to Natalie. His eyes were serious. "He's one of the good guys, then?"

Natalie laughed softly. "Yes, Danny, he's definitely one of the good guys."

Danny frowned as he glanced back over at Jake. "Then how come you got hurt?"

"Oh, Danny." Natalie took his little hand in hers. "Jake is the reason I'm still alive and in this hospital bed. It's because of him that we'll be able to continue talking at my office on Thursdays."

It was Jake's turn to clarify. "I know how you feel, Danny. Not only do you and I need Dr. Morgan, this world needs her. In fact, I'm making it my special mission to protect her from here on out. So you don't have to worry anymore." He smiled gently at the boy.

Danny considered Jake silently for a moment. "Are you really an FBI agent?"

"I am."

Danny slowly smiled back. "Cool."

Melinda jumped in. "Danny, we need to go and let Dr. Morgan rest."

Danny looked back at Natalie and took a deep breath. "I'm glad you're all right," he whispered.

"Me too." She squeezed his hand. "I'll see you soon."

When Danny and Melinda left, Natalie turned back to Jake and smiled luminously at him, thinking that all was right with the world, and then suddenly remembered her promise to Jess.

"Jake, I need to tell you something. Will you promise me that you'll listen to me now? This is really important. I need you to promise."

He looked slightly puzzled, but nodded his head. "Okay. I promise."

Natalie reached for his hand again, needing the direct contact. "You know when you heard my voice telling you where I was? I was having a near-death experience just like I did when I was fourteen. My spirit had left my body, and I was communicating with you from the other side. I know it sounds unbelievable, but it's the truth."

She was still overwhelmed at what she had experienced and knew she would be for a long time to come.

"I talked to an angel, Jake—the same angel I met eighteen years ago. I also saw Whitney." She squeezed his hand. "And I met Jess."

Jake's eyes widened in surprise at her last statement, but he stayed silent, true to his promise.

"She was so pretty, Jake. She looked just how I pictured you at that age, only with long, wavy dark hair. She made me promise to tell you what really happened to her that night, and I told her that I would."

When he just nodded, she continued.

"She said you weren't responsible for her death, Jake. That the fight you had that night was not why she left the house. She had already planned to sneak out and had ground up some of your mother's sleeping pills and put the powder in your soup at dinner. Only things didn't quite go as she had planned, because she used too many pills, and you passed out on the couch before getting to bed."

Jake's brow was furrowed, his eyes distant as he nodded his head slowly in recollection. "I remember waking up that morning after Jess had disappeared and feeling extremely groggy, but I thought I was just tired from school and had just slept really hard. But I've always told myself that if we hadn't fought that night before, and *if* I'd woken up, Jess wouldn't have snuck out and been killed."

He focused again on Natalie.

"And now you're telling me that it wasn't the fight at all, and that I couldn't have woken up no matter how much I had wanted to."

Natalie nodded, seeing unspoken relief in his eyes and feeling her own sense of relief for him. "But that's not all, Jake. One of the older boys in the group that she'd been hanging out with, one who'd been staring at her a lot, came by the house that night alone, which was not the plan. She was supposed to meet up with the group in the park. But he said, 'Let's go,' and Jess got uncomfortable, so she told him that she was going to walk to the park by herself and that he'd have to leave."

This next part was the hardest, and it would be for Jake as well, Natalie was certain. But she determinedly continued, thinking of Jess.

"This boy apparently got angry at that and grabbed Jess, and he attacked her right there in the house, pulling out a knife. Then he suddenly saw you lying on the couch in the next room and started to walk toward you, and Jess realized that he was going to kill you first so there would be no witnesses. Only she knew you couldn't fight back because of the sleeping pills, so she told him she'd go with him if he just left you alone. Jess said you'd always looked out for her, and she knew right then that this was her chance to do the same for you."

Natalie stroked his hand.

"It's time to let go of the blame and the guilt, Jake. It was never yours to claim." She stared at him intently. "You should also know, Jake, that Jess communicated to me that the boy who killed her got what he deserved in the end; he died a slow, painful death in a fire only two years later." She smiled. "I'll give you all the cold hard facts later."

But she still wasn't finished.

"I need to tell you this one last thing that Jess insisted I tell you—she loves you, wants you to finally live your life, and she'll see you again someday. Then she said something that I didn't really understand, just that I had to make sure and get it right." Natalie chewed lightly on her lip, trying to recall the exact words. "Something like, 'I'll see you again someday, but I get dibs on the TV when you get here.' I think that's what she said."

Jake's eyes widened, and then they welled with unshed tears.

"Jake, what is it?" Natalie clutched his hands, concerned.

He swallowed, unsure if he could speak. No one but he and Jess knew of that turn of phrase between them. He realized it was just one more way to prove that Natalie was the real thing.

He gripped her hands and let out a long, slow breath. "It's what Jess used to say to me on the phone when I'd call and say I was coming home from college for the weekend. She was eleven or twelve, and I knew she looked forward to it. We always had this good-natured argument over who got to watch the big TV in the rec room, so she'd start it off by telling me first on the phone—" he swallowed, starting to choke up, "—she'd say, 'I get dibs on the TV when you get here.'" A solitary tear escaped and ran down the side of his face.

Natalie leaned over and put her arms around him and held on tight.

Jake gathered her close, burying his head in the curve of her neck. "Why did she think she had to save me? I should have been the one to save her. She was just a kid."

Natalie thought of Bernie, of how blessed her life had really been since she'd found her, since she'd found Jake. She pulled back and smiled at him, all the love she felt for him shining there in her eyes. "Because, Jake, it's what you do for the people you love."

Natalie finally understood that she had been brought back, at fourteen and now, not only to help her young clients like Danny, not only to assist the victims who had only Natalie to hear them, but for Jake as well—to help him find peace with Jess's murder and to learn to truly believe in the possibilities of life—and the power of love.

About the Author

Danette Kriehn has been a business attorney for many years (more than she likes to admit) but would much rather be writing smart, sexy novels than drafting dry, lifeless contracts. A lifelong fan of romantic suspense and romantic comedy, Danette always planned to write her own stories, and one busy career, a musician husband, and three active children later, she is finally pursuing her dream. Danette lives with her family in a tiny rural town in eastern Washington State. You can visit her website at www.danettekriehn.com.